The Fowler Family Business

Jonathan Meades is the author of *Filthy English*, *Peter Knows What Dick Likes* and *Pompey*. He has written and performed in some twenty-five TV films on such subjects as the utopian avoidance of right angles, vertigo's lure, beer and Birmingham's appeal. He is a columnist on *The Times*.

ALSO BY JONATHAN MEADES

Filthy English
Peter Knows What Dick Likes
Pompey

The
Fowler Family
Business

Jonathan Meades

FOURTH ESTATE • *London*

This paperback edition first published in 2003
First published in Great Britain in 2002 by
Fourth Estate
A Division of HarperCollins*Publishers*
77–85 Fulham Palace Road,
London w6 8jb
www.4thestate.com

2

A catalogue record for this book is available from the
British Library.

ISBN 1-85702-904-6

Typeset by Palimpsest Book Production Limited,
Polmont, Stirlingshire
Printed in Great Britain by Clays Ltd, St Ives plc

For: H, R, L, C – and C

Chapter One

Once it had been Henry and Stanley, Stanley and Henry. Stanley
was the card, not Henry. Stanley was a caution, Henry wasn't,
Henry was cautious. Stanley was his da's boy – all chat, and then
some, such a tongue in his mouth. Henry's tongue was fixed in
the prison of his teeth whose incisor accretions, plaque, molar
holes and food coves were his friendly familiars. You chum up
with those ravines and contours if you're tongue-tied. You go
in for interior potholing. You have friends inside, three dozen of
them, each with its tidemark of salts from forgotten meals, from
grazes taken with Stanley, from wads shared on the way to school,
from midnight feasts when they stayed over at each other's.

It was always Henry and Stanley. Stanley was such a one. It
was always the two of them together, Stanley taking the lead,
Henry gingering along behind whilst Stanley got into scrapes and
scrumped and larked about and scaled the old Victoria plum tree
which Mr Fowler called 'Her Majesty'. Mr Fowler watched in
trepidation as Henry clambered about the lower boughs (Stanley
was already at the top, his head poking through the leaves). He
feared that his precious son might tumble and crack his crown

and so be taken from him and Mrs Fowler – though, heaven knows, it was Stanley's da who had more cause to harbour such a fear for he and Mrs Croney had lost an infant girl to diphtheria the winter before the war ended. Stanley was the hasty replacement, born less than a year after Wendy, poor mite, had perished.

Mr and Mrs Fowler were paranoiacally protective of Henry who reciprocated with a dutiful obedience which masked his timidity: he never ventured out of his depth, he never ran across the road, he was a responsible cyclist. Henry was irreplaceable.

In their family they were, all three of them, fans of Charlie Drake, the squeaky knockabout comic. Knockabout! He surely put himself through it. His weekly television show was a self-inflicted assault course. They howled with laughter in the curtained room lit by cathode blue. Mr Fowler with his Saturday bottle of Bass, Mrs Fowler with her fifty-two-weeks-a-year Christmas knitting, Henry in his raglan and pressed flannels, the three of them wondering what the irrepressible little trouper would get up to next. He tumbled, our Charlie fell. He crashed through walls. He went A over T into porridge vats. He'd better watch out for himself – Mr Fowler said as much. 'Ooh he's going to come a cropper Mother!'

Then he added, he always added, he put down his tankard and added gravely: 'Don't ever – don't you ever – you listening Henry my boy – don't you ever think of trying that. Don't you ever.'

Pearl one, stitch one, take one in. 'And don't,' Mrs Fowler joined in, 'ever do what Stanley was doing up Her Majesty either. I don't know . . .'

Henry Fowler didn't require such warnings. He was a watcher. He anticipated the worst. He observed Stanley's clinging limbs as he did Charlie Drake's flying ones. He observed them with contained blood-lust – the ability to put the limbs together again, nicely, for the relatives, was, after all, the family trade. When Charlie Drake crashed about Henry rocked to and fro on the settee, with his tongue in his teeth, rooting out the rotten holes, laughing with his mouth shut. He got eager, he got agitated. He willed injury on Charlie who lived nearby in Lawrie Park Road – he dreamed of being the one who would make Charlie, our Charlie, look more like Charlie, in death, than he had ever looked in life, so like Charlie that his kith'n'kin would hardly notice he'd passed over. He wanted Charlie to hurt himself that badly so that he might practise the trade passed down to him by his father and his father's father who had founded the business in 1901 when he was just a young undertaker and Her Majesty the Queen and Empress Victoria had only lately died. He dreamed too that Stanley might one day be thrown from weak, ungrippable branches by a high gust and so leave the tree for the ground. The sky would be dazzling lactic grey.

Stanley was his friend, he was such a friend he was a brother – he implored his parents to give him a real brother but they disobliged. Stanley was so much a brother he loved him, he loved him so much that he wanted to break him, the way that adored toys are dismembered. They put toy boxes beneath the carpet in Henry's bedroom to simulate B-Western canyons. The Sioux would ambush the cowboys. The transgressors, defeated, would be beheaded by Henry's fretsaw. When the change from lead to plastic models was made, towards the end of their Indian wars, a penknife sufficed. After he had cut the head off Henry always wanted to reattach it, he always regretted what he had done.

Head wounds were Mr Fowler's speciality. He had the good fortune to work in the golden age of head wounds. Health and Safety legislation was something he gloried in as an employer. He was a grateful beneficiary of its loopholes and of the laxity of its implementation. He had followed a war, in the company of an army padre, burying the still helmeted at Arromanches, in a wood near Rouen where 'the chalk was like concrete', and all around Caen ('Canadian lads – hardly got their bum-fluff some of 'em'). In that war he had risen to sergeant-major, and after it he had dropped the sergeant part. And after it, too, he had revelled in the automotive potency of the age. Cars might not have been as routinely quick as they are today but they still got up a fair lick on roads that were built for old legions, horses, first-generation internal combustion. He had served in a war for his King and he believed from the very bottom of his still undicky ticker that mortal risk was the prerogative of everyone – save Henry, who was precious and irreplaceable.

Mr Fowler was happiest with A-roads, with arterial roads with central flower displays. He loved road-houses which men drove to with their bit on the side to get tight in, to adulterate marriage in a private room secured with a wink and a tip, to drink more after, to exit into the path of an oncoming vehicle. The metalled pelt of roads outside road-houses was frosted in winter, soft in summer (the season of minor mirages). The whole year through it was constellated with the evidence: red glass, rubber, chromium, cloth, Naugahyde, oil, body tissue, blood, especially blood. Every road-house had a bloody road in front of it. There were deaths galore. Racing drivers set an example to the male nation. They led short fast lives: Collins, Hawthorn, Lewis-Evans, Scott-Brown with his two names and one arm. They expected nothing more. In their mortal insouciance and dashing dress they aped The Few. They drove to die in flames and glory. After them young death would be delivered by the pharmacopoeia: no head wounds there.

And there were no seat-belts then, no collapsible steering columns, no impact-triggered air bolsters fighting for space like naked fatties. There was no obligation on motorcyclists to wear helmets. The first British motorways – the very name acknowledges the unsuitability of previous roads – were being dug and levelled when Mr Fowler was in his prime. In his old age he was sad but philosophical about the diminution in road deaths effected by motorways and about the decline of 'random culling', an epithet which, as a child, Henry believed to be in general use rather than specific to his father. 'It's Nature's way. Nature always finds a way. War, disease, pogroms, the South Circular, a faulty earth. You make the place too safe and, well – it's not just the trade that's going to feel it. The world'll be full of old 'uns. Miserable old parties like yours truly . . . Life was meant to be a banana skin. Look at the Bible, my lad.'

The week the M1 opened Mr Croney took Stanley and Henry for a drive up it. He couldn't get the hang of the lanes, but neither could the rest of the grockles – this road was not a utility but a site to see, a novelty attraction to participate in. Every car was filled with children agape at the infantile simplicity of the enterprise, children who recognised that their solemnly playful way of making a road had been borrowed by grown-ups. Here was a model road whose scale had been multiplied by giants. It was so obvious, it was so uncompromising in its totalitarian certainty. It had started from zero. It was the road to the future which was already here, in Herts and Bucks. In the future there were picnickers on a December hard shoulder. They were scudding along part of the apparatus that would take them to the moon. Stanley, who dreamed of becoming a pilot, would by 1980 be an old moon hand, a veteran of weekly trips. Henry, who never considered any trade other than the family's, would by 1980 be burying people on the moon, if, by 1980, people didn't live for ever. Tomorrow: monorails. The day after tomorrow: the defeat of gravity. All mankind will be happy and there will be no lapels. Our shoes will shine for ever. The Queen's means of transport will allow her to visit every one of her subjects each year for a cup of rehydre and a chat.

Mr Croney couldn't wait to leave the future behind and get back to the roads of the present. He slowed in the outside lane indicating right (he was not the only one to do so). It was obvious to the boys, who had never driven, how to exit from the most exciting road they had seen. By the time he had veered across to the nearside lane complaining of a life sentence on this bloody road he was sweating and tetchy. At last he succeeded in getting off it. They crossed a bridge where children stood waving Union flags at the adventurers below. Mr Croney unscrewed the top of his pigskin-covered flask and swigged, relieved, steering with one hand, muttering: 'Now this is what *I* call a road. The M1'll never catch on you know.'

Stanley and Henry knew that overhanging bushes and muddy verges and drunken curves would be eliminated by their generation. Mr Croney drove down labyrinthine lanes and parked on the gravel outside a pub with a red sign and plenty of two-tone cars (baby blue and cream, carmine and tan). 'Church,' announced Mr Croney and went inside. The boys knew the form. He soon reappeared with crisps and ginger beer for them to share in the car. 'I want real beer, Dad – this is for kids.'

Henry was shocked by Stanley's brashness. He'd never dare make such a demand of his father. He was puzzled too by Mr Croney's resigned acquiescence: he returned a few minutes later with two bottles of beer and a couple of pork pies. Stanley, enthused by the motorway and comparing it to American highways, hardly thanked his father but took the bottles and said to Henry: 'I'll have yours. You don't want it do you?' Stanley put his new grey winkle-pickers on the dashboard and lounged with proprietorial abandon listing the attractions of America which is where he would live when he was a pilot: 'They all go on the first date . . . fantastic money even before you've finished training . . . square watches . . . record-players in cars . . . open-plan houses . . .' Henry sat on the back seat masticating the pie's pink meat. Stanley lobbed his from the window: 'Electric windows . . . amazing jeans. It's the country of the foreseeable future,' he said, repeating a magazine headline.

Henry's foreseeable future was already mapped out within a three-mile radius of the old Crystal Palace which his father had watched burn down in 1936, 'a tragic night for Sydenham, son.' But then Stanley had no family business to take over, so had to make amends. Besides, for Henry America was the country of the past, of Custer and Wyatt Earp and Jesse James and William Bonney whose head he had cut off more than a dozen times and whose photograph – was he left-handed or had the print been made back to front? – he had shown to his father who told him: 'That's an Irish face. A bad Irish face, a wicked face. Never trust that sort of face, Henry – bad blood, bad genes.'

When Mr Croney came out of the pub he smelled of whisky. His friend Maureen smelled of perfume made from boiled sweets.

'I'm more of a Mo than a Maureen.' She squeezed on to the front bench seat between Stanley and Mr Croney. She smiled at Henry. She was no oil painting, more a distemper job. She had a puffy pub-diet complexion but was thin with it. There were the ghosts of bruises round her eyes. Her lipstick didn't confine itself to her lips.

'Just giving Maureen a lift home, fellers. Her mum's come over bad.'

'Mo.'

Henry watched her gnawed, knotted fur collar ride high over the seat back as she twisted to touch Mr Croney's thigh. Stanley turned to Henry and winked. Mr Croney reciprocated her gesture, close to where the gear lever would have been had it not been on the steering column. Mo giggled. Henry had her straight off as a disrespectful daughter, out cavorting whilst her mother suffered stomach cramps or whatever, whilst the old lady hawked and spluttered and gasped for breath. The car crunched gravel. They were off on their mercy mission.

Mo's way of showing proper concern for her mother seemed inappropriate to Henry. He considered that it lacked decorum. She sang. She knew all the songs. Her songbook memory stretched back to Henry's earliest memory of what Mr Fowler called the Light Pogrom. Her voice was true, fluid, banal. She could do husky too. She loved a big, powerful, meaningful ballad.

She was more herself when she was Denis Lotis or Lisa Rosa or David Whitfield than when she was Maureen nicknamed Mo.

When she was Mo she was a pub belter, so loud that Mr Croney told her to go easy for the sake of their eardrums, whereupon she exposed a wedge of slimy grey–pink mucous membrane and wiped his ear with its tip. She withdrew it into her mouth and sang '*Que sera sera*' with a giggle. Stanley joined in: Henry felt left out, in the back – he wasn't part of the party. He felt that even before Mo called him 'a quiet one' in a testily admonitory tone and Stanley neglected to speak up for him. Later, as they drove through a town with a swollen river and formal public gardens, Stanley listed for Mo what he aspired to wear: Aqua Velva, a burnt-in parting, almond-toe Densons, Cambridge-blue trousers with a fourteen-inch cuff.

'And he wants a white mac don't you, Stanny . . . That'll turn the birds' heads. What you think Mo?'

'Oh it'd suit him ever so.'

Henry wondered where such sartorial licence would end. He knew, because his father had told him so, that the sort of clothes Stanley would be wearing after Christmas were wrong – which is why he kept his copy of the Denson shoes catalogue with his copies of *Kamera* and *QT* and *Spick*, hidden beneath toys he'd grown out of. He didn't want to own that catalogue any more than he wanted to own those corrupting photographs – but both shoes and flesh shared a lubriciousness, both belonged to the forbidden world of sleek sinuousness. He was ashamed of his thraldom to it, of how it might taint him, of how those possessions debased him, of how they represented the threshold of sinfulness, of how they made him betray the trust of his parents. He was used to the complicity between Stanley and Mr Croney, to their familiarity: it was so unlike the proper relationship he enjoyed with his father. He envied Stanley, yet despised Mr Croney's laxity.

It took Mr Croney a while to see Mo home once they'd

stopped in a lay-by next to the woods. Her mother must have lived in a cottage in a clearing, with a little curl of smoke from its fairy-tale chimney and no road to it. Mr Croney had taken Mo's arm as they set out on a worn path between the trees. He had held her arm to prevent her slipping on the leaves and the bony roots exhumed by years of feet. As they had vanished from view Henry had seen Mr Croney take her by the waist: he needed to support her because she was wearing stilettos and a hobble skirt like a regular piece of homework. It wasn't the kit for a hike.

Stanley grinned: 'That's my mac taken care of I'd say.' He took his father's flask from the glove compartment. 'Just so long as I don't split on him to Mum . . . I saw a beaut with leather buttons in Wakeling's. Swig?'

Henry shook his head. He leafed through a leatherette-bound guide to hostelries, hotels, inns, the entries annotated in Mr Croney's hand. He was a commercial who sought bargain beds and bargain bed mates. He travelled in hosiery and jocular smut. He preyed on what Mr Fowler called the Holy Order of the Sisters of the Optics. He was a saloon-bar flatterer who gave his samples to floozies, in hope. He referred to himself as Knight of the Road.

'He'd buy you a tie if you wanted.' Stanley was already a future man, already drawn into men's deceits and duplicities.

Henry replied, lamely: 'I've got enough ties at the moment.' It had not occurred to him, till Stanley made it plain, that Mr Croney was doing anything other than see the girl back to her infirm mother. To have accepted a tie would have made Henry tacitly complicit. In Henry's family, the universe of three, bribes were not offered because there was no need, there were no secrets shared between two parties to the exclusion of the third.

Mr Croney did not possess his son's candour. Henry saw him returning, saw him brush himself down, trying to divest himself of hanks of earth and moss and leaf meal and clinging twigs.

When he realised that Henry had been watching him he said: 'Had a fall . . . Slippery way . . . Don't want to dirty the car.' He was breathless, he was panting. He had to refuel with air between each lie. He gulped gusts bearing fungal spores and intimations of winter. His trouser knees were wet. His welts were encrusted. His improvisational fluency was polished: 'Hasn't been herself, Maureen's mother, not since she lost her husband. Gets very browned off, it seems, down in the dumps. Takes a lot of ladies that way, their loved one passing on – your dad'd know about that . . . They feel at a loss – it's rotten luck on them. And what with the winter . . .' He shook his head in grave sympathy. 'Maureen's a good girl I'd say, tries to help the old dear keep her pecker up but the old dear's lost her will. It's a horrible sight lads, seeing someone wanting to do away with theirself. Tragic. Tragic. I tell you one thing Stanny – I don't want Mum to hear about any of this. She gets most upset by any talk of suicide. It's a woman thing and us men got to protect the womenfolk. You can bet that Henry's dad doesn't bring his work home, in a manner of speaking. Am I right Henry? Wouldn't be quite nice. Not on. Mum's touchy Stanny . . . They say that women never get over losing a kiddie. A little bit of them dies inside.'

They drove into the early dusk of a thick sky. The fields were flat, the earth was heavy and laden with moisture, mist hung over dully lustrous cabbage rows.

'What,' asked Stanley, idly, as though curiosity was merely an alleviation of boredom, 'did she use? How did she do it? Gas oven, sleeping pills? Barbiturates? Razor in the bath Dad?'

'You're well up on it. You been reading a *Teach Yourself*? Barbiturates – I hadn't even heard of barbiturates when I was your age. Does Mum know you know about barbiturates?'

'Is that what it was then Dad?' he asked sweetly.

'Yes . . . Or something like them. Neighbour come by for a natter and saw her through the window. Thought she was asleep till she noticed the bottle. Had an ambulance there quick as a flash.'

'Didn't they take her to hospital then?'

'She's a veterinary nurse the neighbour. Knew the form. Fist down the neck – brought up the entire stomach contents.'

'Must have smelled.'

'They're walking her round and round her little lounge – stop her nodding off. Very shaky. Keeps bumping into the furniture. And tripping over, oh what-d'you-call – hassocks. Kneelers. She embroiders them.'

Henry watched Mr Croney's scrawny pomaded nape. He marvelled at his off-the-cuff inventiveness. It didn't sound like a story that he was making up . . . it sounded plausible, credible: he wasn't the sort to conjure veterinary nurses and embroidered hassocks out of nowhere.

Could it be that Stanley was ascribing adulterous wickedness to his father to glamorise him, to lend him a raciness that he didn't possess? Was Stanley creating his own father, supplying him with moral deficiencies which Stanley himself hoped one day to manifest and which in the meantime gave him something to boast of in the want of anything else, such as a family business, in which to take filial pride?

Henry said nothing to his parents about the near tragedy that he had so nearly witnessed. He was loyal to Stanley and to Mr Croney and, besides, he knew the embarrassment that suicides occasioned at Fowler & Son. Their burials were grudgingly prosecuted. The specific grief prompted by such willed deaths was more than usually infected by remorseful guilt. It was the denial of fate that took the kith'n'kin so bad – that was Mr Fowler's opinion, and he'd put on his philosophical hat to ponder *the rank arrant presumption* of cheating on chance. And he'd put on another hat, a black topper that shone like metal, to complain of the practical problems of a suicide's funeral. No one enjoys them. That was trade wisdom in those days when shame and disgrace attached to the nears and dears and the welcome death stained the name of all who bore it and the deceased was a skeleton to be buried deep in the family closet and will not, please God, set a familial precedent for we know that it does run in families whether through genetic command or exemplary licence. Not that, Mr Fowler insisted to Henry, it was merely the trade which abhorred such self-abnegation but the entire Commonwealth of Her Majesty's (the Queen's, not the tree's) subjects. Funeral directors do not lead the nation in matters of moral choice. They follow. That is why the state of undertaking perfectly reflects the state of society at a given moment, that is why Mr Fowler considered himself and his peers social barometers. Each year at conference, which Henry would attend from the age of fifteen, speakers would emphasise this point and append the corollary that should the day come when bodies were piled into limeless pits or left by roadsides it would be a mark of society's decomposition and anarchy's abominable triumph rather than a mark of the trade's failure to resolve industrial disputes or to attract the right quality of digger. Henry didn't know then that every trade flatters itself thus; engineers, shopkeepers, bricklayers, quantity surveyors – the state of Denmark is reflected in the state of Danish quantity surveying, now.

Chapter Two

On Monday 28 October 1968 Henry Fowler, just twenty-three, twice a runner-up in the Oil Fuels Guild-sponsored Young Funeral Director of the Year competition and recently the proud bridegroom of Naomi Lewis, stood beside a Greek revival mausoleum close by the entrance to West Norwood Cemetery sniffing autumn in a pseudoacacia's yellow leaves, musing on the greenhouse potential of the seeds in its leathery pods, never forgetting to remember that this was the eighth anniversary of Stanley Croney's death, reflecting thereon, whistling beneath his breath a tune of his far-off teenage when he had been immature, and knew it.

Now he was a married man with hopes of fatherhood, a house with underfloor heating and a picture window which framed the gables and cupolas of houses whose inhabitants his grandfather had buried and beyond them the ordered Kentish fields where his grandfather's father had picked hops and pears before the creation of the family business and liberation from such seasonal slavery.

Henry stood there waiting to direct a procession of Fowler &

Son's (he wasn't the initial son in that name, that was his father, when he'd been the son – but it had passed down, and when he, Henry, had a son and his father had retired, he would be the father and so it would remain in mutating constancy). The procession of vehicles, of Rolls-Royces and Austin Sheerlines, was held up because of a traffic fatality on Beulah Hill. The deceased – the one in the coffin, not the headless motorcyclist – had been something in show business. A manager or agent or promoter – it wasn't a world Henry Fowler was acquainted with. Though when he had visited the bereaved and the brittle bespectacled daughter who was attending her at the big house on Auckland Road he had been impressed by the number of photographs signed by stars he recognised. Charlie Drake was there, and Maureen Swanson who'd married a toff, and Al Bowlly whose death in the Blitz while Mr Fowler was stationed on the Isle of Wight denied him the opportunity of posthumously brilliantining the only crooner he'd ever met.

Henry considered mentioning this to the bereaved but the daughter would keep butting in, talking for her and, anyway, he was not certain where he stood in the debate between formality and friendliness that had riven his trade, the two sides denouncing each other as Robots and Mateys. He knew that with his blond hair, black suit and martial bearing he looked like a Robot but that his gravely worn concern for the grieving might mark him as a Matey. He kept quiet rather than risk what might be considered an unseemly disclosure.

He did suggest, however, that the cortège leaving Auckland Road should best process by way of Annerley Hill, Westow Hill and Central Hill because of the long-term roadworks and temporary traffic lights on Beulah Hill (it was these which were thought to have caused the fatal accident). But the bereaved had insisted on Beulah Hill: 'Cyril loved it. He just loved it. He used to stand there you know and look out across Thornton Heath and Croydon and say thank God I don't live there.

You can see all the way to the downs. No, he wants to go along Beulah Hill.'

That was the Thursday.

The Sunday, Henry did his potting – black tulips (a family tradition), narcissi, three sorts of daffodil. Naomi spent the day inside acting on the precepts laid down by Consultant Jilly Morgan in an article called 'An End To Maquillage Monotony'. When they snuggled up together on their tufty fabric sofa she was wearing oyster-pink lip gloss and Qite-A-Nite mascara. The news was cast by his favourite, though not hers, Corbett Woodall: 'More than forty police officers, including five mounted . . .'

They gaped at the scenes of Grosvenor Square. There were longhairs, moustaches, police macs, police truncheons, police horses, wobbly film frames, inchoate grunts, faces of terror and hatred.

'Vandals,' said Henry.

'Goths and vandals,' said Naomi.

They agreed that should any of the Vietcong who had thrown themselves beneath the ironclad hooves of Emperor, Berty, Throckmorton, Monty and Rex II die in a South London hospital Fowler & Son would not undertake to undertake. They laughed, two as one. And that's how undertake to undertake became a catch-phrase in their family: they were to teach it to the children, when they came along. They cuddled and they thanked each other for each other's love and blessed presence which would endure till one of them was undertaken with due ceremony by their first-born boy, one far-off day at the other end of a fulfilling half century – at least.

Henry Fowler waited patiently as the gatehouse attendant at West Norwood Crematorium Mr Scrivenson listened agitatedly to the phone's earpiece and plaited his nostril hair and gurned and pointed with a Capstan-strength forefinger to the handset and repeated: 'If that's the best ETA . . . if that's the best you can do . . . if that's your ETA we're looking at a log-jam – it's going to be Piccadi— they *what*? . . . Right you are then . . . Okey-dokey.'

He put down the phone, flicked at his collar and its icing of seborrhoea, the dandruff with the larger flake, rubbed his hands to say *chilly*, twirled a tuft of hair protruding from his phone ear, dimped a butt from his great wheel of an ashtray and said: 'No disrespect to your dad Henry – but . . . Beulah Hill, I mean to say . . .'

'That's what they wanted, insisted on. Nothing to do with Dad Mr Scrivenson. Me – me. Mrs Ross has got this idea – you know, it's a road he loved.'

'Henry. Henry. You're a funeral *director*. You direct the funeral. I dunno. Your grandad wouldn't have stood for it. Even the best of times you got problems along Beulah Hill – there's mineral wells there. Tarmacadam's worst enemy. It's why it's always erupting. And all that subsidence in them twinky-dinky new houses. You got to learn to put your foot down – A Generation Out of Control.'

'What?'

'That's what it said in the paper this morning. That's you lot. My God.' Mr Scrivenson stood and gaped through the dust-blasted panes. 'You got a crow. Who's this feller?'

'Uh?'

'The deceased.'

'Mr Cyril Ross he was called. Lived in—'

'What line?' Mr Scrivenson looked at Henry looking blank against the dun wall of this tiny home-from-home. 'What did he do?'

'Some sort of show business. Agent, you know . . . produ—'

'Could have told you. It's only the theatre and the military you get crows with nowadays.'

Crow was old funerary trade slang for a mourner who dressed the part, who outdid the funeral directors in their bespokes from Kidderminster, who turned mourning into black dandyism. The

16

blacker the garb the deeper the feeling – it's like the paint on a Sheerline. A score of coats of jet enamel signals solemnity. Black – figurative and ceremonial uses of. That's an area of Henry's expertise. Henry hurried out of Scrivenson's fug to warn the crow of the delay, inform him of its cause, apologise: 'Excuse me sir,' he called to the man who had his back to Henry and was scrutinising an art-nouveau headstone in the form of an escutcheon. He half turned, raising his toppered head. The crow's garb – black barathea, black satin facings, black frogging, black moiré jabot – subjugated all individuality in the cause of ostentatious or, as Mr Fowler would have it, boastful grief. Henry was addressing a man playing a role, a machine for mourning who thanked him for the information with a nod and a tight-lipped smile. Henry turned back towards Scrivenson's lodge. He had walked a couple of steps before he realised whom he had been talking to. Henry hurried after the crow who was alarmed by the heavy footfalls on the metalled drive.

'I just wanted,' Henry panted, 'to say, if I might, how much "Teresa" meant to me you know. Well, still means to me. It's difficult to explain – my great mucker was called Stanley.'

The crow looked even more alarmed, as though he feared Henry might assault him. 'Stanley?'

'Yes,' confirmed Henry, 'it was today he died.'

'Today,' echoed the crow.

'Well, not *today*, today.'

'Ah.'

'See – I always think of you when I think of Stanley because of "Teresa". *And* Jesse-Hughes.'

The crow surveyed Henry with appalled distaste: 'Jesse-Hughes? The murderer?'

'Oh I thought you'd have known . . . His last request – you *must* have known. I knew because of my dad but it was in the papers. Someone must have told you.'

A shake of the toppered head, a black gloved hand raised as

if to silence Henry: 'I'm sorry – I have absolutely no idea what you're talking about.' He tried to put a laugh in his voice.

Henry grinned *come off it*, mock reproachfully, wagged a conspiratorial finger. He failed to recognise that the crow regarded him as a nuisance, or worse.

'It's all right,' Henry assured him, 'it's just we don't get so many celebrities here – it's not Golders Green or Putney Vale.'

'Of course not.'

'I just wanted to tell you, when I saw you, tell you to your face how important "Teresa" has been in my life . . .'

The trade never reckoned crows to be anything more than vanity and fancy cuffs. Crows were not considered to be *thoughtful* mourners. Nor were they reckoned passionate. No tears, no throwing themselves into the oblong hole, lest they muddy their precious clothes (not hired).

The fourth time Henry mentioned "Teresa" this one, all cold corvine politesse, turned sibilant. Every S was a venomous dart. 'This Teresa, this woman, who is this woman?'

Henry enjoyed a spot of the old joshing. Taking the Michael (thus) was the family way. It was the lime in the mortar that bound the Fowlers. Henry would normally have reckoned the crow to be a misogynist queen because of the way he uttered *woman*, with contempt. But Henry knew a piss-taking joker when he met one, and he respected the ruseful stratagem, admired the implicit knowledge of the game's rules, warmed to the deadpan performance, resolved to play along with it but could not stem his giggling as he mocked: 'So you don't know the handbag shop on Holloway Road then?'

The crow's jaw plummeted on puppeteer's wires.

'Erherch – you didn't know I knew about it did you urchaf? Go on – tell me that Heinz is fifty-seven varieties.'

'Heinz? Heinz . . . Holloway Road . . . hand, handbags?'

'That's you,' Henry winked, archly.

'That's me?' He grimaced, a first try at a grin.

Henry was getting through. He twinkled.

But the crow shook his head in pitiful incomprehension. He turned and strode with his metal heels clicking towards the cemetery chapel.

Henry caught up with him, grasped him by the upper arm: 'Fair's fair, I only wanted . . .'

The crow jerked his arm to secure its release. And then, in an eliding gesture, he briskly flicked at Henry's face. Henry had not been slapped since haughty Miss Gordon had grown exasperated with his inability to memorise his three-times table when he was three times three, equals nine. The crow's black glove stung. Henry clung to his hot jowl, gaped at his antagonist like a hurt animal.

After the ceremony whilst the mourners queued in the foggy late afternoon to shake the hands of the immediately bereaved, to kiss and hug them, Mr Fowler growled from a miserly slit at one end of his mouth: 'I want to talk to you Henry. Later.'

Henry watched dusk crêpe the headstones and the balding branches. He looked out for the crow but didn't see him among the people who by the time they reached the two weeping ashes had ceased to be mourners and were themselves again, free once more to exclude death from their quotidian routine, a freedom which Henry rarely enjoyed, he was born to death, it was his crust. It was death that paid for the ruggedly chunky gold earrings Naomi was wearing when she said: 'You shouldn't put up with him Henry. Why do you put up with him?'

Mr Fowler had just left.

'He's my *father*.'

'So what. That doesn't mean he can just talk to you like . . .'

Henry looked at her so angrily. She'd never seen that before, in all their months of marriage. Henry had never tried to make her cry and now here he was, doing it with his eyes and his tight jaw when all she wanted to do was to comfort him, cuddle him better after the protracted rebukes he had received. She'd heard every word through the thin walls of their first home where there were no secrets. They lived as one. They had lived as one till he made that face at her, till he told her it was none of her business, till he accused her of eavesdropping, of spying, of covert intrusion into a private matter. It was family business.

'I am your family too.'

That is going too far, thought Henry. That is above and beyond. 'In a different sense,' he sneered.

Naomi sobbed. She spoke his name, lengthened it imploringly. 'I'm your wife Henry – that's family.'

'Yes, yes.'

'And when someone speaks to you like that . . .'

'Someone? Someone? You call my father *someone* . . . like, like he'd wandered in off the street. God.'

'Henry you're not a child. They may treat you like you're still ten . . .'

'He was *right*. That's all there is to it. Nothing to do with being treated like a child. He was right. I fucked up. I am his son, and Fowler & Son does not fuck up. I was out of line. No question. He was right. So he gives me a bollocking and that's that. I can take it. No big deal,' he lied, stretching to save lost face with front rather than conviction. She had heard them. She had heard her husband repeat: 'Bobby Camino . . . Bobby Camino . . . Bobby Camino . . .'

And she heard her father-in-law: 'Even if he had been this Bob, Bobby . . . What sort of name's that? Camino.'

'Not his *real* name, Dad – Doug Truss s'matter of—'

'I don't care if he's calling himself Dr Crippen and Ethel le Neve.'

'Dad. You used to hum along to it. "Teresa, Tayrasor, Trasor, Tayrayayaysoar." You used to sing along with me. I still got it – Top Rank.'

'What? Henry – you've got to take control. He gave me his card. Norman Idmiston.'

'It's b'cause he was a one-hit wonder – he's changed his name. Again.'

'He's a barrister. LLB, MA Oxon. Rope Court, Middle Temple.'

She heard nothing. Henry did not reply. He must have stood there with his mouth open.

'We reflect society,' Mr Fowler told him. 'And I'm afraid my boy that the only section of society your behaviour this afternoon reflected was our friends the unwashed jackanapes, the great unwashed, the ingrates. The United States is our ally. You don't burn your ally's flag. We'd be speaking Germ— what I mean is we've got a lot to thank Uncle Sam for.'

'I couldn't agree more Dad.'

'You're not there as Henry Fowler, Henry. You're there in a ritual role. Like the Queen . . . We have to preserve our mystery. That'll be what shocked Mr Idmiston – not that you'd got him mixed up with this Bobby chap but that you broke the spell. That's what it is – I've thought long and deep about our calling as you know Henry. And the one thing you cannot do under any circumstances is reveal what I like to call the human beneath the hat. If you were anyone else Henry you'd be looking at probation. And I'd dock your wages if you weren't a newly married man. It's not just Fowler & Son, it's the whole profession – we're butlers to the dead, we're a caste and we stand together, abide by the caste's code.'

'It was wishful thinking – you know, I let it get the better of me. I suppose I must have wanted him to be Bobby Camino.'

'You haven't been listening have you Henry. What I'm saying is, even if this Bobby Camino does attend a funeral where you're there in an official capacity you do not on any account go running after him asking for his autograph. Not if it's Warren Mitchell or Dick Emery or Gerald Harper or Ted Moult you do not even if you are right about who it is. Do you read me? There's no place for Mateys in Fowler & Son, no place whatsoever.'

'Yeah, of course – but I wouldn't with them anyway – it's just that "Teresa" . . . It's about Stanley. That's what it's about.' And Henry Fowler hangs his head.

'Teresa', written by Doug Truss, Joe Meek and Mike Penny, was recorded by Joe Meek at his makeshift studio above Messrs Kaplan's handbag-and-suitcase shop at 417 Holloway Road N7 in June 1961. Roger Laverne (né Jackson) and Heinz (Burt) played organ and bass. The record's release on the Top Rank label was delayed because of Truss's (Bobby Camino's) contractual obligations to Pye.

The first time Henry Fowler and Stanley Croney heard it was shortly before noon on 28 October 1961 on the BBC Light Programme's 'Saturday Club'. Henry persistently opened the breakfast-room window and flapped at the air with a tooled-leather magazine holder to remove the smell of Stanley's cigarettes – his current and last brand of choice was Kent. Henry kept an eye on where Stanley was putting his feet, shod today in mock-croc almond-toed slip-ons with a rugged buckle. He feared for the cushion tied to a ladder-back chair, he feared what his parents might say if they saw the heeled depressions in the oat fabric and if they detected the sweetish odour of the tobacco. Stanley feigned oblivion to Henry's concern, observed that the song was 'for kids' even though he'd keenly beaten the table in time to the repetitive scat wail.

When the programme ended Stanley went to the toilet, so he never heard the name Jesse-Hughes. Henry, plumping the cushion flattened over two and a half decades by his father's weight, listened to the midday news bulletin: at a special sitting of St Alban's magistrates court a forty-three-year-old grocery company representative had been remanded in custody in connection with the murder of five women. Dudley Jesse Hughes (there was no indication that the name was primped with a hyphen) spoke only to confirm that name.

When seven months later at the Old Bailey he pronounced

the sentence of death by hanging on Jesse-Hughes Lord Justice Killick ejaculated as was his wont and because it was his wont his marshal had a spare pair of slightly too-tight trousers at the ready so that when His Lordship went to dine at his club, a hank of white shirt protruded from beneath his waistcoat, from the top of his flies, prompting murmurs of approval from novice members such as Norman Idmiston.

Jesse-Hughes asked in his death cell to hear 'Teresa' by Bobby Camino. Teresa was the name of his poliomyelitis-stricken wife for whose sake he had polygamously married five widows in the counties of Hertfordshire, Northamptonshire (two), the Soke of Peterborough and Suffolk, had had them amend their wills in his favour and had then over twelve years killed them with atropine, in a dometic accident (shiny stair treads), by drowning (a bath, a river), and by tying a fifth, a jabbering Alzheimer, to a chair in a frosty garden for the night. It was the variety of method which according to former *Reynold's News* crime reporter Claude Vange in 'The Last Gentleman Murderer' kept the police off his trail for so long.

Henry Fowler was to follow the case with scrupulous attention. His father joked that the judge's black cap should be replaced by a topper because the name was a better fit! Not that Mr Fowler was pro hanging. There is, tragically, little that the embalmer can do with a roped throat. The contusions will always show through. They are the brand the hanged take to the other side. The hanged are marked with a blue-black thyroid beyond eternity – no wonder, then, that suicide in the cell the night before is so favoured an option. Henry was never sure whether Jesse-Hughes's request to hear 'Teresa' was granted. He was not sure whether Jesse-Hughes had really asked for it or whether that was a journalistic fabrication. Indeed he was not even sure if he had read it or had been told it by some schoolmate (sychophant? tease?) who knew of his fondness for both case and record. He wondered how the request would have been granted.

Was there an electric socket for a portable record-player in the death cell? Did Jesse-Hughes, a non-smoker with a horror of nicotine-stained fingers, succumb and smoke his first and last whilst he listened to Bobby Camino's song about the imaginary girl who shared his crippled wife's name?

The last cigarette that Stanley Croney smoked was an Olivier, one of a handful he had helped himself to from Mr Fowler's EPNS cigarette box on the way back from the toilet and put in his flip-top Kent pack. He had also swallowed a draught of White & Mackay's whisky from the bottle's neck. When he returned to the breakfast room with one arm into a sleeve of his bronze mac Henry had switched off the radio and was wiping invisible ash from the table with his sleeve before casting his eye about the room to ensure that there was nothing for his parents to complain of. Then Henry checked his hand-me-down wallet's contents of ten pounds, his aggregate sixteenth birthday present from three weeks previously. They left the house at 12.09 to catch a train into central London. They walked down the hill where the big Victorian mansions glared through dripping laurels and rhododendrons. Stanley, anxious about his shoes, walked on the road rather than on the pavement whose drift of wet leaves might conceal a surprise gift from a dog. They passed the forlorn park and the pavilion surrounded by scaffolding and the malnourished trees. A Kent-bound train rattled past the allotment strip where old men hid from life in huts made of doors and iron and wire and string, smoking copious weights of shag. The smoke from their makeshift chimneys was hardly distinguishable from the glary white sky. The road curved after a terrace of railway cottages, and there was the rusty old girder bridge.

Chapter Three

It was going on fifty feet that Stanley Croney fell. It was a seventy-foot drop to the rain-glossed cinders beside the shiny tracks that stretched into oblivion. It was almost a hundred feet high, that rusty old girder bridge. The representatives of the emergency services casually disagreed about how far the tragic lad had fallen – but who, naked eyed, can estimate height or distance with anything more than a well-meant guess when a young life has been lost and there are procedures to follow and the dense nettles on the embankment sting through uniform trousers and speed is vital because all train services have been halted. It was high, that rusty old girder bridge.

The coroner noted but did not question the disparities. He scratched at his eczematous wrists that cuffs couldn't quite hide and listened with sterling patience to the policeman, to the ambulancemen, to the doctor, to the firemen who had surely overestimated the distance because of the duration and difficulty of their haul of the unbruised, uncut body up the steep embankment. And he had heard evidence from PC 1078 Grady in two previous cases and considered him to be a cocky smart alec and careless of details.

Thus he assumed (wrongly, as it happens) that the bridge was seventy feet above the tracks. He heard evidence from Henry Fowler; from the hairdresser Jimmy Scirea whose salon Giovanni of Mayfair Henry Fowler had run into, 'all agitated', asking to use the phone; from Janet Cherry who had talked to the two youths before they turned on to the bridge and who described Stanley as being 'in a definitely frisky mood, you know, sort of excitable . . . show-offy – he was often like that. He was a character.' He had performed 'this funny bow, old-fashioned, sort of like in the olden days if you follow my meaning'. His friend, whom she knew only by sight, had merely nodded curtly and looked ostentatiously at his watch whilst she talked briefly to Stanley about a party they might both attend that night. She had been surprised not to see Stanley there because he had asked twice whether Melodie Jones would be going. 'He was very direct. He wasn't shy.'

Of course he wasn't. He was a one, a daredevil, a cheeky monkey. This wasn't the first time. Everyone can remember the early hours of New Year's Day 1960 when after being ejected from the Man Friday Club (under age, over the limit, we've our licence to think of sonny) he had run up a drainpipe and had scaled a roof of the Stanley Halls and had stood silhouetted against the full-scale map of the heavens shouting to the stumbling revellers in the street below: 'I am Stanley and this is *my* hall.'

He had offered variations on that boast to Henry for so long as Henry could recall. Henry's memories of it were in his ribs. That's where Stanley would elbow him when they walked past the Stanley Halls and Stanley Technical Trade Schools. They walked past so often that Henry suffered costal bruising from his quasi-brother's joshing prods and proud jabs. Stanley's identification with W.R.F. Stanley might have been founded in nothing more than the coincidence of a common name but it had grown from that frail beginning into heroic idolatry. W.R.F. was the odd one out in Stanley's personal pantheon of sideburned rock and rollers, quiffed balladeers, d.a.'d teen idols, bostoned film actors, Brylcreemed footballers. W.R.F. was old, dead, from long ago when they wore the wrong haircuts. But, as Stanley persistently reminded Henry, he was his own creation: he had had no family business to enter, he had started from nothing and had gone so far that he had been able to buy the land and to design and build the loud structures at the bottom of South Norwood Hill. That his philanthropy was boastful is unquestionable – why else make buildings of such striking gracelessness and coarse materials if not to clamour for attention for oneself and one's inventions.

The most celebrated of W.R.F.'s inventions was the Stanley Knife, the *sine qua non* of a particular sort of South London conversation. Although the plump bulk of the handle militated against the achievement of the *bella figura* that Stanley Croney was keen to exhibit, he invariably carried a Stanley Knife: a natty dresser needs protection against the sartorial hun. His knife was his daily link to W.R.F., to the self-made man Stanley longed to be. Stanley Croney was going to emulate him. He too would have a house like Stanleybury, he too would endow a clock tower in his native suburb to commemorate his wedding, he too was on the way to being his own man, and that meant having a way with what Mr Croney called 'the ladies'. Henry despised Stanley's ingratiating charm, his flimsy slimy stratagems.

He knew Janet Cherry by her loose reputation. And he despised her, and her kind, for their susceptibility to Stanley who was never at a loss for a quip. How could they fail to see through his corny ploys? How could they like someone who had no respect for them as *people*? Did they not realise that he was an apprentice wolf, preying? Stanley greeted her with lavish rolls of his right hand and a balletically extended leg as though he were a peruked fop, Sir Grossly Flatterwell making the first step in the immemorial dance which culminates horizontally. They had, Stanley hinted when he had observed Henry pointing to his watch and she had gone her stilettoed beehived way, already culminated. That anyway was how the virgin Henry interpreted Stanley's 'It'll have to be another bite at the cherry if Melodie J doesn't come across. Not that she won't – she's just rampant for it.' *It* was a foreign country, yet unvisited by Henry who'd never been on a Continental holiday either.

'And,' Stanley went on, confidential, man of the world to a mere boy, 'they say she gobbles.'

Henry, morose, didn't know what Stanley meant. He was ashamed that he had not entered the carnal world of which Stanley was now a citizen. Stanley was less than six months his senior: he told himself, without conviction, that six months hence he, too, might . . . might what? Do wrong, that's what he knew *it* to be. Premarital intercourse, as it was then known, was as wicked as electric guitars and didn't happen to nice people, to responsible people, to people called Fowler who attended church. *It* was for gravediggers, not for funeral directors. *It* was not for those who respected their mothers, their mothers' sex, the primacy of Christian marriage, the sanctity of the family, the notion of true love as explained by Tab Hunter who wore neither hair cream nor sideburns: 'They say for every girl and boy in this whole world there's just one love . . .' Just one love. Wait till she comes along. You'll know it's her. And *it* is invariably attended by God's revenges of pregnancy, gonorrhoea, syphilis, gonorrhoea *and* syphilis ('a royal flush' according to sailors, and they know), social disgrace: 'She's had to go away' was what Mrs Fowler said of more than one office help. If the fallen one was a cleaner who couldn't type and wasn't allowed to answer the phone because of her common accent she eschewed euphemism: 'She's gone to have an illegit. No one'll want her now.'

This carnal world was fraught with such dangers – social,

moral, irreligious, medical – that Henry Fowler was not sure he wished to enter it. Yet he was achingly jealous of Stanley who was so confident in his new knowledge, so easy with it. And he broached the subject of that evening with trepidation and with a resentment at what he knew would be Stanley's response.

'You . . . you're going to a party then?'

'Dave Kesteven's sister, Sheila. Parents are away so . . .'

'I thought we were going to the flicks.'

'Yeah . . . look sorry. But we can go any time. Can't we? Eh? You can come. Have a crack at the cherry – never knowingly says no.'

'I'll think about it,' said Henry, meaning 'no'.

'Your choice.'

And here Stanley did one of his party tricks. He put his hands in his jacket pockets and turned a standing somersault. A man, obediently pushing his bicycle from the end of the pedestrians only rusty old girder bridge gaped in astonishment then scooted with one foot on a pedal before mounting the black Hercules with calliper brakes. He has never been traced.

Henry Fowler, the only living person to have seen him, described him as 'quite old, wearing an old man's cap, sort of unhealthy looking, and he had this kitbag thing which was all mixed up with his cape – he had a cape like a tarpaulin and it was all bunched and sticking out funny because of the kitbag; he had cycle clips, and very big feet'.

Unhealthy, how? A sort of creamy yellow complexion. Waxy, you might say, very like some laid-out corpses. Henry Fowler, who often helped out around the family business which he would enter when he left school next summer, was well acquainted with such.

Stanley clapped his hands in self-applause, grinned madly, made Charles Atlas gestures and saluted the horizontal cape which was now astride its saddle and peddling unsteadily in the direction of the allotments. He marched from the pavement on to the rusty old girder bridge with Henry (as usual) trailing behind him. The bridge was just wide enough for three persons to walk side by side without brushing its sides, which were sheer metal sheets – those of average height had to jump to get a sight of the distant track below, a sight which would thus be retinally fixed. The bridge was lavishly riveted, the rivet heads stood proud of the metal like dugs. Each side was topped by a horizontal parapet, eight inches wide, also sewn with rivets. The flaked paint was a history of the Southern Railway's and the Southern Region's liveries – dun, cow brown, algae green, cream, battleship. There were crisp islets of rust, ginger Sporades which shed flakes among the puddles on the threadbare macadam of the walkway.

This is where flowers would be left for Stanley, for years to come, left to die.

The Croney family never forgot their Stanley who, larky as ever, climbed on to the parapet and walked like a tightrope artist until his smooth heel slipped on a rounded rivet head, until he stubbed his foot against an uneven joint, until he overcompensated when the friable rusty surface had him stumble, until he dropped those fifty-five or seventy or hundred feet to the cinders beside the shiny tracks below.

'You ought,' Stanley is now speaking his penultimate words, to the top of Henry's head which is at the same level as his feet, 'you really ought to come. You don't want to worry about your wols. Everyone gets them.' Henry's acne, miniature crimson aureola with milk-white nipples, were his shameful secret. They were for the whole world to snigger at when his back was turned but they were, nonetheless, still a secret because they had never been mentioned – not by parents, not by brusque Dr Oxgang, not by bullies. Their existence was confined to the bathroom mirror. Now Stanley had lifted them from that plane. He had ruptured the compact between Henry and his reflection. Henry was overwhelmed by hurt.

'Just squeeze them. That's what I did,' counselled Stanley, picking his way among the rivets.

Henry's cutaneous ignominy turned to destabilising anger, to a rage as red as those aureola (let's count them: how long have you got? No, let's not bother), to a churning indignation. *By what right?* The words 'wols' and 'squeeze' echoed in his head. Friendship was suspended, blotted out. He felt a momentary resistance to his hand, he walked on, not noticing the depth of the puddles, aware of a bronze streak across the perimeter of his sinistral vision like a light flaw, deaf to the mortal howl because of the thudding clamour in his head. At the end of that moment he became aware of the absence of Stanley's feet a few inches above him. He had gone from A (the bridge's mid-point) to, say, D (the worn metal steps at its end) and arriving there had realised that he had no memory of B and C.

That's when he ran, with his coat inflated by the wind. He ran to the parade of single-storey shops. He noticed how the pediment above the middle shop had lost some of its dirty white tiles, how it was an incomplete puzzle. That shop was a florist's. There was a queue of macs and handbags which turned in unison to gesturing Henry. He stepped out as soon as he had stepped in, his nostrils gorged by funeral perfumes.

The next shop was all dead men's clothes and their repulsive cracked shoes – you can never get the sweat out of leather, that's undertaker lore, family wisdom. Closed, anyway, gone early for lunch, said a note taped to the door's condensing glass. Which is why he hustled past two new hairdos with jowly flicks coming out the door of Giovanni of Mayfair and slithered down the chequered corridor flanked by the stunted cones on the heads of women who would be visitors from the Planet Kwuf. 'Jimmy, Jimmy,' he panted: Henry knew Jimmy Scirea because Jimmy advised the family business on dead hair and how to dress it.

Henry was all agitated. Jimmy had never seen him even mildly agitated, had always considered him a calm boy, so this was unusual. Even so Henry controlled himself enough to act with what his father counselled, with all due decorum: no ears were sheared by the sharpened scissors of the high-haired apprentices who augmented the numbers every Saturday.

They were not privy to Henry's brief conversation with Jimmy, and Carolle the receptionist was used to Jimmy mouthing 'Say goodbye' and making a gesture with a flat hand across his throat when he needed the phone. There was no panic. She told her new love Salvador that she had to go and handed the apparatus to Jimmy and to the pimply boy whom she had thought at first must be the son of one of the ladies under the driers. She couldn't help but hear the name of Stanley Croney, the beautiful boy, the cynosure of every hairdresser's receptionist's eyes.

Henry's face was puffy, sweaty, tearful. There was a film of salty moisture all over its manifold eruptions, there were greasy rivulets between them like the beginnings of brooks just sprung from the earth. He rapped impatiently on the phone's ivory-coloured handset and glared at it as though it might be faulty. He took against a fancifully framed, pertly coloured photograph of a hairdo like a chrysanthemum. He spoke, at last, in urgent bursts as though his breathing was asthmatically impaired. There was a flawed bellows in his chest.

He declined the receptionist's offer of water. He detailed the circumstances with cursory precision. He listened intently, told the ambulance how to get to the bridge. He was calmer when he made his next call, to the police. He used the words 'larking about, having a bit of a laugh'. He rather impertinently added: 'Remember the traffic lights are out by the station there.' He put down the phone, sighed, wiped his face with a paisley handkerchief, thanked the receptionist for the use of the phone and thanked Jimmy Scirea who was putting on an overcoat. Henry seemed surprised that the hairdresser should follow him from the salon. The hairdreser was in turn surprised that Henry, instead of hurrying back to the site of the accident, should amble across the road to Peattie's bakery to buy a bag of greasy doughnuts which he began to eat with absorption as he made his way back to the bridge. He covered his face with sugar. He inspected the dense white paste. He thrust his tongue into the jammy centre. He ate as if for solace or distraction just as a smoker might draw extra keenly on a cigarette. When they reached the bridge Jimmy Scirea hauled himself on to the top of the side to look down at the body below. Then he tried to loosen a cracked fence pale to gain access to the embankment. Henry shook his head and said, with his mouth full, extruding dough, 'Don' rye it. Don' bother. Bleave it to them. Too steep.' He stuck a hand in his mouth to release his tongue from his palate. 'Ooph – bit like having glue in your mouth but they're very tasty. Think I'll get some more later. Yeah definitely.'

Chapter Four

When Henry Fowler married Naomi Lewis his best man was Stanley Croney's brother.

No, Curly didn't forget the ring though for a moment he searched his pockets in the pretence that he had!

No, he didn't embarrass the guests by telling off-colour gags – though he suggested that he was about to do so by talking about the day that Henry hid the salami! This, however, was merely the introduction to an anecdote about Henry removing a pork product from the table on one of Naomi's early visits, before he realised that her family's assimilation was such that they ignored dietary proscriptions.

'My dad's motto,' Naomi never tired of explaining, 'is – the best of both worlds, salt beef *and* bacon, Jewish when it suits!' Not all of Naomi's family and friends were as blithely indifferent to observances as she and her father were. Curly Croney was, even then, at the age of eighteen, canny enough not to stir things between the bride's two factions. Having felt the coolness with which that allusion to the Lewises' casual apostasy was received he made no further mention of it.

He spoke instead, with the persuasive humility which was to stand him in such favourable stead in his professional life, about his debt to his friend, the bridegroom Henry Fowler, his brother and comforter Henry Fowler, who had taken the place of his real brother Stanley. Irreplaceable Stanley – save that Henry had replaced him, as much as anyone ever could.

It was Henry who despite the almost five years' difference in their ages had guided him through the bewilderment and grief that they had both suffered. It was Henry who had been his guiding light and mentor; he had become, as a result of a silly accident, an only child in a shattered family. And it was through Henry's belief in the integrity and sanctity of family that the Croney family had been able to repair itself. (At this juncture Curly smiled with radiant gratitude towards the grey mutton-chop sideburns covering his father's face and to the white miniskirt exposing his mother's blue-veined thighs.) Henry, not least because of his own parents' example, understood the strength of family and the importance of its perpetuation whatever losses it might suffer: a strong family is an entity which can recover from anything, and Henry had shown the way.

Curly didn't know that Naomi's mother had only returned to the family home in Hatch End fourteen months previously after a three-year liaison with a wallpaper salesman in Cape Town which ended when Louis died in the bedroom of a client's house during a demonstration of new gingham prints and Louis's daughters brought an action to remove Naomi's mother from the green-pantiled Constantia bungalow which was now theirs. Nor did he know that fourteen of Naomi's mother's aunts, uncles and first cousins had died at Sobibor and Treblinka and that there is no familial recovery from such thorough murder.

But those in the Classic Rooms of the Harrow Weald Hotel that squally afternoon of 25 August 1968 who had evaded or who had survived industrial genocide were in no mood to oppose the patently decent, patently grateful young man and were inclined, too, to conjoin with him in his celebration of the tanned blond undertaker whom Naomi so obviously loved and had chosen to make her own family with far away, on the corresponding south-eastern heights of the Thames Basin – there, see them there, through the rolls of weather, places we've never been to, goyland, where the JC means Jesus Christ, where yarmulkes are rarely seen, where it may not even be safe to practise psychiatry, where a vocabulary of hateful epithets is nonchalantly spoken, unreproached, in the salons and golf clubs. There are sixty-five synagogues north of the Thames; there are five south of it, and about as many delis. No ritual circumcisers, either – a lack which had not even occurred to Curly Croney, which duly went unmentioned although in later years Naomi's father, Jack Lewis, would sometimes jocularly greet Henry as 'the man the *mohel* missed'. Henry took this in good spirit and was unfazed by the overintimate coarseness, because it was so obviously true – no one would expect a strapping, big-boned blond with almost Scandinavian features to have been circumcised, and, besides, his exaggerated respect for his parents extended to his parents-in-law. It was a respect which Curly illustrated by referring to an incident Naomi had mentioned to him.

On their third date, one Sunday in May, Henry had called for Naomi in his sports car and had driven her first to the Air Forces Memorial at Runnymede to admire 'a properly tended garden of remembrance – tidiness equals respect', then to see the brash rhododendron cliffs at Virginia Water, and on to a riverside restaurant where they ate a chateaubriand steak because it was to share and by such gestures would they unite themselves. They gazed at each other oblivious to river, weir, swans, pleasure craft, laburnums, magnolias (past their best in any case). Henry was explaining the massage procedure that must be applied to a body to alleviate rigor mortis in order to make it pliable for embalming. Naomi leaned across the table, clasped his hands and asked, poutingly, 'Who's your ideal woman?'

Henry was puzzled by this question. And whilst Naomi's pose – eyes fluttering and index finger tracing the line of her lips – might have encouraged most young men to achieve the correct answer Henry contorted his face in effortful recall as though the quarry were some irrefutable slug of information like the chemical formula for formaldehyde CH_2O rather than a softly smiling 'You' or 'You are'. If Henry realised that he was being asked to provide proof of the compact between them he was too shy to acknowledge it.

Suddenly his face cleared. He's got it, she thought to herself, warm with the anticipation of an exclusive compliment He reached inside his jacket, withdrew his wallet and removed from it a photograph which he handed to her. It showed a middle-aged woman, her face partly obscured by the hair blown across it by a gust. Naomi looked at it, as though this was some sort of trick. Then she waited for the clever pay-off.

'That's my mother,' said Henry. 'My ideal woman.'

Curly, whom Naomi regarded as a child, was blind to Naomi's hurt when she told him of that day. He supposed that this vignette was an affirmation of her pride in her future husband's filial loyalty and he recounted it thus, causing his audience to wonder why he should wish to slight the bride at the expense of her mother-in-law. Was he trying to ingratiate himself, in the belief that to be Jewish is to be mother fixated? Was this an expression of covert anti-Semitism? No, it was just gaucheness tempered with Curly's steadfast idolatry of Henry. Do you know what Henry did the day after they got engaged?

The guests awaited the revelation of a passionate gesture, of some act characterised by irrationality and violins. With his father's permission, since it was his father who had bought it for him on his twenty-first birthday, Henry traded in his two-seater, open-topped, wire-wheeled MGB for a four-seater Rover 2000 saloon 'because we're going to be a family and a sports car's not suitable. Not safe either.'

'I really liked the MG, Henry,' murmured the bride, nuzzling her husband of an hour's neck, 'all that fresh air can get a girl quite excited.'

'The Rover's got a sun-roof,' he replied, tersely. 'All you've got to do is wind it.'

Henry had, anyway, made the right car choice in the opinion of Curly's audience. Every one of them was beaming at him. He might not have made a theatrically romantic gesture but he had expressed a long-term commitment by buying, by *investing in*, a vehicle renowned for its craftsmanship and reliability, a vehicle with two extra seats to fill, in time and with God's blessing, two extra seats which seemed to predict a nursery gurgling.

Curly finished his speech with the wish that: 'Next time I offer a toast to these two I hope it will actually be to these *three* – but, for the moment, I give you Naomi and Henry.' Naomi and Henry – their names were multiplied in the gaily decorated Classic Rooms. Curly sat down and Henry gripped him around the arm, patting his shoulder, nodding in satisfaction, a trainer whose dog has had its day. That speech had cemented their brotherhood. Naomi's mother said what others must have thought when she muttered: 'Who's getting married here I want to know? Henry, ob-vi-ous-ly, but who to? I'd never heard it was the best man's role to declare his love for the groom. What did he mean by these three? Is he expecting them to adopt him?' And so on.

Curly would not, at that time, have admitted to loving Henry. Affection, respect, gratitude, guilt – these were the sentiments he allowed. And a sort of relief, an inchoate conviction that without someone whom he could take for granted he would not have recovered from the loss of Stanley. He did not delude himself: Henry was more of a brother to him than Stanley could ever have been, while they were young, at least, and the age gap told. He knew that had Stanley lived, reckless, selfish, apple of his father's wandering eye, Henry would not have been his brother and that Henry would have taken no notice of him, that Henry would forever have been trailing Stanley. His guilt sprang from his having been blessed by Stanley's death, from having been liberated by it, from having been dragged from the shadows by a true soulmate. It was as it was meant to be, according to fortuity and fatidic law. He was thankful that Henry had stuck with Stanley for all of Stanley's life for otherwise he would not have inherited Henry. But why had Henry stuck by his childhood friend? Is friendship, too, merely a matter of habit? Was Henry so desperate that he was prepared to suffer Stanley's routine disloyalty and *infidelity*? Henry was a loner, unquestionably, and not by choice: his parents' age was, no doubt, one of the causes – they were not quite of the generation of his contemporaries' grandparents, but they were of a generation whose children had been born before the war; Henry's father was eighteen years older than Mr Croney whose laments for Stanley included the one that 'we grew up alongside him'.

No mention there of Curly who had come along only five years later. Curly considered himself an afterthought. His father, besotted by Stanley who was made in his image, loved Curly when he remembered to, and when he was reminded to by his wife who clawed the smoky air as though punch drunk when she tried to beat him for his hopelessly disguised infidelities.

She wasn't punch drunk, Mr Croney didn't hit her, she was merely drunk, gin and sweet vermouth, so drunk that she left meat in the oven to turn to charcoal, so drunk that she lost the hang of clock time and would wake Stanley to go to school at 3 a.m. and run a bath for his little brother as soon as she had packed him out the door into the freezing fog and obfuscated sodium light, so drunk that Mr Croney grew neglectful of his excuses. He saw the error of that particular way when he returned one night to find her sober because there was no more credit at the off-licence. Her fury when in that state was focused, hurtful, shaming; he felt he had no right to be alive. So first thing in the morning he hurried to the off-licence, paid her debt and advanced the shop £30, in cash, with a wink. An investment, he said to himself, an investment – and alcoholic oblivion is a blessing to her, it helps her to forget the terrible loss of her baby and should thus be encouraged. No amount of alcohol could inhibit her breakfast screams at yet another boiled wasp preserved in a jar of plum jam.

The Fowlers' old-fashioned house was Curly's refuge from home, his home from home. He first came by one frosty morning six weeks after his brother's funeral (directed by Fowler & Son) having shyly phoned to ask if he could sort through Stanley's electric model train set which Stanley had pooled with Henry's because the Fowler house was big enough to accommodate a permanent layout in an unheated semi-attic bedroom. The .oo octagon of track matted with dust rested on a trestle-table along with a streaky grey aluminium control box, carriages with greasy celluloid windows, an A-4 Gresley Pacific, a Merchant Navy class locomotive, a shunter with a broken wheel, an EDL17 0-6-2 still in its royal-blue-and-white pinstriped box because by the time Stanley had been given it he was past playing with model trains. Mrs Fowler suspected that Curly, too, was past that age. She had a feeling in her waters that Curly was, though he might not know it, in search of something other than metal Dublo and plastic Tri-ang. Mrs Fowler dusted around the track, excusing her negligence, watching Curly as he picked through toys he was interested in only as souvenirs of his brother. He picked up a cream metal footbridge, fondled it with puzzled familiarity, held it out to show her.

'That's the bridge. It's just like the bridge,' he said before he wept.

She comforted him. She made him hot chocolate. She made him drop scones with honey. She held his reticent hands and hugged him. When Henry came in from work experience (at Fowler & Son) she told her son that she and Curly had just been having a little talk. Henry was startled, and it showed. They sat, the three of them, at the breakfast-room table where he had so often sat with Stanley. Mrs Fowler made a gesture to Henry, the sort of gesture a different mother might have made to her son in the presence of a girl, a nodding smile of connivance which implied more than approval, which implied a duty to go for it. So Henry suggested to Curly that they have a kick-about on the lawn. It was frosty all that day, and the ground was slippy. Neither the sixteen-year-old nor the eleven-year-old could control the old sodden ball on the crunchy grass but they played happily, in earnest, straining to tackle, diving to save, deflecting the ball off Her Majesty's trunk, getting up a sweat and blowing white fire from their throats. When the dark came down on the garden they went inside for a tea of anchovy toast and lemon barley water.

That evening's panel on *Juke Box Jury* was Jack Good, Johnny Tillotson, Helen Shapiro and, making his only appearance on the show, Bobby Camino. Curly was also a fan, and hung on every word he had to say about the Dovells' 'Bristol Stomp' before he was shut out by Mr Fowler's chortling joke that 'They're more like the Bristol Zoo than the Bristol Stomp. That's hungry animals crying out to their keepers, that's what that is.' And Henry and Curly longed for the day when they would agree with him, without equivocation, without even a frisson of excitement at the wailing which defied propriety. That was the teatime when the Fowlers taught Curly canasta.

Then it was Henry and Curly, Curly and Henry. Curly wasn't a card, nor was Henry. Curly wasn't a caution the way his brother had been, he was as cautious as Henry. It was always Henry and Curly, in that order, according to age and experience. Henry took the boy they had somehow overlooked off his parents' hands, their cack-hands when it came to their younger one, now, terribly, their only one. They were happy, Mr and Mrs Croney, to let their boy hang around with their lost one's friend.

It never occurred to them, nor should it have, that there was anything mucky (a well-used word of Mr Fowler's) about this friendship. They were right. Henry and Curly never even talked of girls or sex. Stanley's death had relieved Henry of the pressure to compete in an adolescent contest which he'd not wanted to partake in. He was no longer obliged to boast of conquests which he hadn't made, hadn't the nerve to make, lacked the will to make. Had Stanley really believed him when he said he'd fingered Cathy Pelly, when he said that Sally Sanger had unzipped his Terylene trousers? He had only been echoing Stanley after all. Stanley had never expressed incredulity, had never questioned his seductive prowess. So he had believed him? Not on your life.

Henry was happy that the onerous obligations of mucky behaviour had been lifted. He was a loner in most regards – he had few friends other than Stanley and now Curly – so why not be a loner in sex too? It was a private matter, sex, not to be shared, not to be witnessed save by the morosely mocking eyes of the monochrome girls in the discreetly proportioned pocket magazines which he stole from the near-blind Mr Gough, the newsagent whose devotion to such magazines had brought him to that state, had brought him out in brown stains on his skin, had done for his hearing too. Henry could open the door to the shop without causing the sprung bell to ring, without disturbing Mr Gough, frotting and coughing in his cell of tobacco and flesh at the far end of the shop.

Henry knew it was wrong to steal these profane images. But stealing was appropriate because it augmented his shame, it doubled his sin, it increased the guilt attached to his betrayal of his parents with meaty tarts, it made sex conditional on crime even if that crime was venial and the sex was the glueing together of silky pages that were potent beyond their size. These thefts were, so far as he could recall, the only crimes he had ever committed. Try as he might he couldn't remember anything

42

half as bad. He was out of step with his contemporaries' judicious delinquency. He saw the good sense in not jaywalking. He was contemptuous of the kudos attached to getting (a girl) into trouble. And whilst other adolescents were swept along by the glandular revolution within their bodies and allowed it to determine their mores, Henry resisted the hormonal call. At the age of sixteen he was already the victim of a longing for the certainties and stasis of his comfy past.

Stanley had persuaded him to read books by writers with beards. He preferred tales of wartime aircrews' escapes after being shot down over occupied France. He enjoyed the pitch-fork's tynes in a haystack, the shy peasant girls, the radio transmitters disguised as sewing machines, the mortal sacrifices, the Gestapo beating testicles with rubber truncheons. He admired the looks of the men shown in the jacket paintings: tough yet kind, decent and modest, with regular brave blond acne-free features. They were adventurers with right on their side, heroes whose lives were uncontaminated by equivocation and impure thoughts. Henry lent Curly such memoirs as T.D.G. Teare's *Evader*, Bruce Marshall's *White Rabbit* and D. Baber's *Where Eagles Gather*. Curly had only just finished *Fugitives by Night* when Mrs Croney asked Henry to take the boy for a dental check-up.

Curly was soon anaesthetised, soon dreaming that Mr Etherington was the collaborationist dentist to whom Squadron-Leader Victor Wraxall had had to submit. He was grateful when he came round that Henry was with him. His mother so loathed the smells of gas and burning tooth enamel that she might have had a turn. Henry claimed – stoically? genuinely? – to enjoy those smells which are also undertakers' trade smells, the smells of crematoria which are also the smells of duty and profit.

This was not the only dream that aircrew yarns would prompt.

Curly dreamed of Stanley falling, parachuteless, from a fusel-age which burned to reveal an armature of riveted girders.

Stanley's howl as he plummeted through the night sky was the howl that Curly made as he woke before the body made contact with the sinuous lines of a marshalling yard where Wehrmacht troops patrolled between flaming braziers. He woke, twisted and sweating, uncertain where he was – where had the window moved to?

His howl of terminal fear woke Henry in the sleeping-bag along the other side of the small tent pitched beside a stream on a damp Cornish moor. That was the summer they took their bicycles on the train to Exeter and headed west. At Henry's insistence – he was *in loco parentis* and now working in the family business thus a routine witness to the result of quotidian rashness – they pursued his safe-cycling policy. Viz.: ride up hills, tonic for Achilles' tendons and hamstrings; dismount and push bicycles down hills because to achieve speeds of over thirty miles an hour on these precipitous gradients is a risky frivolity, a brief gratification of an appetite that is better suppressed. There were enough dangers without courting supplementaries – there were caravans listing and swaying like the callipygian buttocks of drug-tranced dancers; there were cars performing six-point turns in sunken lanes jammed by caravans; there were bulls sated on meadow grass and anxious to exercise; there were vipers on the heaths; there were sheep everywhere.

They bathed in hidden coves. They lay under the sun on cropped turf incised with rabbit paths. The confectioner's red of sunset delighted them. They learned not to pitch the tent near trees which were contorted and silently screaming because that was the way the wind went, whistling as it bullied. They cooked on a spirit stove and convinced themselves that bacon and beans so prepared tasted miles better. They got used to damp clothes, to rising at daybreak, to lying outside the tent feeling themselves part of the system to which the stars belonged, marvelling at the sidereal patterning and misnaming formations with confident ignorance. When they drank from burbling steams they were,

Henry insisted, refreshing and feeding their bodies as man had done since the dawn of time but without the intercession of engineers who had so denatured water that it is taken for granted rather than regarded as a gift from the Earth to its children, a gift from the Earth's core welling through strata of immemorial accretions to be lifted high as clouds and returned to earth in a cycle of beneficence and generative necessity.

Henry and Curly lunched on crisps outside pubs whose names proudly celebrated the West Country's criminal past: the Smugglers' Inn, the Skull and Crossbones, the Buccaneer, the Pirates' Nest, the Wreckers' Flare, the Slave Master's Arms. The descendants of criminals sported lavish widow's peaks which began between their eyebrows. Their arms were girt as telegraph posts and blue with tattoos from all the world's ports. Their faces were all avarice and cunning. They ran pubs with the same relish their forebears had brought to running slaves. They treated their customers, the grockles and emmets, with bonhomous contempt and smiling malice.

Henry asked a licensee called Dennis Jacka where they might camp nearby. Mr Jacka slid his tongue inside a nostril to think. Then he told them how to reach 'a beautiful spot' further down the wooded estuary. That was the afternoon Curly got sunburned. He stretched out prone squinting through tufts of grass towards the headland and the river's mouth, listening to the narcotic drone of bees in broom, getting the perspective wrong as he grew drowsy and dozed off. Henry sat, all the while, beneath a stunted tamarisk, neglectful.

It was too late when he rubbed sunblock into Curly's back and shoulders which had gone red as an angry glans.

The dogs arrived just after dusk, galloping across the scrubby plateau, their pelts bouncing with belligerent ire, their tongues like horizontal pink standards, barking war cries and followed by Dennis Jacka's cousin Ted Nancecarrow who had no teeth but made up for that lack with a string of convictions for assault,

ABH, GBH, affray, etc. He couldn't remember the number of foreigners he had fought for Cornwall and he never allowed anyone on his land. He carried a torch like a cosh, his stick quivered as though the hand holding it was in the throes of a fit. Henry and Curly used the crossbar of a bicycle as a ladder to the boughs of a sycamore. Curly was sore. He'd have been sorer still had the dogs known how to climb but they didn't because they were dogs. Ted Nancecarrow struck the tree with his stick, he referred to the dogs as 'my wolfs'. He struck them too. 'My wolfs is hungry,' he repeated. The torch's beam picked out a leaf, a grimace, a wrist, a sappy twig broken in the rush to escape the slavering fangs. 'Don't like strangers on my land . . . don't like strangers at all.'

He walked around the tent, prodding the canvas. He tried and failed to pull up a peg with his mud-crusted clumsy boot. He kicked over a jerrycan spilling all the water they had. He picked up a pack of sausages from beside the Primus stove and threw it to the dogs at the foot of the tree. They demonstrated their teeth, their greed, their ingestive urgency.

'They like their scran: don't you my wolfs? They're not too fussy about it neither. Eat anything, they would.'

'We didn't know,' said Henry. 'Please . . .'

Ted Nancecarrow toyed with the fearful rictus in the boughs. He took pleasure in the pleading whine – it meant that he had stripped the foreign trespassers of their dignity and English pride. They were almost as humiliated as victims with bleeding eyes and hairline fractures begging him to put down the adze. He took pity on himself: he couldn't chance it – another offence and he'd go down again, even if he was justifiably exercising a landowner's right. His most recent suspended sentence had fourteen months to run. What would his wolfs do without him? They might attack the wrong people – they had a taste for Meriel Spargo, had to be held back, and they always went for old Bob Nankivell because he'd never washed beneath his foreskin for forty or more years 'tis said. They might even be put to sleep.

'You two. You got ten minutes. I'll be back in ten minutes. And if you're still here . . . You want to learn to keep off of other people's land. Ten minutes I say.' He had saved face. He could live with himself. He clapped his hands and the dogs followed him out of Henry's and Curly's lives.

They cycled through the night, not knowing where they were going, ignoring maps, signposts, stars, anxious only to be far from that flat scrubland. Fear fuelled their tendons, pushed the pedals hard. They were oblivious to the sycamore's grazes and to the stiff hills. Their tyres purred. They passed hamlets, silos, byres, kennels, the illumined windows of hostile hearths. The swarthy bulk of a moor's escarpment slumped against the sky, a beast best left to lie. The world was every shade of black: slave, sump, crow, char. Clumsy clouds lumbered into each other, blind, bloated, slomo, piling up in a piggyback of obese buggers over the terrible trees. The night was loud with the shrieks and moans of creatures berating their fate and their want of shelter. When the rain came it was from a sluice that stretched from one horizon to the next. The road became a tide against them.

It was Henry who took the decision to turn back, to follow a lane beside a bridge across a swelling stream. Their clothes were soaked. The stony surface was no impediment however in the quest for shelter. They stood to pedal. Where the lane diverged uphill from the stream there were grouped trees high above the western bank. Up on the knoll which the lane led to there stood the intact chimney and ruined buildings of a former tin mine's engine house. Along the same contour, 400 metres away there were more buildings, unlit, discernible by the orthogonal pitch of their roofs, by their comforting straight lines. The rain made tympanic mayhem in the leaves above them but the trunks cut the wind. And no stream could rise, they reckoned, by a man's height overnight to flood the tent in a demi-glade. The were right about that.

Curly scrambled down the bank to fill the jerrycan Ted Nancecarrow had dented with his foot. They ate emergency chocolate, failed to tune into Radio Luxembourg because the rain had got to the batteries, cleaned their teeth of the cloying chocolate (at Henry's instruction). While the rain played ping-pong on the canvas Henry reminisced about all the times he and Stanley had got soaked to the bone – great old times. When Curly started snoring Henry hardly noticed even though this was not the boy's habit. He fell asleep and dreamed of rushing clouds, bicycles, coffins, trousers.

It was barely light when Curly howled. He twisted within his quilted blue nylon sleeping-bag. He drew it around him. He cried and apologised for crying. He managed to get outside before he vomited a streak of bile marbled with chocolate. Henry stood over him, tentative arm round the shoulder as he repetitively retched. Soon there was nothing left to express, but his stomach and gorge didn't know that and he jerked forth spasmodically. He ate grass like a dog. By the time that the sun rose over the hill beyond the stream Henry, too, was on all fours shitting from his mouth, writhing, blaming God and Cornwall. He crawled, he moaned as he spewed. When he got as far as the steaming bank of the stream he saw the leucous opacity of the water. It burbled and tumbled like blue-tinted milk, liquid Stilton. He stared at it wondering what had coloured it. He groaned as a ratchet was tightened in his belly. Sweat oozed from him, he was as wet as he would have been from total immersion. There was a hiatus between his seeing the clouded water and his realisation that this was the source of their sickness. Then he spied a dead minnow bobbing. He cursed the stream, he cursed the bully who had caused them to drink from it. When he spoke to say 'We've been poisoned Curly – look at this' his voice was hoarse, his throat was inflamed.

All that day they lay in the sun as pain played with them, now dull, now sharp, now in their joints, now in their innermost organs. There had been nothing in the water's flavour to indicate that it was contaminated – which was a solace of a sort. If it was tasteless then it couldn't be that bad, could it? He didn't want Curly's illness on his conscience, he didn't want the second brother haunting him, too. They hadn't the will or strength to swat the corpulent flies which leeched their blood. They resigned themselves to files of ants passing over their damaged bodies. It was Henry who suffered hallucinations; he'd drunk that much more water the night before. The trees mutated into jagged webs of metal and wire. Their leaves were oxidised blades and the sibilance of the breeze in those blades was deafening, a sussurant din as though conches were glued to his ears and he were being force-fed a Eustachian diet of sea, sea, sea. Each blade of glass owned a hue different to all others. There was a smell of scorched flesh in his sinuses. The soldiers who found them, foetally curved and twitching, were actually two schoolboys dressed in camouflage fatigues skiving from a CCF exercise to smoke Consulates (pure as a mountain stream) and drink scrumpy. Their inebriation and fear of being caught AWOL combined to make it two hours before they called an ambulance, which delivered Henry and Curly to the cottage hospital at Bodmin, whence they were released the next day by Dr Tarpley who advised them to boil water before drinking it. Their bicycles and tent had been stolen. They ran up whopping taxi debts.

Going on twelve years later Henry, a father of two with a throbbing molar, flipped through a glossy magazine in his dentist's waiting-room. In a drink supplement he found an ill-wrought article titled 'The Scrumpy Bar Kid'. The writer reminisced about bunking off from CCF field-days to drink coarse cider poured from the barrel into a jerrycan, about cycling

49

from one scrumpy bothy to the next on a Raleigh Spacerider. That was the marque and model of bicycle that Henry had lost. Henry ripped out the article, pocketed it. That would be a man to hunt down, to trace. He liked the idea of such detective work, of a quest with a cause.

Chapter Five

Clotted cream. Devonport Dockyard (proposed closure of). *Lorna Doone* on telly – 'and did you know Lorna was a made-up name?' Naomi reminiscing about a school trip to Appledore or her dad's friend Nat's Austin Somerset or her protestation that 'you don't have to be Jewish to stay at the Imperial but it helps'. The wreck of the *Torrey Canyon*. Harold and Mary Wilson's Scilly Isles bungalow. *The Boyhood of Raleigh*. Artistic potters. Prisons. Paddington Bear. Messy abstracts.

At any mention of the West of England Henry and Curly would mime ralphing, retching and reaching. No matter how obliquely it was alluded to it was enough to set them off. That holiday was a weld in their fraternal bond. They'd been through it together. They'd survived where minnows hadn't. Ben and Leonora, a.k.a. Lennie, grew up listening to their father and their Uncle Curly making the noises that they had just grown out of, baby noises and bad gurgles.

'I don't know,' said Mr, Fowler, looking over his spectacles from the abridged *Treasure Island* he was reading to Ben and Lennie, 'I don't know, a varsity man and all. I think your uncle's soft in the head I do.' Curly made a wailing bark and stumbled round the room clutching his tummy. Ben laughed and pointed. Curly picked him and swung him to and fro.

'Uncle Curly, Uncle Curly,' Lennie cried. She wanted to be lifted through the air too.

Mr Fowler looked on fondly, proudly. 'You'd have made such a funeral director Curly – you got a way with people. You're a people person.'

'What's a people person?' asked Lennie.

'I'm more a car person,' said Curly.

'People drive cars,' Mr Fowler pointed out.

'I got two cars,' said Ben, holding up three electric model hearses.

'You've got three,' said Curly. 'And what have I got?'

'You got a real Sitran.'

'Citro-ën,' corrected Curly, fussily. His CX GTI Turbo was parked outside. His DS21 was in his garage at home, less than a mile away.

'Two Citroëns, he's got. And they're both black. They use them as hearses in France,' claimed Mr Fowler.

'Ambulances,' said Curly.

'Close enough,' grinned Mr Fowler.

'Nee-nor, nee-nor, nee-nor, nee-nor,' repeated Ben the Ambulance.

Naomi poked her head through the serving hatch and told him to be quiet, to come and wash his hands before lunch.

The *Sunday Express* in the corner armchair was lowered and Henry asked, 'We ready then, I'm extra peckish.'

'Is Daddy going to eat all the crackling?' asked Ben.

''Slamb. No crackling on lamb. Come on!' insisted Naomi.

'Why no crackling on lamb?'

'Cause there isn't,' Henry told him.

'Why?'

'Because.'

'Because what?'

'Because . . . because. Because God gave lambs wool instead of crackling.'

'Can't eat wool – urgh.'

Mrs Fowler sieved flour into the roasting pan and scraped it with a wooden spoon. The noise made Curly shiver. He clenched his teeth and fists. Naomi drained the carrots: 'Butter them would you Curl.'

His knife bounced off the frozen half pound. He emitted an exasperated petulant tush. He flapped the fumous kitchen air with the knife. He inspected it 'Hasn't seen a steel in years,' he told Naomi, reproachfully.

'Ooh dear,' she said with parodic emphasis.

Curly looked hurt. 'It is, paradoxically, blunt knives which are dangerous. It's like keeping your body in trim. If you're fit you're not so likely to get injured. Tools need to be kept in trim too.'

'Well sharpen it then,' she said brusquely, sensitive to her failure to recover her figure after the birth of the children within a year of each other.

For four and a half years since Lennie was born she had dieted, subscribed to fads and partworks, adhered to the principle that if one calorie-free rusk is good for you then two calorie-free rusks must be better. But it hadn't made any difference to her tennis, and her golf had definitely improved – her handicap was down to seventeen, which was partly ascribable to the improved coaching of the new club pro Denny Groebe and partly, as her tactless partner Jill Tann too often joked, to her having 'more meat to put into the drive'.

'These,' said Curly, holding up an electric knife sharpener he'd found at the back of a drawer, 'do more harm than good – they hack at the blade, they leave it sort of serrated.'

'Curly!'

In the afternoon the children and their grandparents got into Curly's bouncy CX, and Henry and Naomi followed in the

Jaguar. They were off to Crystal Palace Park which despite the fire at the end of November 1936 which had consumed the great glass pavilion Mr Fowler regarded as the heart of 'his' London, a site Henry accepted with filial faith. He was keeping Curly's car in view and taking bets with himself on how long it would be before his father gave his eyewitness account of that fire when Naomi, hitherto unusually mute, asked: 'D'you think Curly's all right?'

He was tempted to answer 'Of course he's all right, he's my best mate' but Naomi's tone militated against a pat response.

He asked: 'What do you mean all right?'

'Well, you know, he's always over every Sunday . . .'

'The wine he brings is usually worth more than the entire meal.'

'I don't mean that. He's really generous, we all know that. It's . . . it's just, you know, the way he never brings anyone with him. He's thirty – and I mean, look at his birthday, pathetic.'

'You said you enjoyed it.'

'Yeah, course I did, lovely food and all that, delicious – but you know, ask him what he's got planned for his birthday and it's I'd like to take you both to Chez Nico.'

'So?'

'Well – why don't we meet his other friends? If he's got any. I mean does he have a girlfriend or anything?'

'There was Moira.'

'Three years ago that was Henry, at least.'

'And thingy, ahmm, the French one, Natasha.'

'Natalie. Henry – that was when he was living there.'

'I don't know – it's not the kind of thing I like to talk about with him.'

'Do you think he's queer and that's why we never meet his friends?'

'Curly?' Henry's incredulity was such that he turned towards

Naomi and narrowly avoided a cyclist who yelled an imprecation, waved a sinewy arm.

'God, look what you made me do.'

'I merely suggested that perhaps he is not as other men – apart that is from other men who go for other men.'

'What are you saying – he's a danger to the children?'

'Don't be so bloody melodramatic. And do look where you're going.'

'It's these humps in the road.'

'Well you know who put those there.'

'If you'd paid a blind bit of attention you'd know that Curly is totally 100-per-cent against traffic calming. His whole thing is to make it go faster . . .'

'So more kids get run over.'

'So congestion is – what's the word, alleviated. And if you want to know how I know he's not a homo it's because of your precious chum Freddie Glade.'

(Freddie Glade, b. 21.1.42. Aquarian – but on the cusp, luv. Garden designer, 'exterior decorator', artist in flowers, the creative florist's creative florist. Naomi's occasional tennis partner. Colourful dresser. The front hedge outside the Crittall-windowed house he had inherited from his parents by Sydenham Wells Park was topiarised into the shape of a poodle.)

'What about Freddie?' Naomi's tone was cold, urgent, suspicious.

'D'you know what Curly calls him? The cottage gardener.'

'So?'

'Well he wouldn't call him that if he was one too – would he?'

Naomi cocked her head quizzically: 'Uh?'

Some seconds passed before Naomi, a woman and thus antipathetic towards slang which she regarded as a male-generated pollutant of pure language, remembered what a cottage was.

'Oh that's horrible, that's so unfair – just bloody smug. Offensive.'

'Only the truth isn't it?'

'It dirties everything doesn't it, that sort of talk. Like mucky schoolboys. Anyway just 'cause Curly calls him that doesn't prove anything. Haven't you heard of pots and kettles?'

'I know, I know,' Henry sighed, 'takes one to know one.'

'Quite!'

'As a matter of fact Curly only calls him that because there was a time when every time Curly went to the club Freddie would make a pass at him, want to get in the shower with him, all that. Real pain he was.'

'Hmmhh. He could be exaggerating. I'm sure Freddie's not that bad.'

'How would you know? Or are you going to tell me he's a rampant hetero now? Freddie the lady-killer. The Don Juan of Sydenham Hill. They called him the Dulwich Casanova. Women! Can you resist this man? Thrill to his lithp. Quake as he flaps his writht. See him minth.'

'You're being really cheap.'

'*You* are being really ridiculous . . . I mean, Curly was only saying the other day that he wants to have kids of his own.'

Naomi laughed pityingly. 'And queers don't?'

They were still bickering when Henry turned into the Thicket Road car park. Lennie was high above Curly on his shoulders.

'Grandpa says you been dilly-dallying.' Ben looked at his grandfather to make sure he had got the word right.

They walked up the worn, grassless slope past the noxious blasts from the cafeteria's humming extractor, past the crates of soft-drinks empties and the brimming refuse bins. 'A hearty meniscus on mine if you please,' said Mr Fowler, as always, when his eyes came level with the surface of the boating lake. It was a wonder that the water didn't spill over, it was that high, lapping at the edge where refugees from domesticity sat on their X-folders surrounded by six packs, vacuum flasks, seething bait in jars, telescopic keepnets, alarm clocks, rods on rests. A flotilla of tethered brown boats bobbed on the wind-chopped water. Tiro arms jerked oars from their rowlocks, causing them to dig deep in the dark water, fishermen looked up from their intense absorption in newspaper reports of the disgusting sex acts performed on footballers by unwitting dancers in hotel rooms and screamed at the boat hirers not to disturb the fish.

'You never want to swim in there,' Mr Fowler told Ben, 'on account of the Weil's Disease, from rats. I've seen a few taken with that.'

'Can't swim,' said Ben, 'yet.'

'Course you can't. I was forgetting. You get to forgetting when you get old.'

'And you get to remembering,' said Naomi putting an arm round him and kissing his cheek.

'Oh yes – what memories.'

'He's off,' said Henry to his mother. He'd bet himself that Mr Fowler would start before they reached the Irish elks.

'You're so, oh I don't know,' said Curly with Lennie's hands over his eyes, 'exacting.'

'Kettle pot black,' Henry was quick off the mark. Curly grinned. Henry heard the echo.

Henry took his mother's arm.

Mr Fowler began: 'It was a fellow called Frizzel and you know I'd never have remembered his name otherwise but we put him to rest and then because Grandma was out that evening I went and had a drink with – oh, blimeycrikes whatever were he called . . .'

'Ridley – from Strathleven Avenue,' said Mrs Fowler who'd reminded him so many times before.

'Ridley. Thassit. Ridley. Goshowcaniforget?'

'There're the Irish elks.' Henry pointed to the multiplicity of tines and bezels proud of the araucaria, high above the boating lake.

'Rishells!' proclaimed Lennie, her chin on Curly's crown.

'Rissoles,' repeated Curly, then: 'Irish elks – they lived on the Isle of Man.'

'I didn't go there,' said Lennie.

'And you don't want to go. They beat people with sticks called birches.'

'When they're naughty,' confirmed Lennie.

'No. No – just because they don't like them.'

Naomi smiled a little smile to herself and tried to catch Henry's eye.

'So then this Ridley chap . . .'

'He died in the war,' said Mrs Fowler, 'the Japs got him. His sister married one of those Pook boys.'

'That's right Mother. We went to the new road-house they called it, on the corner of Beulah Hill and Spa Hill – opposite the lodges there. They'd hardly finished building it. Brand new. Very snazzy. Well we hadn't been in there more than about ten minutes when we hear all these fire engines . . . They had 'em coming from Streatham and Norbury and Croydon. Then some chap come in the bar and say the Crystal Palace is in flames. That was one way of putting it. I never seen anything like it. The whole sky. Like Vesuvius erupting – all orange and yellow, colours you'd never have thought of, pink and blue and green. Armageddon it was and, ooh, what's the other one, what's the other one?'

'Apocalypse,' said Mrs Fowler.

'That's the one. Oh yes. If I hadn't known it was the Crystal Palace I'd have said it was the Day of Judgement come.'

They passed the children's zoo with its sad menagerie of guinea fowl, Aleppo cockerels, fancy ewes, lop-eared rabbits, hamsters. Ben began to run. Mr Fowler and Naomi hurried to keep pace with him.

'Careful of the bridge, Ben!' shouted Naomi.

Ben stopped on the middle of the bridge.

'Monsters,' he yelled triumphantly.

Monsters. At the core of the heart of Mr Fowler's London and Henry's London and, now, evidently, Ben's London were the monsters. Triceratops, megalosaurus, megatherium, ichthyosaurus, pterodactyls, palaeotherium – three generations of the Fowler family were bound together by their excitement at the full-scale painted metal models of these antediluvian beasts who stood on hillocks and swam in ponds. It was an hallucination of prehistory, a secret known only by deepest South Londoners. Ben willed them to be real. He wanted the jaws to snap, the teeth to rend, the leathery reptile skin to ripple in predatory anticipation.

'It's here where we watched it from,' continued Mr Fowler. 'All the roads up the hill was blocked. Ghouls! If there hadn't been so many of them they might have saved it but the fire engines couldn't get through. So we got in old Ridley's car, it was a Singer he had, and went all the way round, down Sylvan Hill and Hamlet Road and that . . . Like the *Titanic* it was, like the *Titanic*. Right down here – how far away was we? – half a mile at least, we could hear the metal groaning, terrible sound it made.'

'It was like the monsters coming to life wasn't it Grandpa?'

'That's just what it was like.'

'And tell us about the fire lighting up the monsters' teeth Grandpa.'

'They shone in the light they did. All the colours of the rainbow. And they looked like they was ready to pounce. And the flames they played on the monsters' skin so they looked like they was moving.'

Ben squirmed with fairy-tale delight. Mr Fowler jumped, rather daintily, towards him, hands clawing playfully. The little boy ran from his grandfather who hobbled after him: 'The monsters need feeding, the monsters are hungry, fee fi fo fum.' Ben hid behind his mother.

'Where is he? Where's that tasty little morsel?' Ben squeaked and shuddered as Mr Fowler picked him up and pretended to bite like an ogre, growling, grimacing, crossing his eyes.

'Grandpa's king of the monsters,' Ben told Henry. 'We all used to be like the monsters didn't we.'

'You must ask Uncle Curly about that,' replied Mr Fowler. 'He's a varsity man. So far as I'm concerned I'm not descended from any reptile – but I expect Curly'll tell us different.'

'Whahat?' laughed Curly.

'How many letters is it you got after your name?' asked Mrs Fowler.

'I'm a civil engineer, I don't know anything about evolution.'

'Weren't we like the monsters then?' Ben asked.

'Maybe,' shrugged Curly, 'but so long ago that no one can remember.'

'Want to get down,' Lennie demanded.

'There.' Curly stooped. 'The thing is, Ben, you're like your dad, and your dad's like his dad, your grandpa, and your grandpa is like his dad, your great-grandpa. You're your dad's descendant – that's what it's called.'

'But Daddy's tall and Grandpa's short.'

Mr Fowler stood beside Henry: the six-inch disparity in their height was obvious.

'Yes,' said Curly, 'but that's because of Grandma.'

'She's short too – aren't you Grandma.'

'Oh you're too clever for me Benjy,' Mrs Fowler admonished him. Clever was not a word of approbation in her lexicon. He was right. She was short.

'I'm not *Benjy*.' He stomped along the path beside the pond, clasped the low railing and gazed in defiant wonder at the gleaming khaki paint on the crazed surface of the iguanodon's tail.

Naomi shook her head. 'He's got a real thing about being Ben. It's a macho thing – he thinks Benjy is wet. And Benny.'

'I remember Henry's six-guns,' smiled Mrs Flowler. 'Every day he came home from school he'd put on his holster.'

When they walked on round the pond Curly, straggling back, observed how Henry towered above his parents and gently laughed to himself when the phrase *genetic caprice* came to him.

Chapter Six

Henry Fowler prided himself on his sense of continuity, on his appreciation of the generations' cycles. He anticipated the first day of Ben's apprenticeship with prospective longing and with nostalgia for the lad he had been and for the trade itself in those days when every lichened headstone was sun-dappled and stroked by summer breezes. No sooner, he often reflected to Curly, have we ceased to be someone's child than we become someone's parent. We take our parents' places and play their old roles. We repeat their mistakes – it's in our genes to do so. We learn about their imperfections – not that it lessens our love for them. Some of the stories that Henry's heard about his father as a young man. Blimey O'Reilly! And Mr Fowler didn't deny them, didn't shout down his friends and colleagues who told them in his presence. Indeed he was rather chuffed to be represented as a bit of a daredevil, as a bit of a joker, letting down tyres, peeing in beer glasses, putting on funny voices over the phone (Jews and Arabs a speciality). He made Henry think of himself as a sober sides in comparison. Nonetheless Henry modelled his paternal mores on his father's.

Henry's adult topographies did not diverge from those he had known as a child. His first marital home had been little more than a mile from his parents'. And when they moved, at Naomi's insistence, the summer after Lennie was born they were still only ten minutes' drive away. That took a bit of getting used to though.

It was the view that was the problem for Henry. The megalopolis was spread beneath him. From the house on Ringmore Rise he could look right across the London Basin. It was – and everyone agreed – awesome, magnificent. People'd kill for a view like this, he thought.

That's the Sally Army college on Champion Park – you know, by KCH. Oh and isn't the Barbican tiny. Look at the Nat West Tower – are they ever going to finish the top? Hampstead. Highgate. Holloway. It's like being in an aeroplane. Those vapour trails! That sunset! Sunsets like that are almost edible – they're cassata. The terracotta tower of Imperial College signalled Curly's whereabouts on Thursday afternoons, which was when he lectured. You could sit here all day and just watch the weather. Far far away, far beyond the lucent scum of particulates and emissions which flop across the city, rises Harrow Weald, the woody horizon at the extremity of this scene. Harrow Weald, where they had had their wedding reception. In memory of that day Henry Fowler calls it the Golan Heights.

It was the twin ziggurats of Dawson's Heights which dominated the foreground. Henry was convinced that their inhabitants were work shy if not actively criminal. It was not however the proximity, on the next knoll, of this social housing project which caused him to experience an inchoate unease. It was the fact that the house on Ringmore Rise was linked to London's immensity. Clean Air Acts and kindred legislation had done for smog and London Peculiars. The views were longer, clearer. Petrol haze couldn't begin to match the good old pollutants' toxic gauze – the blanket it spread was mere froth beside the rich head conjured from chimneys' belching ooze. When they used to cycle up here as boys Stanley's promised land of Up West was buried, invisible. Which, so far as Henry was concerned, it could remain.

'You'd never,' pronounced Curly, 'get impressionism nowadays. Would you? No cause for it. You could say, only *could*, mind you . . . you could say that it was painting's coming to terms with industrialisation's environmental consequences. The artist's response to filthy air . . . Looking at the world through a sort of smeared screen.'

'Could just have been that they had bad eyesight,' said Henry, who had recently buried a painter with cataracts.

'Henry! That's Nazi,' Curly reproved him. 'Degenerate art and all that. You know – product of malformed eyes . . . diseased minds. Perfidious bollocks. You need a photorealist for it now – it's so incredibly *sharp*.'

Henry didn't want to look at it. Not simply out of incuriosity but because despite being in the reassuring postal district of SE23 Ringmore Rise was insufficiently hermetic. Indeed it wasn't hermetic at all. Henry abhorred the sheer quantity of light and sky. There was so much of everything.

He thought of himself severally – as father, husband, bearer of the familial tradition, loving son, reputable undertaker, loyal subject of his sovereign, reliable friend in a crisis, member of Dulwich and Sydenham Golf Club, member of Sundridge Park Golf Club, a safe driver (one of his little jokes – he's talking cars, not golf), a sympathetic listener, environmentally responsible, intolerant only of intolerance, etc. He never thought of himself as a Londoner.

That was because he thought of himself as a *South* Londoner, a South-east Londoner. His London stretched across the hills from Honor Oak to South Norwood, it was bounded by Dulwich and Penge. It undulated relentlessly, up and over. Its roads followed the paths of ancient lanes, twisting through woods and across commons. They were yeoman's roads which headed for the promised land of the Garden of England which was also the Garden of Eden (that fecundity, those abundant hop yards, those bulging orchards). These roads were natural. He believed that, and he would say so to rile Curly who dismissed them as pre-Euclidian and who argued that England would remain a backward country so long as it refused to adopt a grid system for its cities' streets. Henry associated grids with central London, with the rectilinear maze of Marylebone and Bloomsbury. Grids were not a feature of provincial life, and it was a provincial life he led among the brick-covered hills which had once been westernmost Kent. We're South Londoners so we wear brick next to the skin: Mr Fowler had instructed him thus when he was just a nipper and it was a dictum which he passed down to Ben and Lennie.

South Londoners are not Londoners. South Londoners are *South* Londoners. They turn their back on the Smoke. When they prosper they buy swank houses in Chiselhurst, Downe, Woodcote Village, Godstone, Brasted Chart, places with plenty of trees, tile hanging and white wicket fences. The Smoke is what is attached to South London, not vice versa. Henry knew that such an assertion ignored the metropolitan bent to centrifugence, that it took no account of chronology, sequence, cause, rail spread. He knew too that he was sentimentally right.

It was with defiant pride that he would look up from his diary to tell Naomi that he hadn't been to the West End for ten months. Naomi was different. She had her shopping, her friends. Their joke was that she would pass on in a boutique's fitting room and that he would go during a service in a chapel of remembrance. Henry Fowler expected to live all his life in South London. He expected too that his children would follow that example. He considered himself blessed in the presence of the trees, the bricks, the slopes, the spires. This was his enchanted garden.

The familiar never ceased to surprise him: the glimpses of

the estuary from between the houses on Honor Oak Road; the palaces of the men who invented beef extract and chocolate biscuits, metal polishes and lithographic processes; the quaint toll-gate on the common; the escarpment of Sydenham Hill and the houses piled on top of each other over its slopes; the ever-tanned Bavarian whose stock-brick villa on Dulwich Wood Avenue had metal spikes along its roof ridge like those which had once protruded from his compatriots' helmets; the railway station buried in a wild wooded gulley; the Horniman Museum's shrunken heads which he had never noticed till the boiling summer night the Tetouan Conservatory Orchestra played there and Curly, then in his Moroccan phase, insisted they all go and watch the musicians with carious smiles and fezzes; the white pigeon lofts beside the allotments off Hamlet Road; the Gothic house which smelled of gas from the old dentist who had lived there all his life – the show hydrangeas around it feasted on the pulp of fifty years' diseased molars in the flower-beds; the forlorn arches which had once supported the viaduct of the High Level Railway, a tardy casualty of the Crystal Palace's destruction, commemorated by High Level Drive from which ran a cul-de-sac called Vigilant Close; the television transmitters at Crystal Palace, Beaulieu Heights and Rocombe Crescent just behind the house on Ringmore Rise, the Eiffel Towers of South London, Henry called them, and we've got three of them. Who needs Paris, eh?

And there was always something he hadn't seen before. Not something new. No, a chipped plaster gargoyle above a window or a weeping tree or a path between garden walls or a railway carriage made into a summer-house exposed by a freshly cropped hedge. There were routes he had taken countless times, whose details were fixed in his memory but which were never entirely known, nooks which had previously gone unremarked. 'Can't remember seeing that before' was so common a cry that Ben and Lennie would mimic it. Likewise: 'There used to be a garage/corner shop/dressmaker just here – didn't notice that it'd gone.' It was like a marriage. The more you know someone the more there is to know, and it's the anticipation of tiny, everyday discoveries that whets our appetite for each other: that, in Henry's opinion, was love's crux, that perennial willingness and need to dig deep, deeper into another soul.

Henry's love for his London, for that London which was the only place he had ever known, was so intense, so normal and of such endurance that he believed that it was reciprocated. He believed that the bond was mutual, that his link to the land beneath the bricks, the lawns, the paving slabs, the hardcore, the shrubs, the pipes, the sheaths of cables, the ragstone, the henges of headstones was acknowledged by the land itself which spoke to him because it was connected to him by paternal and grandpaternal election. This was the land that immemorial Fowlers had chosen, and it spoke to Henry in gratitude for that patronage. It sent him, by means which he could not discern, messages of oneness and fidelity. It acknowledged his loyalty to it.

Henry grew old with his land, he accepted its blemishes. Even changes alleged to be for the better – the filling in of potholes, the clearing of condom sites overgrown with ground elder and buddleia and webbed with torn tights, the renovation of arsoned houses, the removal of the benches where sex offenders sat and masturbated beneath dripping chestnuts, the replacement of the corrugated-iron bus shelter on Gypsy Hill by a glass one which made it difficult for Maddy the Mad Mick to give ten-bob blow-jobs in relative privacy – were blemishes. They were blemishes not because Henry approved of these places and the activities which they had formerly been used for but because they maculated the pure land of his earliest memories, some of which were not actually his memories but syntheses of his infantile remembrances and of his father's, honed by usage and already being passed down to Ben and Lennie. Their mnemonic vaults were filled with matter whose provenance was familial rather than personal.

We delude ourselves when we assume that our memories are exclusively our own: they belong to a common store that we share at different times of our life with parents, guardians, lovers, spouses, children, especially children. They are transmitted by repetition, anecdotally, accidentally: we all remember people we have never met, have never even seen in photographs, who died before we were born, before we were sentient. Henry did meet his Great-Uncle Arth once, shortly before his fourth birthday, at the Star and Garter Home on Richmond Hill where the old man was a tallow head poking from a pile of rugs with wheels beneath them. It was a head which had suffered multiple misfortunes and which bore the scar of every one of them. It frightened Henry who never forgot the way its milky eyes fixed on him and its mouth's working corner articulated the words 'the Boche . . . the Boche' before it got back to its task of dribbling.

Those were the words which Henry thought it had spoken but his parents' memory, when he mentioned the matter at the time of Arth's death in 1958, was different. They were adamant that Henry had misheard: why would Arth have been talking about the Boche when he was a victim of the Boer War? It was at Magersfontein that he had left the back of his head, not Ypres. Henry was mistaken. Furthermore, he was insulting Arth's memory by suggesting that he had even mentioned the Boche.

There was another Arth whom Henry's memory would dredge up, a gay and sprightly Arth who bore his wounds lightly, whose wheelchair was decorated with hop-bines, whose party trick was to spit plum stones the length of a room. He loved to goose the ladies, this Arth did, he always had his good hand up someone's skirt, he was such a so-and-so. Henry could picture him with sureness – there was Arth, with his head on one side, with a basket of plums beside him on a shady veranda smiling mischievously at a woman who had turned to slap him but whose ire melted when she saw his face. This Arth brought out the pity in people. Henry had never met him. But he had known him all his life. And Naomi knew him too though she fancied he was a grubby old bore: Naomi's Arth had a different face from Henry's Arth. Ben and Lennie wondered when they were going to meet Arth who sounded silly and was dead.

And when were they going to the Norfolk Broads where Grandma and Grandpa went on a motor boat two years before the war and which Daddy told them such stories about? And what was the *war*? It was, Ben told Lennie, like work, it sounded a bit like work, or maybe it was like lunch – things happened before the war like they happened before work, people were different after lunch. Breakfast? Yes, Lennie darling, war must be like breakfast. Hickling, Horning, where? Where was it that Grandpa and his friend Cyril got the ducking in the weedy water that made them panic and think they'd die? Why does the water look higher than the land? What's the name of the house where the black-face sheep live? I thought you'd seen them Daddy. Why weren't you there Daddy? It was *before* the war. Weren't you born before the war? Those black fissured bones pushing out of the flat water are broken jetties. You *must* have been there, you've told us so much about it. Please tell us why you aren't in the photos, and why do they have crinkly edges.

There is nothing like black and white for fixing the way a place should be for ever. So much of the South London which Henry wished Ben and Lennie to learn to love and to respect as their familial heritage was now to be found only in black and white, in old leather albums. They were so inculcated with that past that when they drove alongside Peckham Rye Common they wondered where the horse fair was and they berated the wicked gypsies who mistreated their animals and never washed their greasy black hair. They didn't know what *go to the dogs at Catford* actually meant. Something to do with raining cats and dogs? But they choroused the phrase whenever that suburb was mentioned or broached. When Mr and Mrs Fowler had taken the infant Henry to Herne Hill to see their resentful, childless friends Dorry and Bill they would push him in his pram to Ruskin Park where Henry liked nothing better than to watch old people playing bowls. More than thirty years later with Dorry and Bill no longer friends of the Fowlers Henry would drive his children to the road where they had lived (and might still live), put his children in their double buggy and make his way across the park to the bowling green where he would long for an epiphanic souvenir of the child he had been. He hoped too that Ben and Lennie would share the fascination he had once had for the old people's ritual movements, demure uniforms, stooped scampering. He imagined that one day he might play this covertly vicious, emotionally costive game and that years later, in their dotage which he would never see, Ben and Lennie would take it up watched by their children and grandchildren. He anticipated that prospect with a pleasure which was alloyed only by his worry about what Lennie's married name might be. It wasn't a matter over which, he acknowledged, he could realistically expect to have total control: it wasn't every surname that would sit as well with Leonora as Fowler did. What if she were to marry Tim Prosser's nipper who was just a few months older? Or one of the O'Rourkes' ever-increasing brood? Leonora O'Rourke . . . it's too much of a mouthful. Naomi's incredulous indifference to this problem disappointed Henry just as much as her mockery of him for his insistence to the children that they should, on their Sunday walks, go down the street of collegiate diapered houses called Jews Walk – a diversion they tolerated because it took them by Freddie Glade's house and the lonicera hedge sheared with formidable precision into the shape of a poodle.

'Did he really make it himself?' Ben would ask.

'He did.'

'Why? Why did he make it?' Lennie was insistent.

'I suppose he wanted a dog,' said Henry.

'It's not a real dog you know,' said Lennie. 'He could have bought a puppy.'

'He probably . . . just . . . felt like making it.'

'Why?'

'Why? Well. Well, ah, he – he doesn't have a little boy and a little girl who take up all his time asking him questions he doesn't know the answer to.'

'Why doesn't he?'

Even though they were across the road from the green poodle and descending hand in hand towards the ponds in Sydenham Wells Park Henry looked behind him towards the green pantiled house before he replied, *sotto voce*: 'He doesn't have anyone to be their mummy. He's not lucky like me.'

And they skipped merrily down the gentle slope.

Chapter Seven

The flowers at Freddie Glade's funeral!

And, thought Henry Fowler, the pansies! Pew upon pew of celebrity florists and telly gardeners and horticultural consultants and lawn doctors and petal sculptors and rockery gurus and green-fingered gingers and nameless celebs and telly barons and a national newspaper editor whom Henry took for an unsuccessful golf pro and moron journalists who special-pleaded the case that floral arrangement was the new rock and roll.

Henry attended at Naomi's insistence. Busman's holiday, he complained. He was glad, though, of the chance to be there as a civvy and to scrutinise the procedures and performance of Messrs Meckiff & Miller, Funeral Directors. It cheered him no end that one of M & M's junior employees wore cracked black plastic shoes, that another had decorative crescents of filth beneath his fingernails and seborrhoeic epaulettes on his shiny jacket.

'Hullo Henry, old son. Keeping a beady on the opposition then?' Verdon Meckiff joshed him in the shadowy cloisters after the service. Henry grinned noncommittally.

'Wouldn't have guessed that the deceased was your cup of tea,' Verdon went on, falsely innocent. Then, with a stagey drop of his bearded jaw as though afflicted by a sudden *aperçu*: 'Henry! You haven't started shopping on the other side of the street have you?'

Henry grunted, sighed, spoke wearily: 'Leave it out Verd . . . I'm on supportive-husband duty – Freddie was Naomi's tennis partner, believe it or not. She's choked.'

'Spoke out of turn – sorry Henry.'

'Accepted. Weren't to know. They won a couple of cups. Mixed doubles. Club champions. That was a while back, mind you.'

'Oh-huh. Didn't have him down as the sporty type. I didn't know him like you did, of course. You know, seen him around. I'm surprised it's a C of E – I always had him down, you know, as, uh, as a Jew. If you don't mind my – I mean I know Nao . . .'

'It's all right Verd . . . He *was*. I mean he had been. But soon as his parents passed on he jumped ship. Couldn't find a brand of Judaism camp enough I shouldn't wonder.'

'What a bender ch? . . . But I liked that quiz – ufff – you know, he used to be on. Oh what was it called?'

'*Make My Dahlia.*'

'That's the one. Very droll. And she was a bit of an elbow bender that totty.'

'Jane Hare,' said Henry.

'Jane Hare – that's the one. Shall I tug your root Mr Glade . . . Terrible way to go.' Verdon Meckiff's voice nearly broke with the sincerity of his funeral-directorial concern.

'Doesn't bear thinking of.'

'I suppose you could say he went doing what he loved.'

Buggering boys?

No. Freddie Glade died crimping the topiary poodle that was his pride, his joy, his trademark – he had it on his letter-head.

It's the same old story: a blustery day, a wobbly stepladder, a hedge trimmer with a dodgy safety catch.

Henry asked: 'Did he really take off his head?'

'Near as dammit. What's 'e called? Sstt – chum o' yours – copper with the lupus and the squeaky voice . . .'

'Dai Turnbull?'

'*That*'s the feller . . . Reckoned a hit man with a chain-saw couldn't have done a better job . . . He cut an ear off the poodle as well,' Verdon added gravely.

Six youths on community-service orders took four hours to clean the pavement, gutter and road of blood. They never joyrode again.

'Guess it'll grow out won't it . . . Go to seed . . . Turn into just another hedge, any old hedge,' Henry mused ruefully.

His appetite for nostalgia and for its sibling, self-pity, was so keen that he was able to mourn the disappearance of a parochial folly before it happened. No matter that he had previously regarded the ten-foot-long indeciduous poodle, like its late maker, with a grudgingly tolerant disdain. Now that it was to be lost to *him*, now that it was to become another blemish on his patrimonial patch, he discovered a well of affection for it, he recognised its value as an eccentric landmark, he wanted to go and see it, to fix it for ever among the memories he collected and curated for future Fowlers.

'Must have taken a fair old spot of upkeep,' observed Verdon. 'Shame really, fellow of his talents with no one to pass it on to. There'll have been a bit of wedge there too.'

'There will indeed: *Dappled Glade*, *Leafy Glade*, *Ever Glade* – think about it . . . what was it, boof, five? seven? years when he was never off the telly.'

'More like ten, Henry. And all his book writing.'

'All right for some, eh? Do we know the identity of the bum bandit who has copped the wad?'

'As they say.'

'In their line of business.'

'We like to call at the *back* door,' Verdon rejoined. 'Noo – we do not know which particular plague-ridden bender just won the pools. The solicitors are what you'd call terminally discreet. M-A-N-C-H-E-S. Pronounced, would you believe, *man cheese*. You can see why they got his patronage.'

'You know it's something I couldn't never figure – how did he keep it out of the papers?'

Verdon was exaggeratedly incredulous: 'Come on, old son. There's no story is there. Freddie Glade and rent-boy? Freddie Glade takes it up the gary? I mean, it's like, y'know – Gorby discovered to have mark on head, or . . . or Pope shits in the woods. Now, Freddie Glade comes out as *hetero* – now you're talking.'

'And pigs might fly,' nodded Henry.

'Pre-cise-ly.'

'Look. *I* must actually. Fly. Naomi.'

'Self-fulfilling prophecy old son. Be seeing you. Look how you're going.'

The cloister cypresses reminded Henry of an oleographic repro-duction of a Victorian painting on the landing in his parents' house: those trees, a dozen nuns, raspberry cirrus, an intimation of happy death, of heaven even. He hadn't looked at it in years. He felt an unwonted surge of affection for Freddie as he walked along the outside of the brick arcade, which was unfamiliar to him – only two miles from home, yet he'd never previously set foot in the place, dedicated to St Blaise, patron of the throat: one reason, no doubt, why Freddie had stipulated it. Another would be that this Anglo-Catholic church's ritual was even more elaborate than the usual run of such smoky Guignol. Henry imagined that each of the hieratic battalion which officiated wore beneath his chasuble a studded leather bollock holster and a bolt through the glans. And the taste for incense's choking reek must be determined by sexual preference like the taste for poodles, mauve, walnut coffins, art and antiques – all the things that the family man with a proper job and responsibilities has no time to like. Nor the inclination.

Naomi, who had sobbed to exhibition level throughout the service, was standing outside the church's showy west front with a hanky to her face, with Ben and Lennie clinging to her and Curly doing staunch backup work. Henry didn't know the three other people with them, a buxom Titian and two lean, crop-haired men. They formed one of twenty or so groups, passing their germs on to each other's cheeks, gripping arms in competitive caring. Henry, exiting the cloisters, was wondering how many of the mourners had actually known Freddie and how many were what his trade knows as vultures: given Freddie's predilections he had probably known the lot of them.

'Where the hell have you been Henry?' Naomi asked.

Grieving faces turned. Henry winced at her loudness. Ben and Lennie scowled at him with their mother's accusatory eyes.

'I was just having a word with Verd there.'

'It's a *funeral* Henry, not an effing trade convention.'

Henry's expression manifested an evident puzzlement which further stoked Naomi's ire.

'Henry, this is about life . . . death. D'you see? Someone has died. This is not about swapping gossip and . . . and picking up tips from other bloody funeral directors. You're a mourner, not some . . . you're not here to do industrial espionage.'

Henry was mildly affronted. 'I don't think Fowler & Son have got anything to learn from Meckiff & Miller.'

The buxom Titian mouthed 'Whoops!' over Naomi's shoulder.

Naomi sobbed incredulously: 'You really don't get it do you . . . you . . . He's just a number to you. Isn't he? You aren't even working and he's just a number. Another day, another body, another box.'

Henry shook his head at her miscomprehension. He realised

that, in their nineteen years of marriage, he had never previously been to a funeral with Naomi.

He had lived to that day in complacent ignorance of what sort of mourner-profile she would possess, of how such an occasion might affect her. And despite her turning away with Ben and Lennie knotted to her, despite his humiliation in witnessing his adored family stumble like one misbegotten sexiped across the blowy yard so that Naomi might express her grief to another group, he was uxoriously proud of how touched she was, of how wholeheartedly she had entered into the spirit of the event, of how she had responded the way any funeral director would have wished. Verdon was doing something right, then. Henry was jealous.

'Henry. This is Lavender,' Curly said. His hand tentatively contacted the buxom Titian's lower back. 'Lavender Beard, Henry Fowler.'

Henry nodded offhandedly at the woman whilst watching Naomi hugging strangers and dabbing her streaked eyes and stroking Lennie's bob and gesturing. Lavender Beard followed his eyes to demonstrate her sympathy for him and to forgive his brusqueness: 'They're never easy, these partings . . . The English way of death . . . The embarrassment of it all . . . Are we allowed to cry . . . I sometimes wonder if anyone even knows how to cry. Good for her.'

Portings, dearth. Her accent was New England aping the old English of black-and-white films.

'Naomi's Jewish – they've got a different . . . uh. It's a . . .'

'Let's say they're not bound by a Protestant strait-jacket.'

'Something like that,' Henry agreed.

'It's the real English disease,' said Lavender, 'inhibition. It's a cultural . . . it's a behavioural virus.'

'Didn't appear to affect Freddie,' Curly observed.

'Well if he was as much of a nelly as you make out . . .'

'Didn't you know him then?' Henry asked, surprised.

Lavender Beard smiled and whispered: 'I'm a gatecrasher. Promise not to tell.'

'We're going straight on after. It'd have been logistical mayhem if Lavender hadn't come,' Curly explained.

'And I've got this thing about widow's weeds,' she trilled. She was wearing a tightly cut black grosgrain suit with a peplum and a hobble skirt, a sort of black boater with a veil, high black courts, a jet choker above a thick lardy roll of cleavage.

'Ah . . . Where you off to?'

'Newhaven . . . Going over to Rouen for a couple of nights.'

Henry gaped, unwittingly. Curly noticed. He grinned slyly, like a child who has behaved with unprecedented self-determination. Curly . . . Rouen . . . With a vamp, a size 16 vamp maybe – but what a piece of homework, what a piece of liquid engineering, her lips were the colour of the plums on Her Majesty. From the same mould as Jane Russell. Curly . . . How had this happened?

The only holidays Curly took were with Henry and Naomi, Ben and Lennie: he'd join them for a seaside week at Wimereux or Sables d'Olonne, at De Panne or Plougastel – he loved to build model roads in the sand. Otherwise his travel was restricted to traffic-light conferences in Essen, pedestrianisation fests in Chemnitz, hard-shoulder binges in the suburbs of unpronounceable towns in week-old republics: postcard from Brno.

'Rouen? Great!' Henry Fowler had a ready gift for bogus enthusiasm. 'Don't tell me: medieval cathedral.'

'That's the one,' said Curly.

'Lots of scoff and lots of boff. *That*'s the one,' Lavender purred.

Chapter Eight

When an Englishman dies what happens to his personal pewter tankard that has always hung above the bar in his local? Is it reclaimed by his estate? Is it kept as a memorial to him *in situ*, in the place where, so his drinking pals would claim, he had spent the best years of his life? Is it used to toast him on the anniversary of his death so that his name will live for ever more? Does it merely become part of the common store of jugs which mine host jovially fills with a short measure of watered ale for passing trade?

Such questions preoccupied Lavender Beard Croney whose retention of her name was mocked by Naomi Fowler as 'token feminism', as 'having her cake and eating it', as 'precious'. Naomi was also fiercely derisive of:

a) Her so-called profession of social-bloody anthropologist and her use of the title *Doctor*: she doesn't go so far as to introduce herself thus, but it's there on the business card.

b) Her pointless wanky jobs teaching bollocks at the LSE and UCL and doing research, whatever that means, at somewhere called the Institute which is probably one and a half dismal rooms in Euston (it was).

c) Her piddling preoccupation with the Pewter Tankard question, and with countless others like it. She *gnawed* at them, wouldn't ever let go. Talk about curiosity killed the cat – but it didn't, of course. Didn't kill her. The cow's got a constitution like an ox and at least nine lives.

d) Her casual boastfulness about her 'cultivated' background, her parents' taste, her idyllic WASP childhood, her wonderful years at Brandeis, her familiarity with select country clubs – all of which might be interpreted as covert anti-Semitism.

e) Her patronisation of everyone, but everyone, as a case study like we've got saucers deforming our mouths and human bones dangling from our ears and we run around in the buff apart from parrot feathers and lion intestines and have three tits and belong to some tribe for God's sake.

Cf:

f) Her Anglophilia, and her wanting to be more English than the English, to be terminally English – just listen to her accent. She can't *quite* get it right but does she try! She is a walking inventory of castles and moated manors. When she drops names it's like an avalanche. She has memorised Debrett's. Lords, she loves them. But maybe that love is not reciprocated. For, six years after arriving in England as some kind of research student, she has settled for Curly who is indeed a younger son but not in the sense that Lavender uses it. Why is it that when a certain sort of English queer gets married he always gets married to an Anglophiliac American? Don't these women know, or is it that in their anxiety to land a mate they are prepared to overlook the matter of contrary sexual preference? And their wedding! She drove round for weeks looking for the perfect church, like something off a greetings card, and when she found it she dreamed up a lie about her ancestors' links with that part of Kent – or is it Sussex? Near Ashdown Forest and Frant, round there. She even serves you warm white wine because she read that that's what the fridgeless aristocratic English do.

g) Her energetically faked, deafeningly protracted orgasms – which caused the precocious, mock-innocent Lennie to ask at breakfast in the thin-walled holiday bungalow on Noirmoutier whether the previous evening's molluscs and crustacea had disagreed with her.

Forsaking her self-tutored Englishness, evasiveness, discretion and periphrasis she replied, 'Curly – sorry, *Uncle* Curly, is tireless, sweetheart, he likes to keep a girl awake all night. And I'm the lucky girl.'

Henry Fowler, reading a two-day-old *Daily Mail* and dunking a croissant in a cup of British Working Man's tea as his concession to France, raised his eyebrows to Naomi, who wasn't taken in for a moment. She was in no doubt that Lavender's bed opera was occasioned by the presence of an audience, which included, of course, Henry – just as her bulging bikini top and tiny thong with its russet fringe of vermicular hairs were worn for the entire beach.

She and Curly would condescend to join the Fowlers after a punishing daily round of churches, châteaux, galleries, tumuli, salt pans, windmills, canal systems, U-boat pens, bookshops, stationery shops, charcuteries, antiques warehouses. And as for Lavender's French! Naomi was convinced by the courteous bewilderment of waiters and garage staff and by the helpless grimaces of the appliqué-pullovered, silver-nailed, platinum-blonde crone from the letting agency that Lavender spoke the language as a boast, as a means to impress the monoglot Fowlers rather than as a medium of international communication – which it evidently wasn't. Lavender was blithely unembarrassed by the incomprehension which met her most elementary requests and greetings. She ascribed it to the unfamiliarity of south Breton tradesfolk with her Parisian accent. When her telephonic order of, *inter alia*, 2 kilos of onions had resulted in the delivery of 2 kilos of kidneys (and a change of menu) she poured herself a late-morning pastis and with a forbearing smile asked Naomi, standing outside the window with Ben's surfboard: 'What can you expect of people who don't even know the subjunctive?' Naomi couldn't remember what the subjunctive was, and didn't care that she couldn't remember. It wouldn't have surprised her, however, if Lavender was merely parroting a specious polemic in a news magazine headlined '*Les Jeunes: pourquoi suppriment-ils le subjonctif?*'

Both women knew that this first joint holiday, already long postponed, would also be the last. Not that it had been without its successes. They had enjoyed two high tides together sitting with a bottle on the slope at the end of the causeway from Beauvoir-sur-Mer watching as drivers stranded by the surging ocean abandoned their cars to run for the structures like high-diving boards which punctuated the road every 200 metres and offered refuge if not solace as those cars were inundated.

Another day they were in a tailback caused by the fatal collision of two vans and a lorry on a shimmering black road lined with hypermarkets and furniture megastores in the outskirts of La Roche-sur-Yon when Curly uttered a triumphal 'Yes!', scrambled blindly from the driver's seat, causing a screeching ambulance to swerve and its crew of paramedics to wish him dead, and ran across the forecourt of Tiffauges S.A., through the ranks of primary-coloured, factory-fresh tractors, autoharrows and combines and into the showroom where, surrounded by dummies kitted for pest control (apple-green protective clothing, breathing apparatus, sprays, dorsal canisters), generators, pumps, sample fences, cow prods, was displayed a metallic-green Citroën SM, *c.* 1972.

He stroked it, contorted himself to squint at it, was so rapt by it that he started when a mottled nose with moustache attached greeted him.

'He's got a real thing about those,' rued Lavender, watching anxiously as Curly nodded to the loquacious salesman. 'He bid for one at Bonham's – I had to stop him when he got to 12,000.'

Naomi wasn't sure whether this was a pecuniary boast, another of Lavender's fantasies.

'*How* many Citroëns has he got? At the most recent count?'

Lavender, distracted, shook her head: 'Eight? Ten? I don't know – there are some I've never seen.'

'I always,' said Naomi with gauged nonchalance, 'think of them as his children.'

Lavender turned sharply towards where she sat on the back seat and fixed her with angry eyes. They were also vulnerable eyes, hurt eyes.

'His *children*? What do you mean – his children? They're his . . . They're cars. Which he happens to believe are works of art. And collects. Like other people collect . . . Coalport – or netsuke.'

'I know they are cars.' Naomi emphasised each word. 'Doesn't stop them being child *substitutes* though does it?'

'I guess we'll have to wait till we have children to find out,' Lavender replied. 'If he sells them then we'll know you were right.' And she turned to monitor Curly as two police cars screeched past.

He bought the Citroën SM. It's in a lock-up off Gypsy Hill. He drives it a couple of times a month. He hasn't sold his collection; indeed he goes on adding to it. His latest acquisition is a van with corrugated-metal sides which Lavender has nicknamed Ted's Fort after a shack on the Maberley Road allotments of the same material.

He hasn't sold the collection. Curly and Lavender have no children, so the matter of child substitutes has not been put to the test. Why do they have no children when both so want them? When they both so yearn for their life's orderly straits to be breached by noise and egg stains? They have *tried* for children, how they've tried. They have paid rapt attention to Lavender's calendar and diet.

Secretly she rocks old cradles in museums. She'll always offer to tend a buggy for a mother whose baby is making its first steps – such displays of selflessness are treated with wariness by teen slatterns with their white stilettos, stonewashed jeans and blue-veined, maggot-white skin. They clutch their three packs of Raffles and gape at her with victim eyes. She extends the superstition of the empty pram to supermarket trolleys with seat and harness, she wheels them dreamily for hours, an indecisive shopper, talking under her breath, attracting CCTV's attention before she makes her first purchase. She despises her behaviour. She despises herself for brushing against pregnant women in trains, for patting the distended bellies of strangers at parties – she feels an impudent fool when they turn out merely to be fat. She cooks only odd numbers of eggs. She drew the line at vaginal pessaries steeped in the first faeces excreted by a newborn baby, and there are no hayricks to sleep on in South London. She avoids lettuce and parsley, picking the one from mixed salads, scraping the other from potatoes, fish, whatever surface it speckles. She ingests proprietary preparations of ginseng, deeming it to be a form of mandrake.

Covertly, she pores over herbals, encyclopedias of folk remedies, dictionaries of superstitions, collections of old wives' tales, accounts of fertility rites the world over. She debases works of scholarship, transforms them into instructive inventories of quack tips and dubious advice. She gives shameful credence to prescriptions and procedures which she knows to be worthless, which she condemns as founded in ignorance, occlusion, irreason.

The entirety of her life with Curly has been infected by this hysterical want. It's been an invariable condition of her being since she met him. It was occasioned by him. She acknowledges the preposterousness of the programmed conviction that one's own child or children (but let's take it one at a time) will be unlike other people's children. Who are hell. She does not except sullen Ben and the Wisenheimer Lennie. They are the quintessence of other people's children, sibling distillates of hell. She puts up with them for Curly's sake, and for Henry's. And she knows that no child of hers and Curly's could ever display such incipient sociopathy as those two, for their child (Rowan or Robin) would be born of love, raised with love in a house where love's levels were always kept topped up and there were books and Beethoven.

She had watched Curly fall in love with her before her very eyes. The immense flattery thrilled her. They met late one May morning in 1986 during the conference 'Car – Slave or Master?' at Birmingham University. Curly was standing in a drift of cherry blossom, head back, lost in his delight at rushing rolling clouds. Lavender Beard was hurrying across a shower-shined car park to a tower whose all-over glazing swallowed those clouds. She had just arrived in a cab from New Street Station. The driver hadn't known his way around the park-like campus. He had spoken in an accent she couldn't understand – and, she presumed, was unable to understand hers. He had certainly failed to appreciate that she had a very important paper to deliver, that she needed time to settle herself, fix her make-up, prepare her slides, dose herself with codeine, gargle. And pee: she had drunk two litres of water on the train trying unsuccessfully to overcome a hangover incurred by trying unsuccessfully to drink away the memory of Mike the Bike, the courier who had at 17.41 the previous evening delivered a copy of Ariel Quantrill's *The Future of Futurology* which she was to review for the Institute's cracking quarterly *Journal of Mores and Customs* and who at 18.52 began to prosecute a diligent if slobbering act of cunnilingus on her. He brought his head up only once, to apologise for the crackle of his walkie-talkie: 'We're not allowed to turn them off see.' At 19.13, after less than three minutes' coupling he achieved orgasm with a cry of: 'Got the number of the nearest Domino's Pizza love?' She told him she was busy. He said he'd got another delivery to do anyway and, never mind, he'd pick up a pizza en route,

85

a Marinara, probably, but maybe an American Hot, what did she think? She hated herself. She bathed then she showered. She drank a bottle of Jack Daniels.

When she woke at 05.36 she had wiped the previous evening – but only after about 20.30. She had no memory whatsoever of even having watched the T·V movie *The Marlin Gambit* starring Ben Jess Tyte and Lincoln Teme, nor of the chat show O'Biggie & Co. Her recall of Mike the Bike was, however, horribly unimpaired. Oh God! She couldn't forget that his real name was Les: 'But I don't want to be taken for a diesel – eh?' She couldn't forget the tattoo beneath his belly button:

HUNGRY? THIS WAY
⬇

She took inordinate comfort from her sure memory that she hadn't fellated him.

'That was tasty, that was a nice one love.'

His gauche farewell was still playing inside her viced head, still fuelling her ignominy when she first saw the man she would marry. Not that she knew it at that moment. But she did within the hour. And she thought she had given up men for ever.

It began to spit with rain again. She asked Curly the way to the Porter Hobbs Hall because there was no one else to ask. Lost in clouds, he turned dreamily to her: 'It's round the side of . . .' He smiled – a sort of rapturous recognition. 'Lavender Beard?' he said.

'Yesss?' She wondered how this man whom she had never seen before could know who she was – the possibility of an earlier and more complete instance of alcoholic amnesia occurred to her. Oh God!

He didn't say 'You correspond precisely to your photo in the conference programme, the only difference being that I did not fall in love with that photo.' He didn't say that because there is a gap between seeing lightning and hearing a *coup de foudre*. And even had the transmission of sensation from eye through brain to tongue been faster he would have observed the taboo on opening one's heart (that too) to a stranger when that stranger is the object of the heart's desire. He did say: 'I'm coming to your lecture.'

'Knights of the Road: Codes of Gestural Chivalry' was a captious panegyric of the car as agent and promoter of courtesy, fellowship, good manners, goodwill, well-being and social responsibility. Lavender Beard spoke of the car as a domain of individual responsibility and self-determination. For every instance of a driver who believes that he has been wronged, cut up, impeded and who follows his alleged aggressor, forcing him off the road and beating his head to a pulp with a lump of old camshaft, there are tens of thousands of instances of drivers pulling in between parked cars to make way for vehicles coming from the opposite direction whose drivers will acknowledge that routine act of selflessness with an open-palmed salute, a salute that will very likely be reciprocated. This, Lavender contended, is peculiar to England – it is akin to holding open doors for strangers, to giving up one's seat on the underground to the elderly, the pregnant, the infirm *without* an injunction to do so. Which makes the English behaviourally superior to the French who, left to their own devices, would obviously relegate the war wounded and quadriplegics to a heap on the carriage floor.

As she spoke she couldn't help but direct herself towards Curly Croney whose gaze was so concentrated that she felt she was being consumed. He was trying to take possession of her – was that what it was? His fixation with her was so patent that she wondered if he was sick. (He was – he was lovesick, he was the fevered protagonist of any one of a thousand popular songs.) He appeared not to be listening: he certainly failed to laugh when he was meant to and didn't do so until he realised that the rest of the audience was displaying a courteously amused recognition of her after-dinnerish observations on A A patrolmen ('They salute you even if they've just raped you') and V W Beetle drivers ('They shouldn't give each other peace signs, they should give each other a Nazi salute'). He was also the only man in the packed lecture hall who was not the victim of multiple tailoring. She admired his clothes' assertive understatement: bespoke charcoal suit, heavy white Oxford shirt, black-and-grey tie, black brogues.

She would come in time to admire the way he neglected to fold his clothes and slung them casually across the Citterio sofa in his austere bedroom which became their bedroom in such a way that they appeared to have been arranged. He has *to actually try*, she boasted, if he's not to be elegant in everything he does and makes, in everything he thinks and designs. She boasted too that they were never apart from the day they met. She didn't even bother to cash in the return half of her rail ticket. He drove her back to London in his lhd DS *décapotable* that early summer evening when the rain held off and the wind volumised her hair and they knew the very moment that the one was again feasting on the other with pride and beatific wonderment.

The early morning of the following day Lavender woke beside this man whose scent she already adored, whose breath was balm on her collar, whose emissions matted her glossy hair and her lavish bush, whose lack of sexual inhibition delighted her, whose monkish house she wished to remake in her image, whose child she longed to bear.

Curly stirred, nuzzled her neck, blearily rolled on to his back and, as he slipped back into sleep, murmured drowsily: 'Are you going to shave here or wait till you get back to barracks?'

She never told him he had said that. Should she have told him? That was the ghost of his past, a distant past maybe, nothing more. And she was a grown woman, she was a worldling with a tolerance of such eccentricities. Had her father not addressed her mother, whose name was Virginia, as Johnny? Had he not addressed his Princeton friend Harold Van Hage, with whom he holidayed in Europe each summer, as Harriet?

Nor did she tell Curly that the stifled whimper he had enthusiastically mistaken last night for a gasp of pleasure was actually a wince of unalloyed pain caused by his touching a graze in the mucous membrane of her rectum made by Mike the Bike's serrated fingernails. Curly was so pleased that she was excited by this particular exploration that he persisted in making it even when his middle finger, the only one long enough for the job, started to ache with what he imagined to be the onset of repetitive strain injury.

Should she have told him? Of course not. That was her past. That was pre-confluence.

This was already the Second Day of the Rest of Their Life. They went to the races at Kempton.

Chapter Nine

The sixth summer of the Croneys' marriage was the summer of brass name-plates, of stately stone stairwells, of discreet waiting-rooms hung with mirthless cartoons, of doctors who style themselves Mister to elevate themselves above doctors who answer to Doctor, of detached-collar cupidity, of bogus gentility, of effortful levity ('What does an Irish skin specialist call himself?' 'A Dermotologist!'), of the pained, priestly grimace that portends the bad news. It was a grimace whose many variations they came to know and fear.

Every time she found herself in the pedagogic Mecca of Dulwich, Lavender rued her failure to conceive. Here there were girls of James Allen's School, women already, squeezed into the uniform that they would customise by shortening and tightening for the delectation of the local rough. But none of these flirty things was hers to chide and warn and hug.

Posing as a prospective parent (which she was) she would occupy a deck-chair beneath a chestnut to watch cricket matches played in the verdant grounds of the boys' school. Here there were pretend men in cricket whites – private education delays puberty. They wore white like virgins, they were as cross-dressed as molly dancers. They protected their wicket, a hymenal gate, with a bat, a primal shield, against its assault by a groin-polished ball. She made notes for a paper (which she would never complete) on the paramountcy of the game's rites; on the infection of quotidian speech by its jargon, an infection which acknowledges the game's metaphorical potency and variety – it can stand for anything, it can be made to mean anything, it is protean, tirelessly equivocal, endlessly elusive, as evasive as a politician; on its inability to flourish in countries other than those formerly colonised by Britain or formerly as Protestant as Britain (Holland); on its soporific dullness. Her title was to have been *Cricket Stands for Britain*. She dreamed of its becoming a book. But not so much as she dreamed that the little boy who cried when he dropped a catch was her little boy. Even Curly who hated cricket and calumnised it as 'another English disease' would surely come to love it if it was his child who scored the winning run and modestly raised his bat, a primal weapon, in acknowledgement of his feat. If it was his child . . . But it wasn't. And she feared it never would be.

She astonished herself by being sullenly jealous when Henry and Ben Fowler successfully auditioned for the pilot show of a television quiz called *Know Thy Father Know Thy Son*. Of the four sons chosen to participate only Ben was able to identify his father from a childhood photograph, only Ben knew the name of his father's best friend at school, none of them knew their father's birthplace. And the fathers were kindredly ignorant, forgetting their son's first spoken word, and whether their first infantile disease had been rubella or chickenpox or measles, and incidents of nappy hilarity, and examples of supposed precocity; none of them displayed any recognition of 'Famous Family Booboos' (child-eats-firelighter-has-stomach-pumped, that sort of thing). The show was deemed by LWT executives to be ground breaking and courageous but no series was commissioned and the pilot was not transmitted.

Nonetheless Lavender was resentful that Curly should be denied the opportunity even to apply to participate in such familial endeavours, no matter how he despised them. She hated herself for not providing him with the passport to normality.

Month after month after month she bled, and because she bled she wept. She wept anywhere – in her car, at the movies, during a lecture she was delivering on cross-border barter in Pyrenean communities. Her face twisted like that of a newborn whose very absence was the fount of her woe.

It was Mr Lancaster Dovell who, massaging his frontal sinuses with thumb and index fingers, suggested to Lavender that: 'We ought I think perhaps to have a peek at your husband's waterworks. Yah? I'll arrange for him to see Mr Bassett – good man.'

So it was that Curly sat on the edge of a paper-covered couch in a partitioned room above Welbeck Street. Spermatic motes slomoed through the wedge of beam admitted by the clear glass at the top of the sash. A crew-cut nurse with a boxer's face handed him a specimen jar and indicated a bell press: 'Should you require any assistance . . .'

'When you're paying this sort of money – I thought assistance would be included.'

'Mr Croney!' She reproved him with the weary smile of one who's heard it all before, often.

'If you do need some, ah, encouragement . . .' She gestured invitingly to a pile of tooled-leather folders and patted them. 'Ten minutes all right with you? Oh and I know it's a little close in here but don't open it will you, the window. We had a bit of an incident a couple of weeks back.'

(Patient D had been experiencing especial difficulty in obtaining his sample yield. A difficulty he ascribed to the room's airlessness. He managed to force open the opaque lower half of the window. He returned to his solitary endeavour with renewed and frenzied enthusiasm.

Delphine Agah, the new tenant of Flat 71, on the seventh floor of Teck Court, a service block on New Cavendish Street, was busily deadheading the marigolds in a window-box neglected by her predecessor. She glanced down through the grid of the adjacent fire escape's treads and rails, across a white-tiled area, past knots of elephantine telescopic ducts, over a craggy fortress of air-conditioning plant, over the roof lights and lanterns of cramped extensions and into the rear of Mr Gervaise Bassett's consulting rooms.

She dropped her kitchen scissors. She ran to the phone. She dialled 999 and asked for the ambulance service. She was unable to give the precise address in Welbeck Street, just around the corner but she would wait outside the house when she had worked out which one it was. Yes, she was certain. She had nursing experience. She had indeed met her husband when she was a nurse and he was a liposuction patient. She knew an epileptic fit when she saw one.)

Curly had never previously seen magazines such as *Ring*, *Lustsluts*, *Beaverbrook* and *Cockhound* placed in the sort of genteel leather folder which his parents had wrapped round *Radio Times* when he was a child. He wondered whether Mr Gervaise Bassett, if prosecuted for possession of illicit publications, could plead that they were legitimate medical aids. And would the BMA be behind him? He masturbated strenuously whilst scrutinising photographs with helpful captions like: 'Eva loves the taste of Freddi's big mauve lollipop.' He ejaculated into the jar as surely as Freddi did on to eager Eva's face (p. 11).

Mr Gervaise Bassett's mahogany desk betokened his eminence and dwarfed his body. He sat on a castored chair propelling his shoulders and his disproportionately large, smoothly brilliantined head from one side of the desk to the other, like a target in a shooting gallery. The worse the prognosis the faster the target moved. Curly didn't know this. He was transfixed by the speed and regularity of the eminent consultant's cycle. So although he heard what was being told to him he hardly took it in. His distraction was such that he failed to acknowledge its import; it seemed remote from him, notional. Curly surprised Mr Bassett by smiling. Mr Bassett had rarely witnessed a more evident instance of a patient's denial and as he bowled along the three-metre length of his track he observed Mr Croney with unusual interest – the dreamy grin, and the oscillating head as though watching a tennis match, and the disinclination to ask questions: Mr Croney behaved like someone other than the subject of a consultant's tactfully wrapped but definitively gloomy observations, he behaved like a third person, a disinterested party. Mr Bassett, never having treated one before, pondered the case that traffic engineers might be generically dull and backward, the sort of people who, at his distinguished Alma Mater, studied technical drawing for want of academic aptitude. Perhaps best then to spell it out with brusque candour.

'In summation then. What we're looking at here is infertility full stop. Irremediable. That's not just opinion. That's brass tacks, I'm afraid. I'd like to be able to offer some crumb of comfort – but . . .'

'Well you want to know the brass tacks eh? *Brass tacks* – he kept saying *brass tacks*,' said Curly to Lavender mimicking Mr Gervaise Bassett's studiously pompous delivery. They sat at a table outside a pub near the Institute. Curly was framed by geraniums in hanging baskets. Lavender held his hand. Their grief was shared.

He repeated Mr Gervaise Bassett's little joke: 'It can hardly be genetic can it? It's one condition that can't be passed on. Ha! Either it was a fluke of birth he says . . . Or because of some infection I may not even have known about.'

Lavender winced. 'Second opinion,' she said. 'No harm in trying, darling. We owe it to ourselves.'

Curly shrugged. She had never seen him look so defeated.

They sought a second opinion, from Mr William Savage-Smith (detachable collar, soft skin, razor rash, crinkle-cut High Tory hair with special fly-away effect over the ears). His opinion concurred with the first. And he too wondered about traffic engineers. What do they actually do? He asked Curly: 'What sort of *chemicals* do you chaps in traffic engineering use?'

Curly gaped: 'Chemicals?'

'Chemicals. What sort of chemicals . . . You know – in, in your lab . . . In a traffic-engineering lab.'

Curly shook his head in perplexity: 'Lab?'

'Or, ah, when you're building a road – if that's what you do.'

'I'm afraid I go on site once every six months, maybe. Probably less. And labs with chemicals . . . I can't think of the last time . . .'

'So you've never been routinely exposed to chemicals . . . Any sort of fallout? Radiation?'

Curly was proud of his profession and of his achievements in it. Lavender was dismayed that his indignation at being taken for a navvy or a labscout (his nonce-word) should apparently weigh so much more heavily on him than this confirmation of his incapacity to reproduce. His dismissal of his affliction was casual, cruelly offhand. She understood that this indifference was acquired, that it was a tactic for burying the truth, for refusing to acknowledge the enormity of his plight which was also her plight. But he was so swiftly inured to his sterility that she wondered if he had ever really wanted a child.

Third opinion. Further consultation. They can always fix these things in California. Amazing scientific advances. Makes Harley Street look neolithic.

Lavender was pale, distraught, desperate, pleading, and drunk though not as drunk as her husband. Curly's bitterness was consumptive. And it was exacerbated by his having spent the seven hours between the end of his consultation and, thus, of his paternal aspirations drinking manhattans and whisky sours in a series of bars and clubs where he made several new best friends with people whose names he had forgotten when he stumbled out into the bright, baked evening to meet Lavender his love-bucket-honey-pie at La Cannelier where he arrived fifty minutes late.

'California! You're joking. They can't even keep a six-lane freeway moving.'

Lavender gripped the linened edge of the restaurant table. She had never considered what it might be to hate him till then. Her spread, thumbless hands were claws. Curly thought of the beasts in Crystal Palace Park. He had cited them as a reason not to move to central London. He had denied her the postcode she craved. Now he was denying her a child.

'Is all this,' she asked him, 'down to some social disease you once had?'

'Look at this – they can't even spell in English . . . B-E-A-F-S-T-A . . .' He put down the menu: 'No. As a matter of brass tacks it isn't because I've never had one. OK? And I'm not having another fucking test because I'm pissed off with paying £120 to wank into a jar then get patronised by some arsehole with a plum in his mouth.'

A gluttonous plutocrat three tables away stared testily at him over the top of half-moon glasses. Two German tourists turned to watch these volatile English. A con man dressed like a retired army officer adjusted his tie. The stream of conversation in the pretentious, tutti-Louis room was momentarily dammed. A trolley operative halted his vehicle. Throats were cleared. The restaurant manager M Bernard Bettlach, dressed as though for a wedding, glanced at the grave *sommelier* who should have been delighted that his overpriced, floridly annotated wares were performing their rough magic. The *sommelier* considered a moment then nodded, frowning. M Bettlach slid across the mock-Aubusson with a massive show of even teeth: 'If everything's not entirely to your satisfaction . . .'

'It's just dandy,' replied Lavender. She swung her wineglass, an archive of lip prints.

'Good, good. Good. Enjoy the rest of your dinner. Won't you.' And he sauntered towards the next table congratulating himself on not having had to do anything other than exert his presence.

Curly, suddenly lachrymose, shouted: 'The long and the short of it, the bottom line, the ultimate brass tack is that you're going to have to fuck someone else if you want to get up the duff. *Capiscie*, darling? Fuck someone else.'

That was the solution then. Many a true word is spoken in pain, in self-loathing, in self-abnegation, in full hearing of more than forty strangers. Neither of them yet knew that it was true.

'Darling . . .'

'Sir!' M Bettlach had pirouetted. His nostrils flared. He stood over them.

'It's OK,' said Lavender, distractedly. 'Darling, darling, you—'

'I'm afraid it is not OK. I'm sorry but—'

'Oh do leave us alone please can't you see—'

'*Madame*. Your, ah . . . The gentleman. The gentleman is—'

'The gentleman is my husband.'

'He is disturbing my guests.'

'Guests?' Curly looked askew at him.

M Bettlach conjured a wintry smile: 'Your fellow guests have the right to—'

'Fellow? What are you talking about? Fellow . . . I don't know them. They're not my fellows.' He fixed the eye of a curious matron: 'Are you my fellow?' he boomed.

'I think it would be better if—'

'And how did you get it into your little Switzer head that we are *guests*? We are not *guests*. We are parties to a commercial transaction. I am not your *guest*. Got it?'

'Sir, I must insist that you leave.'

'Must you?'

'There will be no charge.' At which point M Bettlach, wishing he'd never left his natal commune near La Chaux-de-Fonds where public drunkenness was met with such obloquy that it was virtually extinct, resolved to help Curly from his chair. He positioned himself to the left side of it and just behind it. Curly, distracted by his audience, six of whom he acknowledged with a grinning bow, was unaware of this gambit till he felt M Bettlach's hand on the back of the chair. He scowled over his shoulder at the determined, anxious face. M Bettlach leaned forward with his arm poised above Curly's shoulder as if he were comforting him.

'It will be better for everyone if—'

'Take your fucking hands off me.'

'I will not be spoken to like that.'

'Get you matey.' And Curly dismissed him with a petulantly flapping hand.

'Are you going to leave us alone – you officious little man?' wondered Lavender with a sweet moue and a winsome eyebrow flutter.

'I have no choice – I shall call the police.'

'Nazi!' shouted Curly as M Bettlach strode importantly across the room acknowledging his guests' sympathetic repertoire of wan nods and pained smiles.

WPC 4721 Pratt had no sense of humour: that was her problem. That's what the lads always ribbed her about in the canteen. She couldn't take a rape joke or a kiddie-porn gag. The crackle of her radio reminded Lavender of Mike the Bike (dead three years now, Volvo and amphetamines – they switched off the life support). Curly rolled his eyes as WPC Pratt spoke, concluding with the words 'so it's up to you sir'.

Curly replied: 'Tell me something. You're a policewoman, right? So when you sit on a bloke's face do you tell him to blow into the bag?'

Drunk and disorderly, obstructing the police in the prosecution of their duty. £100 and bound over by Westminster Magistrates Court in the sum of a further £100 to keep the peace for thirty days. He shared an overnight cell with a charming Cypriot who was charged with the theft of £12,000 worth of leather jackets, who wrote out for him the 'ultimate' taramasalata recipe, who advised against adoption: 'Is like buying a car in auction. You don't know what you're getting. My brother he adopt a boy. He never regret anything so much in all his life. The lad's a no-good. Always in trouble with the police. They give him everything and he turns out a thieving bastard. Don't do it, captain. Anything but adopt.'

Chapter Ten

These two in the moonlit bedroom – conjoined at the groin and filling the air with sweat, mucus, groans and the lapping of muscle against membrane – are Henry Fowler and his best friend Curly Croney's wife, Lavender with the double-F cup.

This is not the first time they have steeped themselves in each other's slippery emissions in the Croneys' marital bed. This is not the first time they have formed a seething machine like a cardiac bellows which expands and contracts. This is not the first time that the boughs which stroke the uncurtained window have taken their impassioned rhythm from the couple heaving like waves in accord with the ubiquitous, omnipotent moon. When Lavender Beard arches and shudders and croaks the knell of little death, Henry Fowler, mixing pleasure with duty, changes gear, grasps her buttocks' buttocks and accelerates with the eagerness of a missionary who has espied heathens on a distant bluff. He makes the last mighty ascent and thuddingly casts himself into his mount's core as though burying something for all time. Listen to his whoops of joy and self-congratulation. Listen to his grunts of effortful release. He slumps prone, pinning her to the sheet which has absorbed all that their open pores can give it. He waits for her signal – the urgent, earnest imprecation which he responds to by withdrawing, by standing on the bed, by bending to grasp her legs and lifting them so that her heels touch his chin and she is supported by him with only her shoulders and her hands, knitted to cradle her occiput, resting on the soaked sheet.

So they remain, mutely absorbed in the callisthenic ceremony, silhouetted against the moon – man with primitive wind instrument. He's detumescent and shagged out. All he wants is to sprawl. He tries to tense his muscles against the tide of his afterglow. He clings to her ankles, he gazes at the benign orb suspended over the wooded heights of South London. It's Lavender's clock, that smiley moon, it tells her when, it told her that this Tuesday night in early May is *the* night. It told her that a Friday night in early April was *the* night too – but forget that. This night, she knows, is the one.

Henry Fowler relaxes his grasp in his post-coital, cigaretteless stupor.

'Henry!' she barks, officiously.

He wriggles, braces himself as well as he can on the supersensitive interior springing the better to maintain her in the counselled position for the counselled duration of two and a half minutes. He reckons it's crazy but he knows the depths of her desperation, he understands her faith in folk remedies and in the lore of old mothers (who would know). He is grateful, nonetheless, when she begins to count aloud for that is the beginning of the end: '148, 149, 150 . . . You're done, sweetheart.'

He lowers her legs gently. They lie side by side. He smokes. She strokes her belly, dreamily, dotingly. While he showers she strips the bed and bundles the sheets and pillowcases into a rattan chest. She lowers the blinds, switches on a bedside lamp. They dress, in silence, in the illumined room whose walls are hung with framed monochrome aerial photographs of flyovers, clover-leaf interchanges, mini-roundabout complexes. Lavender does her make-up in the mirror of a bulbous limed-oak dressing-table which Henry Fowler has known for more than three-quarters of his life – it's a Croney family heirloom, a shrine of a sort, a sentimental incongruity. He can even remember the position of the concealed switch for the strip light above the mirror; he can remember the busily decorated peach bedroom not two miles away, and the electric fire in the shape of a Scottie dog, and the day when Stanley and he opened the drawers to acquaint themselves with the mysteries of smalls and stays, girdles and slips and pink elasticated fabric which flaked in his prepubescent fingers; he can remember the name of a perfume, Ma Griffe, but not its scent. That memory is buried, along with so much else. Atomiser technology has come along the while. So have names. It is L'Autre Femme that Lavender sprays from a cylindrical aerosol.

She flicks back her thick chestnut-red mane so that Henry Fowler, seated on the mattress edge, double knotting his laces, can sniff at her proffered neck. She stands, buxom in a taupe shift, buries his head (hair clasped at the root) in her tummy. 'Strange, isn't it Henry? Isn't it strange what life brings . . . I've done feta salad – so it's feta salad, special taramasalata made from a secret recipe, then pourgouri and – tarum, tarum, from the barby! – marinaded pork souvlaki.'

'Don't get that at home,' repines Henry Fowler, all dressed in uniform black, standing to crisp the creases. 'And it's marin*ated*.'

'Knew you'd say that. That's why I said it. You old pedant. Come on.' And she shimmies towards the door, her slink dissembling her size.

'And that's not all I don't get at home,' he mutters, fretful as a cuddly toy with a wound.

Lavender Beard swivels on her mules and glares: 'That, Henry, is beside the issue. For God's sake . . . That is . . . irrelevant.' She flings arrows from her eyes. He can see that she is close to crying. He makes a big placatory shrug, all palms and hefty shoulders. She moves back across the room to the helpless man, touches the skin that protrudes from the black twill at the wrist, at the neck. She stretches to nuzzle his ear. 'This is different . . . Dear Henry . . .'

He descends the stairs in front of her. She lays her hands on his shoulders as if to conga, the fatuous jollity of which dance ill suits this sternly austere house with its hard edges and polished surfaces and several lacks: no wainscots, no cornices, no carpets, no colours. It is an inventory of eliminated walls, of subjugated ornament. It's the stripped skeleton of the house it once was, that it might be again (bless this house with plenty, bless it with fecundity). Where once there was stained glass representing fructuous abundance now there is cold opaque glass. Where once the hall floor was polychromatically tiled now it is pitted tufa.

Henry Fowler has never taken to it. He considers the style called functional to be dysfunctional, contemptuous of comfort, ignorant of domestic niceties. He believes that this house is, above all, a defensive boast about childlessness, about guaranteed freedom from jam patches and crayon trails. Henry Fowler is a family man and a family fan, as he describes himself, a sculptor of futures, as he also describes himself. This man/fan has lived all his adult life with the lives he has created, with the disorder, noise, tantrums, illnesses, sloth and gaucheness of dependent beings. This monument to tidiness seems like a denial of life, of his life specifically, of the possibility of future lives within its walls.

He is contemptuous of the framed fetishes and mounted trophies. There are prototype traffic lights (unlit) in a perspex display case. There is a traffic cone on a tufa plinth, shown off as though it were a real sculpture. He really wonders sometimes about the way that Curly has made this house a museum of his work. Henry Fowler is all too aware of what his Naomi would say if he made their house a gallery of his professional achievements and he really wonders sometimes how Lavender puts up with, say, the accretion of wall-mounted cat's-eyes and the dado-level frieze of alternating cul-de-sac and no-entry signs. But it's not something he has ever been discourteous enough to mention: an Englishman's house is his archive. And when he and Lavender conga beneath an RSJ into the cook/eat/talk space where the Greek cheese salad and olives and thematically apt bottles of cold resined wines are laid out on a blond-wood table he keeps his perpetual counsel, stays mum as ever. Rather, he picks up a glass, fills it, hands it to Lavender. He picks up another, fills it, swigs, goes *ah*! 'Top-up, Curl?'

He looks over to the grand, vast, stainless-steel stove where Curly Croney is occupied taking slices of *halloumi* from a bath of bubbling olive oil with tongs and laying them on three layers of double-ply kitchen roll.

'If you bear with us a nanosecond,' says Curly, concentrating. 'There . . .' He lifts the last slice, switches off the burner, picks up his glass, offers it to Henry Fowler for a refill, looks at his best friend and at his wife, leans back against a worktop in his apron with the legend CURLY across the breast, in his white T-shirt and his worn Levi's, raises the glass and says: 'To the four of us then . . . How was it?'

Chapter Eleven

'Daaad!'

'Henry! No . . . Really.'

'Imo's coming over,' said Ben. 'I'd come otherwise.'

'I wouldn't,' said Lennie 'I'm not. I mean – *a roundabout*. Cool. Or what?'

'It's not just a— That's not the point. It's Curly's. And it's not like ordinary roundabouts. It's, it's . . . a special roundabout.'

Lennie mimed stifling a yawn.

'Finished?' Naomi, stacking the dishwasher, asked Ben.

'Yeah. It's a bit salt.'

'And it's all pus, all that white,' added Lennie.

'Tell me where you can get proper bacon and I'll get it,' said Henry, hurt.

'I don't know,' said Lennie, 'why we can't have croissants and— everyone else has pain au chocolat, Danish . . .'

'It's because I am an ogre. And my mission on this planet is to clog young arteries with animal fat. And also I *like* fry-ups. And – we live in South London not South Paris.'

'D'you want a daughter with huge white spots like maggots?'

'Of course I do.' Henry tried to hug Lennie as she got up from the refectory-style kitchen table but she wriggled out of his grasp.

'Lay off – or I'll ring Child Line.'

'What did I do to deserve it?'

Naomi looked at him pityingly.

'What did I do to deserve it?' he asked Curly half an hour later, his tone no longer jocular but anxious. 'They're just so . . . unresponsive. I really wanted them to come. I'm sorry.'

'I'm quite glad in a way they didn't actu— Oh Christ look at this!' Curly banged persistently on the horn to alert the elderly driver in front of him that the lights had changed at a pedestrian crossing between Kent House and Clock House Stations: 'God they've got to get these oldsters off the road . . . They're flashing, dear – you can go now, dear . . . They never get the hang of anything – how long have we had lights like these . . . Mandatory re-testing every year, crippling premiums . . . That's what's needed. They're a danger to themselves. Get on, you old boot!'

The experimental mini-roundabout cluster at Eden Park, the first of four such projected complexes, was commissioned by the London Borough of Bromley from Larsen Müller Jago (consultant engineer Roger Croney). It replaced traffic lights at a junction of six roads, one of them dual carriage of the 1930s with a rockery along the middle. The junction's problems were further exacerbated by:

a) An inconstant circulatory balance – flow and volume sampled over a three-month period showed no constant pattern save between *c.* 07.00 and 09.40 on weekdays. There was no complementary late-afternoon consistency.

b) Two (half-timbered) shopping parades, each with a slip road of its own.

c) A petrol station, which offered two means of ingress and one exit.

d) A listed cedar of Lebanon, the only remaining vestige of the late-Georgian arboretum planted by the antiquary and amateur architect Holland Gibson. Its lower boughs had obfuscated the traffic lights and were reckoned to have been directly or indirectly responsible for more than twenty per cent of the accidents which occurred at the junction.

In June 1990 there had been no fewer than seven accidents which the police had classified as 'serious', including two fatalities ('very serious').

In the first three months of Curly's scheme's existence the number of accidents had risen from a weekly average, during the same period of the previous year, of 0.96 to 1.48. But not one of these had been classified as 'serious' and unofficial police opinion was that the majority, which occurred at low speeds, were ascribable to drivers' unfamiliarity with what the designer himself, quoted in *Girder*, called the 'quasi-molecular stratagem of the guideblocks' disposition' and with the introduction of 'ambient riverflow' (i.e. one-way traffic) to all the intersecting roads and, further, to the roads between them.

The *Beckenham, Bickley and Bromley Globe* headlined its report of residents' complaints: BEDLAM COMES TO EDEN PARK – AGAIN! – a reference to the Bethlem Royal Hospital which had removed from Lambeth to its Monks Orchard site, south of Eden Park Station, in 1926 and which had been an object of neighbourly resentment ever since. Interviewed by *Globe* reporter Gavin Stove, 'Jack Bunce, 78, a retired soft-drinks executive of Orchardleigh Avenue, quipped: "We have to go all round the houses to get to our houses now. It's bad enough having all the poor unfortunates lurking on the other side of the fence over there but letting them out so they can re-route the traffic at a notorious black spot – it's like Arnhem all over again."' Mr Stove concluded his report: 'There's no paradise in this Eden. Just a snake of unwanted lorries in residential roads built for yesteryear.'

Curly parked on a pavement. Henry scrutinised the purple-and-orange lines painted diagonally across the roads at intervals which diminished as they neared the intersection. He pondered the curvaceous tumuli, the 'guideblocks', whose differing ground plans were markedly irregular and whose relationships to each other seemed to him to have been randomly determined. He followed Curly across one road after another, looking left, right and left again, and again, unable to get the hang of the layout, fearful that a vehicle coming from a direction he had not considered might wing him or worse.

'What do you reckon?' asked Curly with evident authorial pride, clapping his hands, smiling.

'Yes . . . yes it's interesting . . . very different.'

'I'll say. There's nothing like it in Britain.'

Henry nodded: 'It's certainly unusual.'

'Sculptural engineering starts here.'

'Uh-huh – it's, urm, a whatchamacallit then? A you know . . .'

'Installation?' Curly near sang the word.

'Yes. Installation . . . sorry, I'm not really up on all—'

'Spot on. It *is* an installation. It's a made object. We apply art to cars and to buildings and to furniture, to . . . to what have you – so, why not to roads? Eh?'

Curly was not saying this for the first time. Henry had heard it all before. Bridges, hard shoulders, ramps, railings, crash barriers . . . Curly's vainglorious mission was to make art out of the least-noticed public objects.

'The flowers. What are they? They're nice.' Henry assessed them with a professional eye to future use: they possessed funereal potential. He hadn't seen these before, hadn't been shown them. But that's florists for you: always letting you down.

'They insisted on having something,' Curly sighed, exasperated. 'A design's integrity . . . not a notion they understand. They're canna lilies – they use them in France. Lavender's idea.'

They were standing outside a children's clothes shop at the end of one of the half-timbered shopping parades. They both clasped Styrofoam coffee cups. Curly watched vehicles negotiate the junction. He concentrated with the tense application of a trainer or coach, now biting his lips as he willed on a speeding van, now tutting exasperatedly and clawing the thick suburban air as a Triumph Toledo with four blue rinses came to a perplexed halt among the guideblocks. He turned away, shaking his head. Then, all embarrassment and shyness, he mumbled over the shriek of an accelerating motorcycle: 'I'm infertile Henry.'

Henry was preoccupied by the ostentatious slink of a Chiselhurst wife from her metallic pink Shogun to the premises of Wax'n'Tan With Max'n'Fran. He marvelled at her ability to be simultaneously overdressed and underdressed. 'Gosh! Look at that. D'you think she has to have a licence to wear one of those?' He turned to Curly: 'If you're creative – it sort of goes with the territory . . . The child in the man. All that. Part of you's bound to be.'

'Wha . . . ? What do you mean? Part.'

'Well, you know, ah, Picasso – or was it . . . Thing – the one you lent me the book about. Always on about genius being infantile.'

Curly smiled pathetically. 'No! No! I said, I said: I'm in*fertile*, Henry. In-fertile?'

Henry's brain went immediately to work to decode the syllables which it believed it had misheard. Curly could see his molar fillings, his tongue, and the elastic saliva strands extending from top lip to bottom on the point of snapping but just holding. Curly spoke with the jittery gabble of a tiro paying court with rehearsed words: 'I've been talking this through with Lavender. In fact we haven't been talking about much else . . .'

Curly continued while Henry fixed on a carved neo-Tudor bressummer. The wood was faded, flaking. It could do with a tosh of paint pretty sharp. And that herring-bone brickwork really did need repointing a.s.a.p. The eyes of a child mannequin in the shop window fixed on his. They were lavishly lashed, liquid brown, pleading: they begged him to bring her to life, so she might go to the ball for which she was dressed in a sequinned bodice and satin puff sleeves with a velvet bow in her verisimilar Titian tresses. She would do anything to be brought to life, would pay whatever price he named.

Curly stopped speaking.

Henry knew this time that he had not misheard. He was startled, incredulous. He half-expected Curly to signal that he was being invited to participate in an elaborately perverse and circular practical joke whose primary victim was its author. But Curly was unquestionably in earnest. It was like being asked to assist in a suicide. But that, Henry told himself, is an end and this is a beginning. In his shock Henry was capable of realising that the ramifications would be manifold, knock-on, domino. The first domino had fallen with Curly's extraordinary request. He tried to unpick the matted compress of the love called friendship, uxorious trust, charity, duty, favour, loyalty. But all Henry could actually think was: Is this the way that Curly should have approached him? Is this the correct way, the socially sanctioned way? Is there an approved form of etiquette for asking your oldest friend to impregnate your wife or is it nowadays like, say, what to wear when it says smart casual or addressing strangers by their Christian name – a free-for-all where anything goes?

Curly took him by the arm. They walked away from Bedlam Corner as it would come to be known, past the pink Shogun and the copulating rhinoceroses on its spare-wheel cover, by a circuitous route of roads whose gardens were gay with rose trellises and smiling gerbera and flowering lavender and lawns so green they seemed dyed, back to Curly's car.

When he saw a metalled surface whose aggregate was composed of ginger pebbles Henry could not but think of the Start-rite mites setting out hand in hand along life's highway in the old advertisement. They'd be getting their bus passes soon. Had their journey fulfilled its promise of happiness and safety and chiropody-free radiance?

His had – he could put hand on heart and swear to that.

There had been setbacks, sure, messy blots here and there, an ingrown big toenail in '77 and the same one again in '82 since when he had followed Mr Scalby's advice to abjure toecapped Oxfords no matter what the trade might say. But these had been the exceptions. Yes, the far side of his horizon was always going to be as unknown as that which the mites had approached all those years ago. Yes, it was always going to spring surprises. The trick was to make sure they were nice ones. That was an important part of Henry's philosophy. It was always other people who got divorced, who had Down's kiddies, who got into financial scrapes. It was other people who had the skeletons – the embezzler grandad in choky, the jabbering aunt in the bin, the schoolgirl daughter in the club. And Henry had sought to keep it that way. Such problems, conditions and fates were for other people. He didn't want his life polluted by the grubby disgraces that other people were so prone to and which they increasingly failed to recognise as disgraces. Curly was proposing a future of conspiracy.

He admitted as much when he suggested, in a calculated aside, that it would not be necessary to tell Naomi, that indeed everything might be easier, 'less pressurised', were she not privy to this compact between the three of them, this bond of blood and trust, this clandestine rendezvous of secret seed and discreet egg. But, of course, it was up to Henry and if he reckoned that his marriage vows decreed . . .

No. Mum was, aptly enough, the word. Whatever he decided his lips would be sealed.

'It's between us,' Henry agreed, digging himself in deeper. 'Us three.'

Curly smiled and started the car.

'I could,' Henry suggested modestly, 'fill a jar – you know . . .'

'You wouldn't enjoy it. You don't want to be a sad wanker. That's the *very* point.'

Curly posited his and Lavender's theory of surrogacy which included the paradox of proxy paternity: that a man who has engendered a child by artificial means, without carnal knowledge of the mother, will, even if he knows the identity of the child, suffer a greater and more abiding sense of loss than one who has fomented conception by the usual means and he will attempt to overcome that loss by seeking the child whom he regards as 'his own' and taking possession of him/her. This is because his emissive gesture, which might not otherwise have been made, had a specifically procreative intent. There existed a willed link between cause and effect. A man who has, on the other hand, impregnated a woman as a result of enjoyable, recreational and apparently irresponsible concupiscence will regard the gratification achieved in the prosecution of that act as an end in itself and will not expect or desire to extend the relationship to one of joint parenting: the history of the world and of the Child Protection Agency suggest that man is an animal who is as likely to scarper as to nurture. Surrogacy is thus best undertaken in circumstances in which causal sex and casual sex are as close as the adjectives which describe them.

Curly relished that juxtaposition, those scrambled letters. He repeated: 'Causal, casual, causal, casual – Christ!' He stamped on the brake to avoid a teenage girl who had stepped in front of the car. She hurried gauchely back on to the pavement and into gaping blimey denimed arms. 'Look at her – look. They always do that . . . avoid mutilation by a hundredth of a second then have a giggle with their mates about it. Amazing. It's genetic. Must be.'

Chapter Twelve

Month after month after month she bled, and because she bled she wept. Lavender Beard Croney's menstrual pattern attained the uncanny invariability which she had yearned for when young and single, when she had occasionally been careless of contraception, when her diaries were pocked with red runic devices, underlinings and marginalia executed with such anxious intensity that their imprint carried through the page from one Sunday till the next. The memory of those prodigal years and their lost children reproached her now.

Every month her breasts grew heavy on her and weighed dully with a pain that increased as she grew older. This was her body's harsh means of telling her what she knew so well – that it was not fulfilling its function as an apparatus of reproduction, that she was not allowing it to fulfil that function, that she was fighting the instincts she was imprinted with. Her body had it wrong. She wanted what it wanted. She longed to be filled with a version of herself, with a being who would be *their* child, who would belong to her and to Curly, even if he did deprecate himself as the non-playing captain and as the loving nurse who almost thinks the child her own. He referred to their putative son as Blenheim and to their trinitarian enterprise as Operation Blenheim. It was a coinage which did not amuse Lavender. Anything which made light of their predicament combined with her frustration at her inability to stem her menstruation to render her fractious, snappy, ratty.

Henry irritated her in many ways. When, as he entered the kitchen one night, he heard Curly say Blenheim he asked: 'Is that Blenheim as in Blenheim, Ramillies, Oudenarde, Malplaquet? Or Blenheim as in Blenheim, Lancaster, Wellington?'

'Neither – it's as in Blenheim, Seaton Delaval, Grimsthorpe, Eastbury.'

'Ah,' Henry grunted, puzzled, and stuffed a chilli-red merguez in his mouth, retched but didn't fetch, quite.

'Why d'you say that in front of him?' Lavender complained when he'd left. 'It's our secret. It belongs to us. Us. Why do we have to share everything? Isn't it enough – me having to fuck Henry without letting him into every last cranny of our life? Christ, Curly – it's not me, it's not me, it's not my being, it's not my, my, *self* that he's . . . It's only my reproductive organs he's meant to be . . . attending to. My ovaries. Not that he's making much of a job of it. Is he?'

'How – uh, how many . . .'

'How many free fucking fucks has he had without delivering do you mean darling? Weell . . . By my reckoning – and *I was there*, remember – that makes, ooh,' and she sighed with a profound weariness, unable to sustain her anger, 'fourteen . . . fourteen times. It is never going to happen is it . . .'

Curly scraped couscous, leek, smeared turnip and gamboge, harissa-stained lamb fat from a plate into the kitchen bin. He felt like scraping himself too into that bin (stainless steel, domed, overpriced). His life was now defined by his generative nullity. And it was measured by the very mark of Lavender's fertility, her periods. He was, he told her, beginning to get the hang of what it was to be a woman. The two days each month when she ovulated and the day before them and the day after were like holy days, feast days, days when oblations were made to Henry, the harbinger of fecundity, in the form of post-coital slap-ups: souvlaki, paella, sauerkraut which Curly insisted on calling choucroute and which was Henry's favourite: 'A splendid reward for a task assiduously prosecuted,' Henry pronounced tactlessly, pompously, whilst dog-sniffing the wine chosen by Curly to complement the fermented cabbage and smoked pork and cured sausages and junipers. 'Umm, yes, that, as . . . as what's-his-face, you know, on the telly, would call dry as a nun's minge. Well he wouldn't, actually – not on the telly so to speak . . .' Lavender glared at the ceiling and the low-voltage lights. Curly bit his lip.

Henry irritated her in many ways. She didn't want her little Blenheim or little Eastbury (a girl's name) to talk like his or her birth father who blithely referred to couscous as tar brush grub, and who cracked tiresomely unfunny gags like: What do you call an Arab with a suitcase? A terrorist. What do you call an Arab without a suitcase? A terrorist on a budget. It wasn't so much the ugly sentiments that she objected to as the coarseness of their expression. And what if this was not learned, not culturally acquired, but a genetic trait that might be passed on, might prove uncorrectable – like gesture or handwriting or voice?

She was vexed too by the self-righteousness and piety of Henry's philo-Semitism. Years of marriage to Naomi had turned him into a doggedly intransigent supporter of Israel (which he had visited once, pronounced 'heaven on earth', and had never returned to). Any act of belligerence or state-sanctioned terrorism perpetrated by that country met with his enthusiastic approval. Any action which threatened what he perceived as its interests would be characterised as Fascist and appended with the observation that Syria shelters Nazi war criminals. He was ostentatiously sensitive to real and imagined slights on his children's maternal heritage. He was eager to take demonstrative offence on their behalf.

It would have been insolent and ignominious to fault him. He was proudly loyal, paternally protective. Although he had never considered converting he had grown into the cliché of the zealous convert. Yet Lavender recognised a strain of sententiousness, of smugness, of moral aggrandisement through his very proxiness. He seemed to presume that his not belonging to that faith and race rendered his championship of Jewry and Zionism (which he didn't differentiate) all the more laudable, all the more deficient in self-interest. It was as though Jews were 'his' tribe – which he had elected to support as someone else might choose to support a soccer team.

If only he would impregnate her! If only she could be full with him! She could then be shot of him. She realised how contrary to her sex's immemorial wish this sentiment was. But these were singular circumstances. What had been audacious in its conception was in practice trite and frustrating. 'I do not,' she told Curly as she lay beside him watching cars thrown across the ceiling by the camera obscura of a gap in the blinds, 'enjoy getting banged by other people. For whatever reason. And nothing's happening, is it?'

He didn't reply. She repeated: 'I said *nothing is happening*.'

'I heard. I was thinking, perhaps we should try someone else.'

'Please . . . We've been here before. *Who* else?'

Curly sat up and switched on the light. 'I mean, maybe we ought to get Henry to see someone? One of the quacks I went to. Give him a boost. Shot of something.'

Lavender's cackling laugh ascended the scale. She bit his ear and exclaimed: 'Darleenk, you is a gen-ee–us!'

'Never know – might do the trick.'

Chapter Thirteen

Henry Fowler's worst day yet was a bright blinding day.

It was the hottest day of August – temperature: 31 degrees, humidity: 82 per cent.

There was a look of murder on cabbies' faces and a hose-pipe ban in the offing. The air was thick with particulates, with emitted grist, with gaseous suspensions which curried eyes and mucous membranes. The flies were the size of bees. In central London Henry felt like a foreigner.

Who were all these bounteous girls with so few clothes on? With bottoms that had been poured into dangerous skirts. Oh there was so much skin, from tender biscuit to cooked crazed leather, from cleft chest to painted toe, from bra to mule. It was skin to devour. Henry wanted to be at the feast. No matter that his face was shinily self-basting. No matter that there were saline deposits describing arcs beneath his oxters and fretting his collar and spangling the chest of his royal-blue shirt. No matter – for this was Henry of the soon-to-be-reawakened appetite. He strode through the jellied air with inappropriate friskiness towards his second appointment with Mr William Savage-Smith.

One professional to another – that's how he conceived of his relationship with this consultant whose sobriety and respectability were such that he must have *something* to hide, some grubby buried vice, probably inherited from his father and practised in anonymous apartments at signal expense. He was so proper and, Henry reckoned, fee-greedy that he would not prescribe Henry the miracle drug Cocksure (not its real name, merely a ribald sobriquet) without Henry submitting to the test which had humiliated Curly, which had indirectly caused Henry, after years of near abstinence and meagre rations, once again to consider himself a sexual being.

During their recent holiday in the northern Auvergne Henry had twice persuaded Naomi to agree that they should make love and the fact that at the last moment it hadn't happened was due to the advice given to her by the thalassotherapist at the spa in Vichy rather than to her own unwillingness. Henry thought this promising. His brief disappointment was lifted by his delight in the verdant grandeur of the primitive post-volcanic landscape – it was as though the breasts of buried Amazons had been painted by a megalomaniac called Greenfinger. And there was solace to be had, too, in his anticipation of an appointment with Lavender the day after they returned to South London.

He had, as Curly cannily believed he would, begun to forget the real purpose of the monthly trysts – the child, so far as Henry was concerned, would merely be the unfortunate by-product of the exercise of his lust, of the permitted adulteration of the Beard-Croney marriage: Henry would feel no more attachment to little Blenheim than a carefree rover would to a wild oat germinated far, far away over distant hills in a passing womb to which he could no longer fit a face or name.

Henry sweated in Mr William Savage-Smith's waiting-room. He had been disappointed on his previous visit to discover that the photographic assistance which Curly had incredulously reported was not provided here. It was, a nurse had told him, the 'signature speciality' of Mr Gervaise Bassett (currently holidaying at his villa near Urbino and so unavailable to see Mr Fowler). It was a speciality eschewed by Mr Savage-Smith not because it might be considered offensive to his all-female staff (their sensibilities were, anyway, perennially ignored) but because he was anxious not to be accused of plagiarising Mr Bassett, a man jealous of his reputation as a pioneer and innovator.

'It's very small, the genito-urinary world,' the nurse had explained. 'I mean, everyone knows everyone else's business.'

On this boiling day she brought Henry a cup of sweet tea. 'There – that'll cheer you up.'

Henry shrugged quizzically as she left the room. He hoped that his demeanour was already cheerful. He was indignant that his cheerfulness had not been recognised. He had beamed at her with what he considered an appropriate interest – appreciative, certainly, but far from leering, well this side of lupine. Yes, with a smile that said 'all's well in the world of which we are equal (and only incidentally sexual) citizens', with, indeed, a smile composed of good cheer and zealously tended teeth.

Mr Savage-Smith hardly looked up. He mumbled a greeting. He shuffled in his chair – a gesture towards a gesture at standing. He continued reading a printout. He kneaded an ear lobe. Mr Savage-Smith's professionalism impressed and enervated Henry. All this show to convince his patients (and himself) that he was more than a mere pill pusher. He was a past master at being an eminent consultant: his voluminous gamut of ties and his stagey business with his bifocals advertised the gulf between his side of the desk where an initiate of a profession's arcana sits and the other side. Exclusion, Henry recognised, was what defined every profession. He practised it himself. It was what differentiated him from civilians. Without exclusion and the stamp of expertise it brought . . . well, the unthinkable might occur: the bereaved might realise that they could do it themselves, take the law into their own hands. They'd conduct backyard cremations. They'd dig graves in their gardens as though burying the family pet.

Henry ran an eye over the silver-framed family photographs on the desk. The Savage-Smith children were animal lovers: they bestrode ponies and stroked labradors – experiences which had been denied to Henry's family because of Naomi's distaste for quadrupeds, their smell, their moult, their feed. There were group portraits at christenings: Henry's children had not been baptised, nor, reciprocally, had they been bar mitzvahed. Here were the Savage-Smiths at one of their daughters' weddings. That'll come soon for Ben and Lennie, Henry thought fondly, smiling to himself about how quickly they'd grown up, wondering how he'd get on with their respective partners. He feared the prospect of being a grandfather but knew equally that he'd take pride in that status. He hoped that his parents would live long enough to see their great-grandchildren. Four generations of Fowler in a silver frame – now that will be something to celebrate.

'This—' Mr Savage-Smith cleared his throat: 'This is difficult . . .' He clenched his hands as though at prayer.

What a performance!

Henry was due later that afternoon to see a client, a Miss Moodyson, a septuagenarian spinster whose brusqueness and rudeness to him were inexcusable despite her having lost both parents (ninety-seven and ninety-nine) within three days of each other. It's often the way, it's the shock at the first's fatal stroke that does for the second. Her manner at their previous meeting had been condescending, she had evidently been under the illusion that she was addressing a tradesman. Henry would borrow from Mr Savage-Smith, he would treat her to a magisterial display of professionalism. He felt inspired.

'You're married . . . Ah, what's that, twenty-four years.' His delivery as he read from a file was slow as if resolving a conundrum, as if speaking to himself. 'Good innings nowadays,' he added in a smiley aside, actually addressing Henry. 'And two children . . . seventeen, sixteen . . . Uhmm. What did you, ah, *do* about the children? If I can put it that way.'

Henry pulled a face of bafflement, regarded him askew: 'Sorry but you've lost me there. I'm not quite with you.'

'I'm loath to invoke our friends the shrinks . . . the chippy brigade. Trouble with most of them is they neglected the Airfix side of their development: you'll never be a surgeon if you couldn't glue models. Yah? Still, they may be on to something with this notion that, how shall I put it, that a continued appetite in middle life is dependent on fecundity in youth . . . comparative youth. Of course there's no absolute proof of a causal link, never is with Jimmy Shrink . . . But circumstantial . . . Thing is I suppose *we* have tended to overlook the possibility that infertility and impotence could be connected simply because they're so routinely connected by the layman.' He spoke the word 'layman' with an amused sneer.

Henry nodded complicitly to signal that he, too, knew all about laymen a.k.a. the non-professionals, a.k.a. the pitifully uninitiated who demand to be led like lambs.

'The new thinking on this one's if a chap's conscious of his infertility or a low sperm count it acts as an inhibitor. One's touching here in a way on . . . on very big questions. What are we for? And the answer that our bodies seem to give us is that we're for reproduction. And if we don't reproduce our generative equipment takes industrial inaction, ha! Bit of a conundrum . . . If we don't do our bit to increase the human race then it looks as though we're supposed to forfeit the pleasures of sex – that's the message I'm afraid. Not a very cheering one. Especially not for the gay tendency: astonishing the incidence of impotence in middle-aged homosexuals – they're not necessarily infertile of course but they're pretty much all childless, goes without saying.

Electively childless . . . which is different. Haven't reproduced by choice.'

'I'm not homosexual. Never have been. And I wouldn't describe . . . I mean it's not impotence . . . not *per se*, nowhere near. Not actual—'

'Course not. Course not. Appreciate that. What I'm suggesting is that your condition – I must say you've done jolly well to spot it, nip it in the bud. Early bird! Ah? It's nothing that InterVene can't sort out p.d.q. Indeed yours is *precisely* the sort of case it's intended to treat. Childless . . . Symptoms of prospective impotence in middle life – hints at what's to come. Eh?'

'Yes . . . ?' Henry was ever more bemused. 'But I'm not childless. I've got two children. Like you said. Sixteen and seventeen.'

'Young adults . . . Their maturation, becoming sexual beings themselves – it's just the thing to set off the sense of inadequacy which manifests in partial impotence.'

'I don't feel inadequate,' replied Henry, stiffly.

Mr Savage–Smith smiled: 'Of course you don't. The children. Boys? Girls?'

'One of each.'

'There you are then. They're getting to the age when they're going to reproduce and – well it's like a worm isn't it? Working away at you, that knowledge. Their generative capability is going to be a reproach to their adoptive father. Going to make him feel inadequate that he couldn't have children of his own.'

Henry shook his head long-sufferingly. He laughed. 'No. No, I'm not their *adoptive* father. I think you've got your files in a twist.'

'Ah . . . Ah, so you took the donor route. Heavens – that makes you something of a pioneer in . . .' He scanned the file: 'What? '75?'

'I don't quite . . . This donor route. How's that relevant? They're our children. Our own – they're not adopted. There weren't donors involved. I don't . . . I think there must be . . . It's probably a computer error. Usually is.' Henry grinned reassuringly.

The grin dissipated as he witnessed Mr Savage-Smith's aghast reaction. The consultant seemed to be suffering a turn. He cradled his forehead, covered his eyes. Then he worriedly studied the window – four panes, one so warped that the house opposite was all bendy bricks and vorticist cornice. He distractedly chewed the ball of his right thumb. He scrutinised Henry as though he had never seen him before. He was looking at a different man, at a man whose life he was about to change for ever, who was gaping at him with an inquisitive show of filled teeth. He fixed him eye to eye. He spoke slowly and warily with no attempt to dissemble either his shock or the gravity of what he had to impart.

He could have spared Henry Fowler. Another consultant – Mr Gervaise Bassett, perhaps – might have allowed the man to live on in ignorance, in the comfort of his lie. Mr Savage-Smith didn't hesitate. He took a momentous moral decision in a split second, in the conviction that to have evaded it would have been a hippocratic dereliction which he could never have forgiven in himself.

'Mr Fowler, there's no easy way to put this. You are infertile.'

Henry's disbelieving laugh was an articulated wince.

'I hadn't realised,' continued Mr Savage-Smith, 'you weren't apprised of—'

'Ridiculous. It's . . . What . . . What are you basing it on? Infert—'

'The test results are unequivocal I'm afraid . . . The samples you deposited—'

'They'll have mixed them up. They do it with babies. Do it all the time. You can't pick up a paper without some . . . If they can do it with babies they're not going to have any problem doing it with specimen jars are they?'

'I only wish there had been a mistake – but they're fail-safe, our procedures. Samples are split, they go to two laboratories, independent, no contact between them.'

'Tell me this . . .' Henry repeatedly jabbed a finger. He swallowed before he could speak again. There was a lachrymose catch in his voice. 'How many infertile men . . . do you know . . . who've got two children?' He stared at Mr Savage-Smith whose face was obscured by his hands. Was the man trying to hide? 'Two children. How can I be infertile?' He was accusing. He was pleading. Mostly he was pleading.

Mr Savage-Smith's sympathy was engaged. He murmured through clasped hands: 'Ah, perhaps . . . perhaps you should have a talk with your wife.'

Chapter Fourteen

The scissors glimmer in Henry Fowler's hand.

The nocturnal city's penumbra seeps through uncurtained windows. He steals through this house which is his house, which he knows so well, which is a history of more than a quarter of his life: here's the parquet tile which clicks even when stepped on softly; here's the stair-rod with the kink which wasn't there one day and was the next; here are the prints of oasts and elms at the turn of the stairs; and here, invisible because of reflective glass, is the hand-coloured, yard-long photograph of the Crystal Palace.

He opens the door of Leonora's room, a door he used to open on all fours as Barry the Bear, roaring, when she was little, when she was a lost princess squirming with delighted fright. He used to open it as Thargul the Kreblonite when she was the doomed space maiden Zurgtrene. He was her father then. He longs to be her father still: he is her father, surely. The bedroom admits no light. He closes his eyes to prepare them for the solid blackness. Lennie insists on blinds and lined cutains. She smells the way young girls will, of warm laundry and newly baked biscuit, of downy skin and chewing-gum. Her breath fills the room. It guides him to her. He moves gingerly. As his eyes adjust to the darkness he begins to discern the disposition of her body beneath the single sheet's pleats and folds. These are the soft contours of her shoulder. She lies diagonally across the bed, almost prone. How tall she has grown, a stretch-Naomi, fine and equine, long limbed with her mane of chestnut hair sweeping across the pillow as though fixed by a head wind. He looks down on her with a love that's unconditional even though its very foundation is in question. His grief numbs him. He stares at her and wonders – who are you?

Clenching his teeth in anxiety lest a cracking joint betray him Henry Fowler squats beside the bed, clutching the scissors. He fears that his balance is impaired so he slides his right leg behind him, kneels on that knee in a pose suggestive of chivalry. He lifts her thick hair from her pillow with his left hand, resisting all temptation to stroke it, grips a hank between thumb and forefinger, manoeuvres himself wrigglingly on the carpet, lifts the scissors and cuts. He puts them into his pocket and takes from it an envelope in to which he slides the lock of hair. And as Lennie stirs, murmuring in her sleep, Henry creeps from her room. He closes the door, sweeps his brow with his cuff, seals the envelope with what meagre spittle his dry mouth will yield, replaces it in his pocket and, a thief in the night, tiptoes away. He hears Naomi's car draw up outside.

There's that old familiar screech when she clumsily engages reverse as an auxiliary brake. It still brings a smile to his face, the way she can never get the hang of it, it still has him shaking his head in a pipe-and-carpet-slippers way, fondly.

'Ooh. What a . . .' Naomi sighed as she dumped her bag on a chair beside the kitchen table. 'How are you?' she asked Henry who sat at it pretending engrossment in the new edition of *The Right Box*.

'OK,' he lied, 'all right. Yeah.'

'I had to play with Sheila. Wuss – she's so *timid* . . . No sense of adventure. Never taken a risk in her life. Still, I made a small slam – hearts. No thanks to her.'

'Well done.'

'I'm going to – d'you want a Cointreau or something? B and B?'

Without waiting for his reply she walked from the room. Then her head reappeared round the door jamb: 'Oh 'fore I forget – They've asked Ben to stay on . . . That's good isn't it. He's going to come back after the weekend. Is that all right with you?'

Henry raised his shoulders noncommittally and spread wide his palms, in one of his now unselfconscious 'Jew-ish' gestures. He cursed silently. She walked through to the dining-room where she kept an ebony-and-ormolu-effect trolley loaded with sweet liquors of the world. She raised her voice: 'I did ring. At about four. But Horse Face said you were out.'

He heard the chink of sculpturally extravagant bottles.

'Mistuh Foalher hez en h'ppointment,' she exaggerated Mrs Grusting's parade-ground enunciation. 'Did you?' she yelled.

'Did I what, love?' He heard himself call her love. It formed on his tongue without his leave, exited his mouth before he could stop it.

'Have an appointment at four o'clock. I never know with her. She might just be being difficult.'

'Yes. I did.'

He had had an appointment at four o'clock with Dai Turnbull who had overcome the handicaps of a facial lupus the size of a fist, a fluting voice, two aborted corruption inquiries, a dismissed charge of causing death by dangerous driving, a dismissed sexual-harassment suit and perennial alcoholism to achieve the rank of Detective Chief Superintendent.

Dai's catch-phrase was 'never kick a nigger . . . till he's down': he was a legend for the way he extended the pause. It had made him a sought-after after-dinner speaker on the South London circuit because, as every Rotarian, Lion and Mason agreed, the Super after-dinner spoke as he found.

They met in a not-very-French café in Upper Norwood where Gordon the owner knew better than to present Turnbull with a bill, and the waitresses in horizontally striped tops knew better than to complain about Turnbull's octopus hands. Hands which when Henry arrived were occupied tearing up a cake and dipping the pieces into a stiffly corrected coffee.

They small-talked:

'How's the lad then Henry?'

'He's at Solihull this week.'

'Shacken are son goo.'

'No. The N.S.R. . . . whatsit. Centre of Excellence – for squash . . .'

'Oh that's right yeah. Yeah, remember he was a bit of a player. Course his mum was—'

'That was tennis.'

'Same basic skill though. What I mean, Henry, is he doesn't get it from you, does he?'

Henry winced.

Turnbull ordered more coffee. 'And bring the bottle this time if you would. I dunno – optics, measures. In Spain they've never heard of them.' He leaned back. 'So . . . ?'

'Now Dai. This is strictly, uh . . .' And he brushed the side of his nose.

'Ontrah noo. Course it is Henry. You know me old son.'

'Thing is, well, I, I need to get some DNA tests done. And I was wondering if there was any way you could discreetly bung 'em through one of your labs . . .'

'Oh dear Henry. Oh my. You been playing away haven't you . . . and someone's saying you've stuck one in the back of the net.'

Henry did his best to grin his roguish grin.

'Whoops-a-daisy. I feel for you Henry I truly do. But the

answer is no. No can do. The flesh is willing but my hands are tied – there is ab-so-lute-ly no way round the . . . It's watertight you know. The procedures. Don't think we haven't conducted a thorough . . . Why d'you need the Met to do it?'

'Well . . . I guess . . . Well suppose I don't. Really. Not specifically. The Met. I mean I don't know how you go about . . .'

'Aaah. Haah. Someone Else's Baby! That's what you need Henry. Just the ticket. Someone Else's Baby.'

He observed Henry for a sign of recognition that didn't come.

'No? All that fuss over the advert? No? Doesn't ring a bell?'

Two weeks before Christmas 1989 Shaun Memory, a former Detective Inspector who had taken early retirement, sometime celebrity security executive and currently the managing director and sole employee of AAAA Investigations, was unable to afford even the services of the equally unsuccessful one-man advertising consultancy which rented the neighbouring plasterboard-and-asbestos partition in a Tulse Hill office block. He was 'just another struggling trace agent going under for lack of curiosity, for criminal lack of interest in the where-do-I-come-from factor'.

He wrote his own advertisement and took a display space in the personal classifieds of two broadsheet and three tabloid national newspapers.

> You're Dark. She's Blonde. The Kid's Ginger.
> How Do You Know It Wasn't The Milkman?
> SOMEONE ELSE'S BABY
>
> 0(8)1 674 1910

The response was immediate and various.

By the third week of January 1990 Someone Else's Baby was

investigating seventeen cases in which a husband or male partner suspected that a child which bore his name might have been conceived of a covert liaison of the mother. In four cases the child had already attained majority, and in one the client was the paternal grandmother, acting without the knowledge either of her son or of the daughter-in-law whom she suspected of having betrayed him.

Shaun Memory was obliged to take on extra investigative staff, one of them a former colleague who had paid his debt to society, the other a moonlighter still employed by the Met. A further partition was rented and a school-leaver hired to answer the phone, open the mail, paint her nails, etc. It was this girl Vandella who excitedly told her boss one late January afternoon that a researcher from BBC2's mid-morning flagship *Hare Dares Share Cares* was on the line.

It was his appearance on that programme which made his memorable name. Memory was quick-witted and canny, and in an agitated studio discussion with representatives of angry women's groups and resentful men's groups and wronged family groups and fearful children's groups he convincingly refuted the accusation that he was preying on the basest of fears and was pandering to the paranoia of the sort of men whose appetite for domestic violence was whetted by the aggressive selling of his agency.

No one was obliged to seek Someone Else's Baby's services – he was a small business, not an arm of a police state.

Was he not creating problems where none had existed? asked Jane Hare, the grossly over-promoted telly gardener (who had made her début as the simpering, sexy [for a gardening programme] trug interest on *Leafy Glade*).

Of course not.

Was there not the possibility that his investigations might touch people's very identity?

Of course there was: that was their point. Wasn't a father's identity bound to that of his children, was it not even defined by the sureness of his paternity?

And surely children should not in this day and age live in ignorance of their natural parents as he had done . . .

It was here that Shaun Memory broke down and tearfully recalled in agonised detail the agony of his very own personal agony.

The evening of the day they had buried his father (Dad) his mother (Mum) had taken him aside and had confessed to him, her only child (Son), what she had had to keep, Son, all these years from Dad: that he (Son) was, how can I say this, in fact the son of Angelo Bravin. Remember him – the half-Italian chap – who used to come down with his wife Augusta to visit once a year from Scotland when you were just a nipper? Angelo who had been with Dad in the REME during the Berlin Airlift. Angelo who always used to give you a florin and a slice of the dry salami he kept in his pocket.

But then Augusta died and Angelo remarried and we (Mum and Dad [who wasn't Dad]) never heard from him again but they heard about him, not, evidently, directly from him but from other REME veterans Dad was in touch with, that he had had a family with the new wife and they must be taking up all his time at that time in life.

Shaun Memory almost held back his tears, but not quite.

The special pleaders and the studio audience were silenced.

Shaun Memory's parents, Shaun Snr and Betty, would not have been surprised, would indeed have been gratified by their son's performance.

They were in their apartment above their nest-egg-cum-golden-goose, the Bar Crystal Palace in Estepona, bought for a song when Shaun Snr had taken his early retirement from the Met in 1972, and although they had a nice satellite dish among the characterful tiles they weren't watching.

Dai Turnbull was watching. Not normally an avid mid-morning telly potato, he was having to wait on a tired shiny sofa because his Thursday masseuse Avril was taking her time with her eleven-o'clock gentleman, a mug payer, apparently.

Having served with both Memory father and Memory son he had a bit of a titter to himself. He began to calculate the odds against the creation of a new pass number into the Central Police Computer being uncovered. Then he thought through how he could put it to Shaun Memory Jnr who was as bent as the day is long. He swiftly buried his head in *Slutlust*'s centrefold when Avril's eleven-o'clock gentleman at last appeared – the Metropolitan stipendiary magistrate Mr Robert Edwin with a fresh bloom on his failed-barrister face. Dai noted this for future reference.

The vein stood proud of Henry Fowler's skin, a worm gorged on blue cheese. It shone when a dab of spirit was applied. Then the needle went in. The dropper filled with crimson of such splendour and chromatic richness that Henry told himself of course it's all right, of course it's the right blood, it's just a cock-up, with blood like that how can I be infertile.

That blood has signs within it. That blood is a message, it's the book of my life, it's what I inherited and what I passed on, it's the vector of my essence.

'I hear you – I know what you're looking at,' Shaun Memory, himself, told Henry. 'This is one for me personally . . . I'll look after this one myself . . . any friend of Dai's . . .' Bloke to bloke, geezer to geezer. 'I'll get you a result . . . Didn't get this little lot by not getting them.'

Shaun Memory congratulated himself by stretching back like God in his padded leather recliner and swivelling to include everything around him in his office on the ground floor of the fancy Gipsy Hill villa where he now employed a staff of twenty-two. There it all was, all that other people's misery and suspicions had bought him: the heirloom range of furniture, the ancestor paintings, the heritage features (age-old putti at the corners, deep cornice moulding all around the ballroom-size room), and through the long windows an abundantly sylvan garden whose boundary was invisible, which might, thought Henry, have stretched to West Norwood Cemetery.

'So – we got your blood sample, we got the girl's hair and . . . what we got of the boy's?'

'Wristband,' Henry reminded him.

'Wristband! I like it . . . That's how we slapped one on that heavy-metal feller. See it in the papers? *Krait* – Darryl Fox. Refused to give a sample . . . So we had Vandella there liberate one of his sweatbands. After a gig. Souvenir for a loyal Krait fan eh?'

Shaun Memory's laugh was vicious.

'OK Henry – if I may – you just leave it to us and we'll be in touch . . . should be Friday. Oh – and the girls know to give you a Dai special: 12½ per cent discount.'

Chapter Fifteen

Another lazy afternoon for them, but not for me, Henry told himself. Another ignorant afternoon for them. Maybe the last.

He fixed a sandwich of thickly buttered bread and ham. He stared out into the drowsy garden where bikinied Lennie was sprawled behind a stockade of sunblock bottles. Ben and Ben's fellow squash prodigy, keen, bulgy-muscled Nolan Oates lolled side by side on a striped recliner and a Portofino chair chosen by Naomi and bought by Henry out of the fruits of his labours burying and burning the dead for the children of the dead.

The last time he had looked Nolan had been rubbing tanning oil into Ben's thighs with what seemed to him like undue zeal.

A glass jug sweated on a table shaded by the thatched South Seas parasol. The carmine fluid in it was evidently iced. He wondered what combination of sticky liquors they were drinking.

Then he wondered why he cared.

He tried to persuade himself that he was indifferent to them and to their behaviour, that he didn't care if they turned into teenage drunks, thence into pocked derelicts, diseased runaways peddling their bodies at King's Cross for the price of however many grams of crack it took to achieve blissful oblivion. But he did care: the thought of them screaming as their most intimate quarters were ripped and bludgeoned by drunken middle managers from the soot towns sickened him. The habit of worry was not one that could be quashed at a whim. He was going to have to learn lack of concern, he was going to have to work on post-paternal indifference. His fatherly instincts were not going to die of their own accord. They would have to be smothered. He needed to perform a psychic excision.

His unconditional love for Ben and Lennie had initially surprised him with its stealth and then with its steadfastness. No matter how bolshie, no matter how sarky they became he tolerated them, excused them, told himself that he had behaved that way too at their age (he hadn't – and he knew it). Ben's selfishness was of course singlemindedness. Lennie's petulant sulks were expressions of her high standards. She was bound to be bitchy because she was so much cleverer than her contemporaries.

He remembered the squashy batches of Pampers and the smells of powder, of pink ointment, of Milton steriliser which he, who had lived a lifetime with formalin in his nostrils, could still not abide. He remembered the brief period when they had been of a size to share a double buggy which slithered on slimy bronze leaves on Fox Hill and how they all ended up in a pile against a none-too-steady fence with an excited spaniel on the other side. For years after they'd ask him to tell the tale of how he'd stopped their buggy racing down the hill, of how close they'd come to a terrible accident, of the dangers in wait at the bottom. Fifteen years ago, fifteen years! It seemed no time at all. The spaniel was called Biscuit, it must be dead by now.

He hadn't thought of them as cuckoos then. He had believed then (or would have done had it ever occurred to him) that they had every right to the most precious place in his life, every right to his heart. And to his pocket: how much was it supposed to cost to bring up a child?

All his love, all his energy, all his money, all his care and kindness and forbearance and sufferance – all for what?

For two counterfeit children. For two bastards with a wobbly provenance. For two gets got on his strumpet wife by . . . ?

Now, there was the question.

Who's your father?

Should he be consumed with hatred for the unknown seedsman? Should he confront him whilst *his* wife and children (and God knows where they came from) cower behind him down the hall when truth comes rapping on the door.

In his wallet, stapled to two flimsy slips of indecipherable printout bearing figures, percentages, arrows and ratios, was a personally written note from Shaun Memory himself on paper bearing the Someone Else's Baby logo:

It's a sickener but as anticipated. But it'll be best at the end of the day for one and all if you can clear the air. The analysysis conclusion there's no profile compatibility between your profile and the kids. It also is 99% certain that the two kid's have the same father. I have instructed further tests of this instant to ensure 100% watertight but take it for read that it is the same father. This fits with the circumstantial closeness of them being born so close to each other. Formal breakdown of analysysis and explanation follows but I have taken the liberty of informal message in as much as you wanted the results double quick time. Speak soon to pursue how we proceed the matter from here. Cheers. Shaun.

Henry ran his hand over the front of the fridge where magnetised sheep, cows, trees and fences had once been ranked. Those attachments had constituted the children's rustic world. He had used them to teach Ben and Lennie about the countryside which they seldom visited because of Naomi's antipathy to the smells and her appraisal of mud as inconvenient and her fear of quadrupeds unless they were tinned or in a packet. He could list all her foibles, all her whimsies, all her enthusiasms: he had lived with them half a lifetime.

And nothing could dissuade him from being charmed by them, vain and trivial as they were – nothing. Not even this epic betrayal which Henry Fowler knew to be the stuff of the old Greek myths and on which shrinks had founded their trade: 'Their fraudulent trade. You might even call it freudulent! They'll still be at it come the millennium. They give a different meaning to Grecian 2000.'

That was one of the gags he had made in his address, 'Special Concerns Prompted by Filial Grief for a Mother', to the Lowestoft conference the previous autumn. It won him two big laughs and a round of applause which he reckoned to be genuinely felt, well deserved.

It would have been his absence at conference all those years ago that had allowed Naomi the opportunity to conceive and gestate the two insults in the garden.

He hadn't always wanted to go but it was duty, it was family tradition. What was conference without a Fowler?

No wonder Ben lacked an appetite for funeral direction. No wonder when he had spent a week in the office during his Easter holiday to get a feel for his future he had moped and had treated the staff with an offhand indifference as though the very notion of contact with the business was beneath him – the very business which was starting its tenth decade, which had provided him with all that he had ever asked for, which bore his name. No wonder – it wasn't in his blood; the boy lacked the genetic pattern which had made generation upon generation of Fowler supreme in his field between Streatham and Beckenham. Henry had instructed him that his hauteur was despicable, that Fowler & Son would be around long after they were both dead, that the family business was bigger than any single Fowler. But then, Henry told himself, at Easter Ben had been a Fowler. Now he wasn't. That was his problem. That was the burden he was going to have to bear throughout life. Henry had spent hours deliberating about how he should break the news.

You are not you.

No. No. How could he hurt them thus. They were his children.

Even when concentrating on the very matter of how to tell them that they were not his children he would forget that they were not his children. He was so much a prisoner of paternal habit. He had defined himself as a father above all else. And now he was an ex-father, a father who had never been a father, a delusory father. He was a cuckold duped into caring for a family of cuckoos. He was no bodily part of the family which had been his family, his life, for seventeen years; it was more than eighteen since Naomi had told him with a sly, proud smile that she was pregnant.

Had she believed he was the father? She must have known.

The day of Ben's birth had been the most thrilling of his life. He had himself felt reborn. He had been granted a further identity. He was no longer just the son who had become a husband. His accretion of roles had further swollen: he had driven excitedly, but observing the speed limit, from graveside to bedside, from a finished life in Hither Green to a fresh one in Denmark Hill.

He feared that he might cause confusion at the hospital. He didn't want this special day adulterated by presumptuous hospital staff directing him towards the mortuary. So he stripped off his jacket and waistcoat and tie at successive traffic lights, folding them with exhilarated abandon so as not to crease them and stacking them neatly on the passenger seat beside him. He was smiling rapturously, humming a tune, a soaring, hymnal tune whose name he had never known. He told himself I am a father now, I am a father now.

I am not a father now.

And he couldn't remember the way the tune went.

He wanted to hum it again to recover what he'd lost – that day zero of the most beautiful baby he had seen, his baby, coated in silky hair leeching the narcotic breast milk of the wife whom motherhood had transformed into a serene mammal. Mother and child formed an exclusive pair amongst the abundant flowers in baskets and vases and bouquets and cellophane which filled the small room. They were tied to each other. Naomi smiled at him from within a far state of dreamy detachment. Her absorption in the child was entire.

Henry took the boy when he was sated. His eyes filled with terror. His face contorted like an inbred dog's. He screamed. He wriggled. But Henry got the newborn's rhythm – of course he did, they worked to the same blood clock, father and son – and the boy calmed. Henry claims he smiled. Then Henry began to sneeze with rhinitic spasms, shuddering uncontrollably.

'You're allergic to him,' announced Naomi with proprietorial satisfaction.

Henry passed his son to Naomi and struggled to pull a handkerchief from his trouser pocket.

''Snot *him*,' he insisted. 'It's all these flowers. Like a florist's in here it is.'

He stepped back from the bed and tripped on a plastic bucket of exotics, breaking the stems of two parrot-beaked heliconia and making a puddle which he stooped to mop with clumsy paper towels.

Naomi sighed and spoke to the baby: 'He's spoiling our lovely flowers.'

The miracle of life. That baby could now bring a carbon-fibre racket into contact with a rubber ball travelling at 90 m.p.h. in such a way that the ball's speed would be so reduced that when it touched the front wall of the court it would plummet vertically to the floor. That was a miracle. And so was the human ingenuity which made the connection between that ball's terminal trajectory and a dead bird and advertised that ingenuity by the use of the figurative construction 'to kill a ball'. Telephones, butterfly stroke, nylon-tip pens, the emotive capability of music, the way some people are blond and some are left-handed, the shapes of faces in clouds, water's inability to flow uphill, the tastiness of animals' flesh, pain, bustles, reptiles' poison sacs, sinus drainage, cantilevering, DNA testing – miracles of life, all of them.

Henry was in an ontological slump with his feet up, the curtains drawn and a cup of tepid tea when he heard Naomi return home.

'What you up to?' she asked through the gloom. She put down the shiny boutique bags she was carrying. 'You got a headache or something?'

Henry didn't speak. He shook his head, stood and reached for his jacket, draped over a coffee table. He withdrew his wallet from an inner pocket.

This was it. The moment he most feared. The moment whose anticipation had nagged at him fretfully. It was the moment that he couldn't stop himself trying to foresee, trying to call.

It wasn't too late to pull back. He could continue to lead this life of lies that he had led for eighteen years. He hadn't of course known the nature of the life he had been leading: thus it hadn't been a life of lies. But once a dupe knows he's a dupe he ceases to be a dupe. And if he doesn't reveal his knowledge of the bad faith he has been subjected to and mutely plays along he colludes in his own betrayal. He blesses the hand that grips the hilt.

Henry silently handed Naomi Shaun Memory's memo and the attached test results.

She peered at it in the half-light. 'What's . . . Someone Else's . . .'

She walked across the room, drew a curtain. She stood to read in the window bay. When she had finished she held the paper by her side and stared through the window. She scratched at a spot on a pane.

She turned and spoke with wistful candour: 'I'd almost forgotten . . . So you *didn't* know . . . It's funny – I often . . . I often used to tell myself that you knew, that you'd guessed and you didn't say anything because you didn't want to upset the apple-cart.'

'What!'

'Well, they don't look like you do they? You might have guessed. You probably *should* have.'

'Lots of kids don't look like their parents. I don't look like *my* parents. Doesn't mean to say that my mother was off with all and sundry getting knocked up.'

'Henry! Don't be coarse.'

'That's ripe. This, this is incredible.' Henry hadn't known what to expect but he had certainly not expected Naomi's blithe and guiltless admission of her infidelity. But then Naomi had lived for years with the two consequences of that infidelity: she was acquainted with her mores – he didn't doubt her protestation of near-forgetfulness. He had only the other day watched a telly programme about unsolved crimes in which a psychologist had claimed that the majority of murderers who go undiscovered forget their crime after the passage of years. Murder, though, does not generate lives.

Henry wondered at her shamelessness.

Sometime as that day worn on and vapour trails were scrawled across the blush in the West and the window-cleaner's neligence became ever more apparent Naomi asked him brusquely: 'What do you want to do?'

'I don't think we can go on like this.'

'We have for years – gone on like this.'

'You have. *You* have. I haven't. Not me.'

'What are you going to say to Ben and Lennie?' she asked.

'What am *I* . . . ? That's up to you isn't it – they're your kids. I don't feel inclined to say anything.'

'Henry. Henry. Don't be so . . . old-fashioned. You're being like some sort of Victorian whatsit.'

Henry remembered the print of Augustus Egg's triptych *Past and Present* in his parents' dining-room. A stern Victorian husband, despite her pleas for mercy, casts out his adulterous wife to live rough with her illegitimate child, rendering his own children by her motherless and bereft.

'What are you smiling about?' Naomi accused him.

Henry shook his head. It was too complicated to explain. She would misunderstand. How times had changed.

'Henry. How else did you expect to have kids?'

'What d'you mean?'

'*What do you mean?*' she parrotted. 'I mean I couldn't get pregnant by you . . . Seven years. Not on the pill. Seven years it was, Henry, seven years we were trying. I wanted children. I longed for children.'

She comes now to as near tearfulness as she will get.

He made stumblingly towards her.

'Henry – I don't need these . . . things.' She waved the analysis strips. 'You don't need to give them to me. If that's what they're saying . . . It's infertility isn't it?'

'That's not what they're for. You've just read it. They're DNA matches.'

'But you are. Aren't you? Infertile.'

He stood still, he cast his eyes down, he nodded.

Naomi stretched out a hand to him. It rested on his forearm.

'I think I've known for years,' she said.

'I don't understand how you could do this.' He flapped his arm to push her hand away.

'They're *your* children – just like if you'd adopted them . . . or I'd been married before or something.'

'What! Oh don't insult me. Please. *My* children. *My* children.

My children don't exist. I don't have any children.' Henry looked out into the garden where Ben straddled prone Nolan Oates and was anointing him with Tanfastic-Lite, rubbing the lotion into his fellow prodigy's abdomen.

'Whose children are they, matter of fact?' Henry tried to sound indifferent, unconcerned.

'Henry – don't.' She mistook her cue, simpered sweetly: 'Don't be like that. They're *our* children. You're just—'

'Stop being so fucking cute. You know what I'm talking about.'

Naomi walked across the room. She tapped the corks and screwtops of several bottles before pouring herself a kümmel.

'Do you want anything?' She put on a little girl's voice.

'Just tell me,' he replied brusquely.

'The . . . *their* natural father—'

'Cut the crap. Their *father*. Without the bleeding euphemism. Their *father*, all right.'

'I was just going to say. Their *birth* father . . . is dead.'

'Have a name? Did he have a name? This *birth* father.'

'Oh Henry you were always so naive. I mean it's not the sort of thing you discuss—'

He hit her.

That was the first and only time he thus contaminated their union. He smote with an articulate open palm, he stung with his wedding ring. She staggered back dropping her kümmel glass.

She enquired incredulously: 'Henry?'

She could not believe what he had done to her. Nor could he.

But his appetite was aroused. His big scrubbed pink hands grasped her by the neck.

'Don't!' she yelped.

She had never before seen the veins that rose like subcutaneous roots in his forehead. She had never before seen bedlam in his eyes.

'OK. OK,' she gasped.

Henry relaxed his grip. She might have tricked him with her womb but he knew now that he could better her with his limbs. There was potency in his infertile body.

'Well?' he insisted.

'He's *dead*,' she panted.

'So you said. Do you want to go through all this again? I'm sure I'm more up for it than you.'

'It was Fred.'

'Fred?' Henry pondered the curt syllable. 'Fred?' He was nonplussed.

'Did I know this Fred?'

'Fred . . . *Freddie*. Freddie Glade?' She bit her lip.

'Freddie Glade. You're joking. Ahahaha. And pigs might fly . . . Stop messing me about. Who was it?'

'Henry. Freddie Glade was their father.'

'Like fuck. Freddie Glade was a screamer, he was a pillow biter.'

'We had an affair for three and a half years.' She spoke with such cold authority that Henry's doubt evaporated. 'I stopped it because he wanted me to leave you . . . And I . . . I didn't want to. I loved you. I couldn't . . . That's never going to come off the carpet.' She looked down to where the unbroken glass had spilled its sticky contents.

'So that's where Ben gets it from.' Henry gestured towards the garden where the two glistening boys were now gently wrestling each other under Lennie's bored eye. 'Solved that little mystery eh? The bender gene . . . Think about it . . . Your son's a Jewish arse bandit. I'm glad he's not mine. I've some packing to do.'

Chapter Sixteen

Henry Fowler, aged forty-six years and ten months, left his marital home which he soon came to understand had never been anything more than a provisional home, a home which he was surprised not to miss.

One spore-ridden autumn evening he sat in his car down the road from it, watching as a spurned spouse is meant to. The moon wore a shred of defiled nightie. Naomi pulled shut the sitting-room curtains. Lennie returned from school in an unlicensed cab with a smoking exhaust. A few weeks previously that would have worried him, and he'd have instructed her not to take risks with Nigerian taxi pimps. Now he was not so much concerned with her safety as with the lost opportunity to exercise paternal authority, exhibit paternal love. It wasn't the children themselves he missed, it was being a parent, it was the way the children affected him. That was what Naomi had taken from him – his status, the role he defined himself by. The loss he suffered was not that of three individuals but of the composite unit of which he was the fourth part – the family, *his* family. He was no longer Henry Fowler, Family

Man. His honorific had been stripped from him, and that shocked him.

He went Home to his octogenarian parents and to the room he had inhabited till he left Home to get married. He went Home to a room that was a museum of his former self. A museum made by his mother who, in the way of mothers, still thought of him as a child. To his mother Henry was a Meccano boy, a Denis Wheatley reader whose wet afternoons were passed with plastic cowboys and lead Indians. He was a boy who communicated with his mother and father through the medium of board-games: Monopoly, Halma, Scrabble (for which the familial name was Squabble).

It wasn't that his mother ignored the evidence of the white tidemark round his blond head and of his cheeks' paunches and of the overlapping labial folds his eyes peered out of. But she believed that within every grown man there is a little boy fighting to get out – and only his mother has the key.

In that room she had recreated a synthesis of his childhood, a generalised remembrance. There were toys from age eight alongside clothes from age sixteen, his first driving licence, a torn duffle bag filled with ticket stubs and cigar boxes, stamp albums and copies of *Photoplay*, extinct fountain pens, an equestrian statuette of the Queen side-saddle, a money box in the form of a crown, a cricket bat with a perished rubber handle and Stanley's name inked on its splice.

Henry showed it to his father.

'He's going to come a cropper up Her Majesty if he's not careful. He's such a climber Stanley is. Have you washed your hands for lunch?'

Mr Fowler suffered the immemorious state called CRAFT – Can't Remember A Fucking Thing. (The BMJ's Acronym of the Month prize went to Dr Tim Le Vasseur of the MRC, The Ridgeway, Mill Hill, London NW7, for that one.) CRAFT is the still smily end of Alzheimer's, before the rage sets in. Before the jabbering and scowls.

'I don't know why we have that fellow in goal when we've got Sam Bartram.'

That Charlton Athletic goalkeeper had retired forty years previously, in the days when Brentford's goalkeeper was Gerry Cakebread, a name that was a household joke because Mr Fowler had noticed a baker in Letchworth called Cakebread – 'With a name like that . . .' He ascribed Gerry's supposed fumbles to his hands being slippery with dough. Forty years later he sat close by the TV screen on a Saturday afternoon watching the classified results with his tea and his dripping-soaked toast, with his Littlewoods coupon and chewed HB stub. He would chuckle if Brentford had conceded more than one goal: it would compensate for his never winning the pools.

Forty years later . . .

Why, it seemed like only yesterday.

Literally like only yesterday.

And that was Mr Fowler's problem. The longer he had held a memory the clearer it was. The more recent the event the more CRAFT-affected its retention would be. His late middle age, his old age, his dotage had been scrambled without regard for sequentiality. The mnemonic store of a third of his life existed in a single plane. The trivial and the momentous piled up regardless of moral paramountcy and temporal linearity. The randomness of his remembrance rewrote his history.

His life had been dominated by a stone in his shoe which had caused him discomfort throughout many cremations. His life had been marred by his embarrassment at having addressed the Duke of— by the wrong style at His Grace's former butler's funeral. He reminisced persistently about a perfect sunset, stripes of baby pink and baby blue, which he had witnessed near Bridge of Allan on his Scottish honeymoon. It had set an unattainable standard. No subsequent day's end had matched it. He railed against the raggedness of orange clouds and the untidiness of modern sunsets. Unleaded petrol doesn't smell right. Cars today! He compared his tinny apple-green runabout to his stolid subfusc Rovers, he never forgot a car he'd owned, nor its registration number. This one, G849 ALB, it's a Noddy car, a can on wheels, that's all it is, not fit for a senior citizen – and apple green! He had forgotten that he had chosen it himself. He asks when Old Cyclops, a 1953 Rover, is going to be back from the garage. Plastic shoehorns break. Why can't phones have proper dials so you know where you are with them? It's always tricky dealing with women like that dog woman – you never know where you are with them . . .

Mrs Fowler hurriedly shushed him when he talked about the dog woman. Henry hardly looked up from his dinner on a tray. He was tired of feeling obliged to express curiosity about a cast of nicknamed walk-ons promoted to starring roles. Most nights he stayed Home and ate TV Toastswitch, a favourite recipe of his early teens gleaned from a 1959 edition of *TV Times*: toasted sliced bread, grilled streaky rashers, chopped tomato, sprig of parsley to set it off. It tasted as satisfyingly delicious as it had when he had first eaten it. It took him back to those times of simple comforts in the overheated, brown house, times that seemed effortlessly to repeat themselves. He embraced the old routine. There were differences: in the morning he left for work in his car rather than for school on his bicycle; when he went out in the evenings it was to Curly's house, not to Stanley's.

'Just popping over to see the kids,' he'd lie to his mother.

He didn't reveal to Curly and Lavender the reason why he had left his marital home.

Had he admitted to his infertility Lavender would have had no cause to copulate with him, he had no doubt of that. He lied in order to prolong the arrangement, to safeguard his thrice-monthly emissions.

He claimed that Naomi 'was seeing someone else'.

Curly giggled at the euphemism: 'To see. Verb, transitive. To register ocularly. To understand through the sense of sight. To fuck . . .'

Henry smiled wanly. His resignation was well practised. He had slipped into the role of the cuckold who does the decent thing for the sake of the kids. He hadn't forced his adulterous wife from the house. He had provided for his family.

'Who is he? Do you know him?' Curly asked.

'Some Jewboy from Edgware.' Henry relished the racial slur of his lie, the breach of decency. There was an almost physical sense of release in speaking thus: it was like swearing as a child. Lavender glanced at Curly.

Henry added: 'I haven't had the pleasure of meeting him.'

Lavender trilled: 'It's brilliant isn't it? It's classic Arends and Page.'

She excitedly cited those authorities' 'classic study' of the breakdown of marriages between partners of different races, colours, religions, nationalities. They had investigated 500 or perhaps 900 such broken marriages (Henry wasn't hearing well, he had neglected his earwax routine since returning Home). One of their conclusions was that women who have contracted exogamous marriages and who subsequently conduct adulterous liaisons are three times as likely to conduct them with members of their own tribe/race/sect, etc, than with members of their husband's or other alien group. Such liaisons may be regarded as redemptive. By entering into such a union the woman is reaffirming her link with the group which she has betrayed and whose genes she has depleted.

'That's pretty deep . . . Yeah, thought-provoking,' said Henry.

Is that why Naomi had slept with Freddie Glade?

It didn't make him feel any different about it. He remained, more than a month after the revelation of the deception practised on him, numb and peculiarly invulnerable. Hurt? Hurt was to come. He had yet to appreciate the weight of his loss. He was rehearsed at telling himself that he was no longer obliged to endure Lennie's aspirantly worldly sarcasm and her brother's sullen sexuality. He was spared the burden of commenting enthusiastically on Naomi's purchases of the day. Just how many ways were there of murmuring appreciation whilst hinting that pecuniary prudence might be in order tomorrow, or next week – fairly soon anyway?

'Could be, though,' he suggested, 'that they're just homesick – so to speak.'

'But why are they homesick? What are they homesick for? Obviously,' Lavender observed, 'there's the question of . . . of the identification of the lover with the father.'

She was into her stride. A Jewish woman who marries an uncircumcised gentile will suffer difficulty in deluding herself that she is marrying (and re-enacting the primal scene with) her father. And things are even harder for a black woman married to a white man. How can she pretend that it is her father's flesh which she takes within her, which surrounds her, when that flesh is the wrong colour.

Henry thought, she can wear a blindfold. People do.

'All sex aspires to the state of incest,' Lavender murmured as though her contention were beyond dispute.

Curly smiled: 'I'm your Daddy darling. And later, my sugarsweet, Daddy's going to leave you to play with your Uncle Henry here. And you're to do just what Uncle asks.'

Henry eurekaed to himself, loud enough though to be heard: 'Of course – *that*'s it.'

Lavender was surprised and alarmed before she was flattered. This was different. Henry's swollen mauve top looked dangerous. This was different. On every previous occasion he had sprawled on her. He had covered her as a practised stallion might a mare, with a hireling's brisk efficiency. The end had been the thing, not the means. Indeed the procedure had been almost chaste. He had been there on generative business: a gent from the fertiliser trade, spraying. His embarrassed jocularity was anaphrodisiac.

But tonight his behaviour is that of a lover. He doesn't envelop her in an embrace as if to conceal his sex and to avoid meeting her eyes. He kneels. Their only contact is genital. His eyes feast on her dark aureola. She responds by grasping his scrotal sac, by digging her nails into its tight skin, by trying to pierce it with their almond tips. She can't stop herself. This is dirty sex. She tells herself so even as she is in her gasping throes. This is outside their procreative compact. Limits have been exceeded. She is enjoying this – she feels that she is committing an adulterous act, that the pumping is more important to her than anything in the world, more important to her than the putative fruit of the seed which Henry declines to release into the womb whose neck he bruises with his ceaseless thrusting: an obdurate cyclops roving on urgent business attempts to batter down a door which opens the other way.

That night Lavender feigned sleep when Curly returned, murmured his surprise at finding the light out and slipped into bed beside her. Her body was a plausible liar: the rhythm of her breathing, her susurrus hum, the roll of her limbs as they swam in dreams. It didn't occur to him that she might be keeping her eyes tight shut against the memory of the preceding hours, against him. It didn't occur to him that she'd been crying at her infidelity.

It would have shamed her to face him. She despised herself for having permitted Henry to treat her like a lover. She despised herself further for having acted like a lover, for having conjoined him in a manner determined by concupiscence rather than by generational urgency. No one ever got pregnant by ingesting sperm: indeed the Second Vatican Council (1962–65) specifically proscribed fellatio, 'lunching off the cardinal' as novices in the

Holy See have it, as an inadmissible form of contraception.

The next night was even worse.

Curly was green from drinking. He was red from crying. He had his chin in his hands at the kitchen table. A bowl of melting ice-cubes stood beside an almost empty bottle of pastis.

Lavender, a ziggurat of supermarket bags, gaped in alarm.

'What . . . Whatever's the matter? What's happened?'

Curly shook his head.

'Darling!'

She dropped the bags and kneeled beside him.

'What is it?'

He put his hands on her shoulders. He wore the expression of a wronged pet. He persisted in shaking his head: 'I can't . . . I can't believe it. Oh . . .'

'It's OK. Just . . .'

'I've never felt so fucking betrayed in all my life.'

A skein of wool filled her throat. Her heart capsized.

How did he know? What had she done to give herself away? Had she spoken in her sleep? Are there no secrets?

She flung herself against him, hugged him, beseeching forgiveness.

She pleaded: 'I'm so sorry. I'm so sorry – I never meant . . .'

Curly wasn't listening. He sobbed. His speech was snuffly with thick vibrato: 'How how could he? How could he do it? He knew . . . It's the most . . . most grotesque abuse. It's me. It's my fault. I should never . . . God, darling please forgive me, please . . . I must have been mad . . . dream up an idea like that. And him just take fucking advantage . . .'

A shiny squeezer in the open dishwasher glared accusingly at her.

'Darling it's not your fault,' she said. She stroked his cheek. His face was tear blotched. 'It's mine.'

'All you wanted was a child . . . God what a . . .' Curly's hands suddenly frisked his body questingly. He looked around him, as though dislocated, as though intoxication had so amended his perception that his everyday surroundings were alien when they were merely askew. He stumblingly rose from his chair, tripped on a disgorging polythene bag, crushed a tub of double cream without realising he'd done so and steadied himself on the chair where his jacket was slung with a sleeve inside out escaping from itself. He struggled with the writhing garment. He eventually extricated a quartered sheet of writing paper which he thrust at Lavender at the second attempt. He was bustled backwards as if a burly gust of gale had struck him. From his position buttressed by the wall he gestured and exhorted: 'Look at that. Look at it '

She hesitated. Whose poison pen? Was Henry so consumed by guilt that he must confess? Still kneeling, she winced at Curly, an imploring 'Must I?' which also hinted at her helplessness. She unfolded the paper.

The name William Savage-Smith was printed in Baskerville at the top. She did not immediately recognise it. She read the slightly smeared script – trust a pompous doctor to use a fountain pen she thought.

Dear Mr Croney,
I should be grateful if you would telephone me in a matter of the
utmost confidentiality.
Yours sincerely,
William Savage-Smith
6ᵗʰ November

This man apparently had a role to play in their life. He had already been a harbinger of ill tidings. Now he was a scarlet-letter man, a whisperer. She sensed his shadow over what was left of their marriage. This is the end she told herself. And all for what? How cheaply we sell what's precious. How biddable we are. How . . .

What was that date? That was last week. That was nine days before last night.

'Went to see him. Know what he told me. Didn't actually tell me. No, no, no, no. Oh no. Far too discreet. Hippocratic . . . the privacy, all that. He sort of left me to discover – uh, obliquely. We, you and me, are not going to have a baby. No mewling, no . . . no nappies – look on the bright side, eh? D'you know why? Because Henry is infertile. We're two of a kind. No baby juice. He's betrayed me, he's betrayed us, worst of all he's betrayed you. And it's all down to my fucking stupid . . . Never going to let him in this house again. Next time he calls . . . I never want to see him again . . . I never thought I'd say that of anyone.'

The table edge moved in and out of focus before Lavender's eyes. She was buffeted by a rush of indignation, by all-consuming anger, by massive relief. She was sorrier than ever for her sullied self. She could see a way to hating Henry. Traitorous Henry. Contemptible Henry. Infertile Henry.

She rejoiced that Curly had no idea that she had deceived him with her lubricious abandon. He didn't know that she had adulterated the marriage which meant the world to her: he was ignorant of last night's transgression. It was better for both of them that way.

She flung herself across the spilled bags and through the smeared puddle of cream and clutched him and repeated: 'You're my love. You're my love. You're my love. Darling so long as I've got you . . .'

Curly recounted as much of his day as he could recall whilst Lavender mashed potatoes and grilled mackerel fillets for his stress and heart.

Mr Savage-Smith had haltingly small-talked for an embarrassed while. Then he mentioned 'the fellow you sent along to me: your friend?'.

He pointedly avoided using Henry's name.

He spoke of 'the extraordinary coincidence of a shared condition – not only shared, but unprecedented in my experience'.

He asked Curly what diseases they had suffered in common. Curly shrugged, shook his head, rubbed his jaw as though it were the site of memory and might be urged to yield up some fragment which, like a photograph developed but never printed, had failed to find a place in the album of his life.

'Did you ever, ah, go abroad together?' winced Savage-Smith: he was, morally, a member of a far-off generation which was disgustedly fascinated by Port Said's dirty postcards, which considered French to be a synonym for gross licence complemented by retributive disease.

Curly wondered if he had asked this because he was too inhibited to ask if they had ever had sex together.

'France a number of times. You know there's one thing . . . we both got poisoned, when I was ooh fifteen, fifteen I guess, something like that. Contaminated water – we were camping. We drank from this stream and next morning – 'cause we drank out of it at night and couldn't see – next morning we found it was full of dead fish and it was this sort of, uhm, bluey green, very opaque.'

'And what reactions did you have to it?'

'This was years ago . . . Delirium, fever . . . We vomited a lot. Cramps. Terrible cramps. And I had headaches for weeks after, maybe months.'

'What treatment did you receive?'

'Spent a night – two nights? can't remember – in some sort of backwoods hospital.'

'Uh-huh. Where was this? There may be records still. I have no idea whether the French keep records as diligent . . .'

'Wasn't France. Sorry I . . . No. No. It was Cornwall. Bodmin Moor. The doctor, the one at the hospital, he thought it might have something to do with some tin workings, tin mine.'

'Tin! Oh fuck!' exclaimed Mr Savage-Smith in a most unlady-like way.

*   *   *

The next day Curly sat in his office, dehydrated, with a mouthful of felt, composing a letter to Henry. He wrote and deleted for going on an hour:

> *Dear Henry,*
> *I think I understand why you did what you did . . .*

Too placatory.

> *Dear Henry,*
> *I cannot tell you how hurt I am by . . .*

Too polite and long-suffering.

> *Dear Henry,*
> *Friendship involves and depends on companionship, compatibility, mutual appreciation, trust, tolerance, indulgence. But there are limits and I fear that you have perhaps overstepped them . . .*

Too understanding, too reasonable, too qualified: this should be hate mail proclaiming a severance, not a disquisition on the nature of camaraderie. And why address him as 'dear'?

At 11.40 he wrote:

> *You have abused our trust. You have abused my wife. You have treated her like a prostitute. You have exploited our vulnerability and our longing for a child. Your deceit is unforgivable. We entered into a contract which you have dishonoured. You have forfeited our friendship. We do not want to see you again. Do not attempt to contact us. Curly.*

He stared at the screen, astonished by his directness and hostility. It was as though someone else had written it. He pressed Ctrl+P. He watched transfixed as the page emerged from the printer. He didn't sign it in his hand, reckoning that its authority would be mitigated by that gesture. He typed an envelope in Reception.

He attached a stamp. He didn't want it franked with his company's name. This was personal.

It was whilst he was sauntering back from the post box that the matter of Ben and Lennie's paternity occurred to him. He stopped, pondered a moment then laughed so violently that an approaching aggressive beggar started and gave him a miss.

Chapter Seventeen

It was a boy of Ben's age that had just been buried in the sluicing rain. Mr and Mrs Legge, the parents, hadn't got beyond the stage of numb bewilderment.

Rudolph had been trouble in life. Rudolph was grief in death. He had self-mutilated since he was twelve, punishing his body for its pubescence. Then he had taught himself to hide in the boots of cars parked at supermarkets. He'd sidle down the ranks till he found an unlocked one.

When Mrs A— and her two daughters returned to their family Fiat with a laden Tesco trolley they opened the boot and screamed at the blood-smeared moaning boy inside. He wasn't fussy. Asda, B&Q, Safeway, Sainsbury, Comet . . . so long as there were cars he could pursue his obsession. He was never more excited than when anticipating his discovery, during those moments when the footfalls ceased and he could hear the voices, the puffing, the click of the trolley, the struggle for keys and, in the final second, the mutual blaming when it was realised that the car and boot were unlocked. The subsequent shriek caused him to ejaculate then to enter a profound comatose sleep.

Rudolph Legge died unrequited in the boot of an old Escort which had been joyridden and abandoned. No one remarked on the long-stay banger in a far corner of the Dog Kennel Hill car park where rust-coloured weeds erupted through the tarmac and dog roses climbed the thick wire fence and polythene bags blew like wind-socks in the bare boughs.

He had chosen badly. No one came to proffer his release. He was missing for sixteen days.

Mr Legge's moustache was a decomposing roll-up. Henry watched the bedraggled couple whose hair was tight to the crown. Their stoop-shouldered clothes shone dark with rain. They weighed like ill-fitting pelts. He wondered whether their grief was tempered by the relief that they were no longer parents to an aberrant son and by the knowledge that he had perished doing the thing he loved. Henry saw the very lack of release from the boot of JWW 583S as a greater release – from a consuming possession, from a cupboard demon which could never be sated.

Mr and Mrs Legge were spared. They might have been victims of fate, of minor crime, of a car-park attendant's lack of vigilance and curiosity. But they were also beneficiaries. They would no longer be dogged by Rudolph's behaviour. They would no longer inhabit a world of perpetual anxiety. Blessing in disguise thought Henry, yes, blessing in disguise. Best thing that could have happened to them – and to Rudolph too: what sort of life was his? Where's the quality of life in a life like that? There *are* lives that aren't worth living.

There are people whom we can learn not to love even though the consequent void hurts and the loss makes us pine. Henry wished he had not exhumed Naomi's secret. He had been so steady, so modestly content in his ignorance. His heart ached. He was working on learning not to love. There was no one to show him how. To how many parents is it vouchsafed that they are not parents? How many men have fatherhood torn from them? The very rarity of Henry's predicament militated against its alleviation. There was no form to follow, no etiquette to ape. The erasure of paternal love is not among the practices and customs which comprise the common store of moral gambits. Henry had to teach himself, had to find his own way and finding his own way had not hitherto been Henry's way. He was a man who went by the book. But this book was unwritten.

He sought, then, lessons from life. He was eagerly on the look-out for families more rent than his own. The Legges fitted the bill. He was proud to grief-manage such people. And he hoped that he might learn from observation and understanding of them. He was looking for other parents whose presumed equivocation about their children (live, dead or imposturous) would sanction his own. He sought to legitimise his willed antipathy to Ben and Lennie. He wanted to hear that the unconditional love of parent for child was a sentimental invention, not a law of nature. Henry wanted to persuade himself that his indulgence of Ben and Lennie was more than adherence to generational orthodoxy. He told himself that his paternal laxity was an expression of his indifference to them and to their well-being, that it was neglect by deep wallet.

The last of the seven drenched mourners had shaken hands with the bereaved parents.

The car that would take them to their childless home drew up beside a threadbare cypress. The wipers groaned against the rain's tide. The driver's condensed breath obscured his face. Droplets posing as mercury slipped across the profound black enamel.

Henry opened the door for Mr and Mrs Legge.

'Are you going to be able to get off somewhere . . . bit of a break?' he asked chirpily. 'Without the worry . . . You deserve it. Must have been difficult – getting away when you, ah, never knew what Rudolph was going to be up to . . . Free agents again . . . Berlin?'

Mrs Legge snuffled. Mr Legge peered incredulously at Henry.

'Good choice this time of year they say,' Henry was anxious to assure him as he crouched to get in the car. 'City break. I had a dream about Hitler the other night. Quite jovial he was. Talked about the improvements in drinking chocolate.'

Henry, stooping, felt the door handle jerked from his grasp. He raised his hat as the car rolled gently away. Mr Legge's expression was that of a man concerned for his own safety.

Henry was thinking, I'd like whipped cream on top of mine.

'Mr Fowler! Sir!' Erskine the Work Experience, a mite lost inside his coat, knock-kneed across the puddled asphalt from the Crematorium Superintendent's.

He spoke as loud as he dared. 'Urgent phone call sir. Can you phone the office sir.'

Henry rolled his eyes, wondered what it could be this time and, as he followed the cowering boy to the stuffy room, rued his ban on his staff even carrying mobiles (but you really can't have them going off during a service, especially not the ones which ring by playing 'O Mein Papa' or 'Mamma Mia').

Everyone blamed the rain.

'It was so heavy I couldn't see across the road.'

'I'd just had my hair set – had to go back and get it done again.'

'Like Thailand.'

Everyone blamed the rain apart from Henry Fowler (who regarded himself as the third victim).

Henry didn't blame the rain. He had no doubt about the real cause. He knew the reason the eggs got broken in the meridional gloom and how the yolks, mixed with blood as though just fertilised, eddied in a nacreous pool of petrol and rain. How many eggs had there been?

He'd warned them against getting egg bound. He'd warned

them against being tempted by the prices – 'We Must Be Clucking Mad' – at the farm beside the road at Biggin Hill. Constipation can be a real danger in the elderly. A killer even, what with all the straining. It's an undignified way to pass on, with your smalls round your shins and your veins popping out, all for the sake of an omelette.

He'd buried some that had died like that. He'd been to fetch them stiff off the Armitage Shanks – rigor develops quicker in the smallest room because the smallest room is the coldest room in the older-style house. The smallest room is often so small the door needs sawing out.

They had at least died instantly. This was supposed to be some consolation. They hadn't *really* suffered in the tumbling box, nothing but death, anyway. This was supposed to be some consolation. Henry knew it. But it didn't lessen the shock. His initial reaction was that this call was a malign hoax. When he realised it wasn't, his anger was complemented by helpless grief. He was glad that it had been instantaneous, he was thankful for that – but *what about me*, he screamed to himself.

There was no breath left in them when the first horrified witnesses arrived at the overturned car. Every one of these witnesses showed off gums in rictal extremis. That's how incidents take you. The wheels were still spinning. Like a stranded, struggling turtle the car rocked precipitously on its roof on a guideblock. No breath, but blood all over the old folks' faces and dribbling down their chins as if they were messy eaters, blood smeared across the windscreen. Eyes like fish eyes in a freezer. Surprised at what is happening to them, at what has just happened to them, that nothing's going to happen to them again. Faces pressed up against the windows the better to see the void beyond. There was no doubt that they were dead. Nonetheless a red-headed mackintosh returning from the PDSA with her cat in a basket, a retired fireman with a rucksack full of tinned soup, a limping chiropodist and a solicitor's receptionist's stalker attempted to pull them from the hardly dented vehicle. The four of them ignored the danger to themselves. It was when the nearside door was opened that the cargo of eggs was released. It flowed and flowed. Yolk lent colour to the scene. It combined with the blood and the rain and the seeping petrol. The amalgam formed pools where the road was painted with orange-and-purple stripes.

Mr and Mrs Fowler were the fourth and fifth persons to die at Curly Croney's experimental mini-roundabout cluster in Eden Park.

The two previous fatal accidents had also occurred during periods of limited visibility. The Sikh sergeant who drove Henry from the police station to the mortuary for the formal identification told him that the irregular shapes of the guideblocks made them difficult to discern in heavy rain and at dusk before the street lights came on. 'Bits crop up where you're not expecting them. They won't do anything about it. They keep going on about the integrity of the design.'

They hadn't been an overtly emotional family.

In the fluorescent chill of the bare tiled room which he had so often attended with professional disinterest, Henry held his father's hands.

He whispered: 'Thank you.'

There was work to be done on his father's face and head. The sparse hair was pompadoured by blood.

'I'll see you right Dad,' Henry told him.

He nodded to the young attendant who hurried to shut the drawer that was an undignified resting place no matter how temporary it might be. Henry turned away: purgatory is a filing cabinet.

He kissed his mother's cold forehead as he ever had.

Again he whispered: 'Thank you.' He meant thank you for bearing me, for giving me life.

Her mortal serenity should, he knew, console him. Perhaps she hadn't even screamed. He was going to have to work out how to take solace from their presumed lack of pain. *They won't have felt a thing.* But right now that happy failure hardly impinged on his startled grief.

Henry felt cheated. He felt robbed. He had been robbed of the opportunity to say one last thing to them. Years of loitering at death's door had taught him that the bereaved always secreted something they had wanted to impart to the deceased. Indeed there was an apparent obligation on the bereaved to complain that Mum's/Dad's/Gran's death meant they could never tell Mum/Dad/Gran that . . .

Henry had no idea what might have caused him to converse with his parents. Since returning to live with them he had had every opportunity to tell them whatever he wished but, irritated by their invariable incomprehension or mishearing, he sat with his supper on his knee, doggedly silent, staring at the telly. And so it might have continued.

But weeks or months hence there could have occurred to him a momentous observation he wished to share with them. He would have been prepared to bellow slowly, to explain it to them as to imbecilic infants.

Then again, he could very well have had some vital question for them. There was no doubt in his mind that he had been denied the opportunity to ask them that question, whatever it was, just as they had been denied a future of rages, chair-lifts, incontinence, slobbering aphasia, fright, wind, butter on the rug, soup on the cardi.

Chapter Eighteen

The house was unlit. It was the first time Henry had seen it thus since he had returned Home.

Every previous evening that he had walked up the chequered path towards the front door and buttery toast the stained-glass lozenges in the fanlight had shone their welcome, pinchbeck jewels promising hearth and safety.

Tonight he shivered in the damp night air. He was reaching in his pocket for his latchkey when the phone rang inside. He hurriedly turned the key in the tumbler. Oh dear! They've forgotten to double-lock again.

He picked up the phone in the dark hall. 'Hullo.'

'Edgar?'

'It's Henry.'

'Ooh! Ooh you do sound so like him. You've got the voice all right. It's Marge, love. It's your mother I was wanting to speak to – about Saturday. If I may. Has she told you about Saturday?'

'I'll just call her.'

He was jolted to a halt.

My mother is dead and cannot come to the blower (as she

called it when Henry was just a bundle in nappies). Henry gripped the Bakelite handpiece to his face. It was not as black as it once had been. Where it had been most held it was stained by the long decades' accretion of salt, imperceptibly mottled like a stone scraped of lichen. It smelled of his father's breath, this old blower. It had always smelled that way. He pressed it to his chest like a favourite soft toy.

'I . . . Madge . . .'

'Marge!'

'Marge. Sorry. Sorry. Mum an' . . . Mum and Dad are . . .' He lapsed into a locution of his trade, his voice dropped in register and volume. 'They aren't with us any more. There's . . . there's been an accident. Eden Park. This aftern . . . It was about lunch-time it happened. In the rain. I'm so sorry to . . .'

He listened to the gulp, the gasp, the glottal revulsion. This information was bitter to receive. And, he realised, he was going to have to impart it over and over. He was going to have to utter those words repeatedly or, according to recipient, a variation on them. He was going to have to listen to variations on Marge's distended ululation: 'Oh you poor boy you poor poor ooohh . . .'

'Oh Henry – what can I say . . . I can't believe it. I really can't believe it.'

'What'm I going to tell Cecil.'

'It's like a bad bad dream it is and no mistake.'

'Anything we can do for you Henry – anything, you just let us know.'

'If you need a shoulder – I say would you like Jack and me to come round? It's a good three hours before I have to put him on the whatsit.'

'You have our deepest sympathy, deepest sympathy – they were parents in a million old boy. Most heartfelt.'

And so it went on.

It was way past supper-time when he realised that he'd been

reading the numbers in the tooled-leather phone book without a light. Thanks be for the clarity of Mum's hand then. He smiled and shook his head, remembering her despisal of early Biros, her contempt for throwaway Bics. How she'd tutored him in ledger clerk's copperplate with his Platignums and Osmiroids and, ultimately, the cowl-nibbed Parker he'd always craved. Neatness. Slope to the right because otherwise people will think you're left-handed and where's that going to get you? Don't cross a T before it's joined to an H. Never cross a seven like *them*, it's foreign, never, or you'll be taken for one of *them*. He laughed. Out of affectionate memory for his young self as much as for her.

He walked to the kitchen and opened the fridge to get a drink. He gasped, he moaned tearfully. There in the cold white light they stood, brown fists in their sea of snowy lard, speckled with pale caul, all ready to be heated up. He had for weeks been beseeching her to make faggots the way she made them when he was a child. Here they were. And the flour, pea and potato mix for the fritters? Maybe she hadn't got round to it yet. He still cried even though the promised meal was incomplete. She had made such an effort. He wanted to thank her with a hug. She must have spent the morning before she set off on what was to be her last journey devotedly chopping the pig's pluck and wrapping it in its membranous web. The dead are always with us – their actions and gifts stretch beyond their last breath. His mother would be with him in the fat he wiped from his lips and the strands of minced spleen he flossed from his teeth. That is a meaning of legacy. Henry wondered where his parents' wills were. He must make a start on Father's roll-top desk in the morning.

He wasn't hungry. Shock suppresses appetite. He went back to the phone with a can of beer and a bottle of whisky. He had his speech off pat now. It was a hardly varying litany that he recited into the mouthpiece long into the night, till eventually he heard himself pausing for portentous effect and letting his words dissolve in cadent melancholy. How the undertaker makes the man! The prowess Henry displays in implying sympathy for the recipient of his sad tidings is founded in a lifetime's negotiation of grief's thin ice.

If only he had his family which was not his family to comfort him in this sad dark house of cold tiles and human absence.

He dialled without consulting the phone book.

Naomi said: 'This is a funny time to call.' She said: 'Oh Henry ... I am so sorry. Oh no ... I can't believe ...' She sobbed as though suffering whooping cough. She snuffled forlornly. 'I really liked them. You know that don't you Henry. I really loved them. They were family to me ... Oh excuse me I know how it must be for you the last thing you want is me getting all weepy.'

Ben was playing in a tournament in Cardiff. Lennie was sleeping over at a friend's.

'They'll be upset. I'm sure they will. I'll let them know first thing in the morning.' Then she paused and asked: 'Do you want me to come round? I'm not all that asleep.'

'It's nice of you,' he replied, 'it really is but no, no. No this is one I got to sort out on me tod love. Know what I mean? Yeah?'

His lapse into stage cockney surprised him. It was a shared habit of their long marriage, an affectionate bent which he had forgotten and which had sprung unbidden from wherever it was buried. He rued the implication that a bond survived between him and Naomi. He thought he had excised her from his life.

He readopted a brusque tone: 'I'll keep you posted about the service then.'

It was one o'clock when he called a bemused, drowsy Curly.

Henry could sense him trying to extricate himself from sleep's trammel, wriggling this way and that, wiping his eyes with one hand whilst listening guiltily with the other.

Henry whispered the word again: 'Murderer . . . Murderer. You killed my parents. It was all for vanity wasn't it. To satisfy your own precious—'

'I told you never to get in touch with us.' And Curly put down his bedside phone.

Henry tardily rejoined: 'Get you dux!'

That was the first of the nights that he wandered through the house, listening to it, trying to fit it to him now it was his, trying it on for size as he never would his diminutive father's suits. He stroked the handles his parents had grasped, he ran his knuckles across the rough and the smooth of their lifetime's accumulated dressing-gowns which hung as a headless humpback from their bedroom door. Had there ever been a time when he didn't succumb to the reassurances of candlewick and quilting? His parents belonged to a generation which lay under eiderdowns separated by an arm's contraceptive length. When did they make love? Where? Who visited whose snug estate? In which of these two suddenly redundant beds had the procreative act occurred?

Every bed is a coffin in waiting. Henry slumped on his mother's. It was like throwing himself into the grave beside her. He hugged the pillow. He suffused himself in the smell of her oldness, the smell of exhaustion, bone fatigue, systems winding down. He wondered how much longer she would have kept going. How long he would have had to prepare himself for the embalming job of a lifetime, how long he would have had to watch as all dignity left her and she became a machine for processing soup into diarrhoea. It might be painful watching them turn into veg, decline into insentient senescence before our eyes but at least it's a process that acquaints us with loss gradually.

*　　*　　*

He was touched and surprised by his staff's solicitude. Mrs Grusting manifested near-human emotions for the first time in her twenty-three years' service and attempted, despite being his senior by only a month, to position herself *in loco parentis*. She offered cooking, sewing and a shoulder to cry on whilst persisting in addressing him as Mr Henry. Few other employees were left from his father's era. They were, however, familiar with the old man, they knew to doff their hats with due respect. But it was him, Henry, they felt for.

He had never realised that he was held in such affection. All this on top of his recently changed domestic arrangements, which although he had never even mentioned them, were whispered about, which were the reason, it was reckoned, why Miss Royston was taking that much more trouble with her shaving and personal hygiene.

By day he embalmed his parents, rendered them more like themselves than they had ever been. He glossed their cheeks and blancoed their teeth, teased their hair and clipped their nails (he painted Mother's the lovely shade of violet he remembered her wearing on holiday in Bonchurch, the superior part of Ventnor IOW).

He did away with the wounds Curly had inflicted on his father.

It was a time of ecstatic concentration, of joy at a craft practised with a purpose that it had never previously attained. Only in such extremis does a craftsman become an artist, only then is his work infected by a meaning that is more than a sum of its techniques. Henry remembered the young carpenter who had carved for his four-month-old baby girl a coffin which represented the cot she had died in – every fold of the sheets and the asphyxiating blanket was hewn from a beech block.

Whilst Henry laboured, Mrs Grusting and Miss Royston phoned the nation's most distinguished funeral directors with the double funeral's date, time, location.

They sought and received Henry's permission to hire a temp to help arrange the function rooms, the catering, the horses, the countless little details that would make the big day one to remember, one that would set the standard for funeral directors' funerals for the foreseeable future.

They didn't expect the agency to send someone like Miss Sullivan.

'Mr 'enry,' simpered Mrs Grusting, hurrying to him as he wriggled from his car in the yard, 'it's ever so embarrassin' but Ai'm not quaite sure that this new girl has the skills concomitant to 'er position. I wonder if you'd be so kaind as to . . .'

Henry had several of his mother's mothballed dresses laid deep across his forearms. He believed that the one on top, an amethyst grosgrain ballgown, her life's one ballgown, would best suit her. But he carried options: her elaborately bodiced, rustily watermarked wedding dress; a floral suit as garish as a senior royal's; a little black number for the cocktail parties she never attended. Laden, he grudgingly went with Mrs Grusting through the side entrance into the office. He put his head round the door. Miss Royston's smile was a Chevrolet radiator.

Miss Sullivan sat with her big buxom back to him at the desk his mother had used. She was talking indignantly on the phone. Her hair was a chaos of combs and grips, tussocks and wisps, faded stains – it was a history of failed chromatic indulgence. She was an ample size 16 squeezed into a size-10's day-release clothes which corrugated her flesh. She wore a turquoise cardigan that had turned to felt, a bursting *and* seated ochre skirt, old woman's man-tan tights so abundantly laddered they might have been woven in obeisance to a forgotten fashion, a pansy vandal's pink patent Doc Martens.

Henry glanced at Mrs Grusting with for-the-life-of-me eyebrows.

Miss Sullivan was on the point of turning when she heard them come in but was irked into throwing out her phoneless hand in exasperation. Her speech was childish, impeded – and, at that moment, indignant, as though she had just suffered an insult: 'That ith *bot* what we're athking for. If you doan wob to do it pleath juth tell me and I'll get ob to thumwub elth. Fowler & Thub have give you trade for fifteen yearth – the very leath you cab do . . .'

'Blimey O'Reilly,' Henry whispered to Mrs Grusting as she followed him across the yard to the Body Block where he was working on his parents. 'Poor girl . . . You got to thympathise though eh?' he laughed. 'Still no slouch is she . . . sounds like she's getting on with it.' Then he halted and asked: 'Any other problem is there? Apart from her dress sense, that is?'

Mrs Grusting shook her head at the child Henry. 'Didn't you see?'

'What you . . . ? See what?'

'Didn't you really? She's, uhmm, she's blind.' Mrs Grusting, to whom euphemism was second nature, could hardly bring herself to enunciate the word.

'Blind?'

'You know. Blind. Her *eyes*? She can't see.'

'Oof. You sure? Oh God that's all we need. Christ . . . Where'd we get her from?'

This, Mrs Grusting pronounced, is the last time Fowler & Son would ever hire from or pay a commission to Hang-On-A-Sec (Upper Norwood) Ltd.

'Gor – that's the last . . . Isn't it just eh? Gee-suss! Oh well – grin and bear it, have to.' Henry sighed. 'No choice . . . Not on, in this day and age, is it, letting people go for being blind. Protected species. Like the Yids . . . *The unsighted*. It's the way they always bump into you: that's what gets me. Remember that . . . Clock House – oh what was he called? Dry cleaner he'd been. Daughter was an ugly little miss.'

'Mr Root?' suggested Mrs Grusting.

'That's the one. Spare me. Still this Miss Whatsit . . .'

'Sullivan.'

'Yeah this Miss Sullivan – sounds like she's getting on with it . . . And it's only a week.'

'Two, I'm afraid, two weeks' engagement,' corrected Mrs Grusting through guilty teeth. She added, conspiratorially: 'Of course – she may prove to be unsuitable for reasons not regarding her infirmity.'

By night Henry prowled the house which would never be his.

He might own it, it might be his to sleep and eat in, his to live and die in – but it would never belong to him save by the letter of probate. He was at best a steward, at worst an unwitting usurper.

It was no longer Home.

That state had been conditional upon his parents' presence, upon his being their son whom they had not noticed turn into a man.

Now they were gone it pained him to realise how little he had impinged on the place's fabric. He had lived there all those years, he had been back all these months – and it remained their domain, their bespoke shelter.

It was a sloughed skin, a doffed overcoat, a voided carapace.

He grew used to its echoing emptiness. It's not till they're not there that you realise what a noise they made, busying themselves, backchatting, talking at the wireless, opening doors and cans, oiling locks, hoovering, blowtorching ancient paint, slapping the newspaper on the table, grunting when the milk boiled over. Their absence fomented an inchoate guilt which he ascribed to his appropriation of their property, to his inadequacy as a son, to his failure to succeed his father as the Undertaker's Undertaker (which he aimed to rectify, in pomp, in style, with his father's funeral).

It calmed him to loiter in the house with undrawn curtains

and extinguished lights, to move through it like a burglar reliant on the moon and street lamps. When caught in the searchlight sweep of passing cars he cast leaping shadows which morphed up the stairs, slipped across the landing's ceiling, glided round the cornice to oblivion. It had never been like this before. The house had forever been bright lit because his mother feared the dark and slept with the door ajar. It had been headachingly hot because she feared the cold. If it couldn't be his house it could be an eerily unfamiliar one, it could be rendered strange. He suppressed the heating too.

There were the objects which had surrounded him whilst he grew up, which had once been special because they belonged to Home, because they had been chosen by his parents. They were his early life's inanimate familiars, invested with a greater authority than toys. Even though he could discern only their dim outlines and momentary reflections he had them off by rote, he knew where each one was, in its immutable place:

An amber-eyed brass owl money box whose head turned to reveal a slot for pennies.

Seven beersteins with hinged lead lids and low-relief representations (bucolic carousers, hop-bines, lusty *Mädchen*, pointy hats, etc) – souvenirs of the Black Forest and Freiburg holiday, summer '37.

A statuette of a jolly, bald friar in a habit the colour of polished liver which was, perhaps, another souvenir of that momentous holiday.

An electric repro Georgian lantern clock smelling of metal polish.

A kukri in a scabbard of leather so thick it might be wood.

A Widdicombe Fair musical box in the form of a tankard illumined by a representation of the seven revellers on Tom Pearce's grey mare and inscribed with the song's verses and chorus: 'Bill Brewer, Jan Stewer, Peter Gurney . . .'

A porcelain caricature of a fish, probably a John Dory.

A framed and glazed print of chalky downs, plough horses, seagulls, windmill.

A framed and glazed print of a wintry track, leafless hedges, skeletal elms, rookeries.

Each of them was chipped or tarnished, faded or cracked – done for, one way or another. And without the eyes which had selected them and the hands which had received them as gifts, without the sentimental pride that had patinated them and had lent them value their purpose was gone.

Had they been some other dead people's cast-offs on a totter's barrow Henry knew that he would have looked at them with contempt. All those years of Naomi's sniping at his parents' taste had affected him, and these objects were measures of the change. It was as if he was seeing them naked, deflated. They were correlatives of self-satisfied paltriness and aesthetic nullity which he had refused to acknowledge whilst his parents were alive and which he was ashamed to discern now they were dead. He was as repulsed by his disloyalty as by the threadbare gewgaws. It was an illness, it was invasive and disfiguring. Nonetheless, in the dead hours of night, when few vehicles passed by, when the world was silent save for the aubades of birds with bad timing, he found himself gathering objects from shelves, stripping them of their half-century of familially acquired preciousness. He shoved them into cardboard boxes which he piled in the middle of the room.

In the morning he loaded the boxes of what was henceforth deemed junk on to the car's back seat.

They lay in adjacent drawers of the fridge in the Body Block. They were dressed, crimped, tweezered, rouged, powdered, plugged.

Henry sat slumped close by them at the long chemical-stained table. He had completed the first stage of his professional and filial obsequies. His eyes were shut in perfunctory self-congratulation. He exhaustedly contemplated tomorrow's tasks.

He acknowledged that they were a welcome distraction. To how many is it given to grieve through deed – that was a perk of the trade. How privileged he was to be a Fowler, preoccupied by an exigent craft which by day allowed no time for reflection on the void, the mapless void. Sooner or later, he realised, he would, as we all must, turn cartographer of parental loss. He feared for himself, he feared how civilian grief might strike. He was grateful for its postponement. The greater the welter of tasks he set himself the longer it would be before he was forced to contemplate it. He feared it. Even the contemplation of contemplation caused him to scratch at the exematous crust on his crown till it bled and deposited ruddily flecked grease beneath his fingernails. He dissolved a granular quoit of ultramint beneath his tongue. He sought to relieve its anaesthetic sting with a swig of tea. This was cold and bag-in tannic.

He picked up the phone to the main office: 'Mrs G – can I have a cup of tea please lot of milk and a chocolate digestive? Oh – so it is. If you could manage – before you go. Ta ever so. Two chocolate digestives.'

He distracted himself with the composition of a list:

> *Jesu Joy Of*
> *Gather Lilacs in the Spring*
> *My Special Angel*
> *Oh Mein Papa*
> *By a Babbling Brook*
> *Jerusalem*
> *Elizabethan Teresade OR Green sleaves*
> *Al Bowley*

He put a line through 'Jerusalem'.

He added to the list 'My Boomerang Won't Come Back'.

Would Charlie Drake's squeaky shrieks of indignation detract from the dignity of the occasion?

The door opened, too slowly.

His pen was poised above the paper. He asked without looking round: 'Charlie Drake, Mrs G. Pro or . . .' He turned. He had sensed a different presence: 'Oh – hullo . . . Miss ah . . .'

Mrs Grusting's space was occupied by a paunchy golden labrador in an elaborate harness and, behind the creature, Miss Sullivan clutching a mug in her leashless hand.

'I've brought you your tea. Where thall I put it?'

'Here, let me, let me,' Henry clambered across the room. He gripped the mug tight then eased it from her.

'And,' her hand reached deep into her cardigan pocket, 'your bithcuith. Excuthe fluff eh? They're a bit sticky.' She licked a tache of chocolate from a finger. 'Pawph. Orrww. Whath *that*? Itham half whiffy im here.'

'Preserving chemicals.'

'Oh ith that what it ith. Whoog! Muth take a bit of gettib uth to. What d'you reckob Jane?'

The bitch Jane wore the expression of indignant resignation. What a job. What a fate. What a name.

'You don't smell it after a while. Don't notice . . . Goes with the territory, as they say. You make yourself take it for granted. It's like . . . ah . . .' His search for a simile was stillborn by the sight of Mrs Grusting across the yard Nosy Parkering without dissemblance, attempting to gape through the half-open door of the Body Block.

'Like a blime perthon hath no choith about beem blime.'

Henry only half-heard. He was waving his hand to decline Mrs Grusting's gestural offer to come and fetch Miss Sullivan.

Then he recoiled from the oblique accusation of the message stored in his head: 'No, no, no. That wasn't what I was thinking.'

'I dint thay you wath. What you doon?'

'What d'you mean?'

'Why were you boovim your armths like that? I cab feel, I cab. The air it booves too.'

'I was just waving to Mrs Grusting.'

'Thee thent me acroth here hoping I wath gomb to drob your tea dim't thee?'

Henry spluttered into it. It seeped down his chin. Foam formed on its surface.

He knew that Miss Sullivan was right. This was Mrs Grusting's means of proving the temp's incompetence. The sly old thing. He realised he need not bother to keep a straight face.

'What on earth makes you think that?'

'Obviouth innit. Dithabilitith cam't be fired, not for beem dithabilitith. Juth 'cauth I'b blime duddon meab I'b dumb.'

Jane farted.

'Wha . . . ? No. Of course not. Christ what is that . . . Of course not.'

'Amb it duddon meab I'b deaf. I 'eard 'er. Pathing notes to Mith La Dee Da. 'Bout be.'

'I'm sure Mrs Grusting didn't wouldn't you know.'

'It's OK: there's always subwun tryn' it ob. Achually I tell you what, it's bot OK. But – gothe with the territory, *ath they thay*.'

'I'll – I'll look into it if you really . . .'

'I woobm bother. Not om by accord. Eberywun taykth the pith owb uf dithabilitith. Uthed to ib. Uthed to do ib mythelth.'

Henry Fowler stared at Miss Sullivan, at her fat redundant eyelids, at the indignant head jerks, at the bodily lassitude learned, maybe, from the farting bitch Jane via the once-white leash. She might have just come out of hibernation.

He thought about her whilst he was hauling old encrusted sauce bottles and solidified packs of flour and greasy tins from kitchen cupboards around 19.50 on the 24-hour clock which had been bought despite familial objections to the EEC, the Fourth

Reich – as Father was liable to call it before Mother urgently shushed him.

What an aggregate of misfortunes Miss Sullivan is. How massively insulted, how harmed, how resentful, how vulnerable to exploitation.

The next day Miss Sullivan crossed the yard again. She was still led by Jane but was less dependent on the drooling bitch. She walked steadily as though she retained a pedal memory of the path's idiosyncrasies, of the sites where the asphalt was worn and the cobbles laid by Henry Fowler's grandfather showed through. She had brought him a slice of Mrs Grusting's cake. And Henry Fowler had dared say what he had never said before, never would have said during his parents' era, during the thirty years of Mrs Grusting's weekly cake which was an 'office tradition'.

He said: 'No wonder it's called *sponge*.' And he dipped it in his tea.

Miss Sullivan grunted quizzically.

'*Sponge*? Like in the bath.' he explained.

'Oh! Thoap–yourthelf–down thponge.'

Hoops of mucus were suspended from Jane's gums. He exhaled in repulsion.

'Can't be that bad,' said Miss Sullivan.

Mrs Grusting phoned to remind Henry she was leaving early. He didn't need reminding. This was another, more recent, office tradition. No matter how much work there was to do Mrs Grusting left an hour early every Wednesday to do her duty to her mother at a sunset home for the hard of hearing beside Gatwick Airport. Henry admired the logic of that enterprise.

'Ai was wonderin' if you wouldn't maind as a special favour draivin' Miss S. there to the station. Ai been attendin' to the matter misel'. There's no obligation. Just a little common kaindness – so long as she's with us.'

Henry sighed yes.

'Ai knew you would. It's off to the hurlyburly of the M23 then. Byee.'

Miss Sullivan stretched to pat Jane's slobbering nose. The bitch, off duty, was snoring on the back seat of Henry's car.

Her hand stumbled. 'Whass tha'?'

When he stopped in a traffic-lights queue he turned to watch Miss Sullivan kneading the fabric of his mother's wedding dress, aquainting herself with the slub, the stitching, the sheerness of the satin puff sleeves. The Fowler wedding he had not participated in. 1933. How they'd waited to make him, how they'd waited twelve years till the world was safe for their precious child.

'Wedding!' She explored the raised, beaded bodice: 'Feelth lubbely. Ith't white?'

Even with functioning eyes she couldn't have seen what he saw: the album's pages interleaved with crisply creased tissue which he'd lift to reveal the fine grained prints of the severally textured dress, his monochrome mother's plump radiance, his father's bashful pride, the inky morning suits, the bouquets, the snag-toothed bridesmaid, the best man (drowned in a torpedoed submarine), the families united by love's happenstance.

The van behind flashed its headlights.

'Yes,' he told her as he declutched, 'it's white. Always were in those days.'

'Fwhat fwhite?'

'Uh? What d'you – well, *white*. Sort of . . .'

'Ivowy? Polar?'

'Yes.'

'Fwhich?'

'Bit of both?'

'You woulb't make much of a fwitneth to a cwime.'

'Dear me, suppose not. Oh Jesus.' Henry braked hard.

A bald head and a vestful of belly held up a lavishly tattooed arm to stop him whilst it guided a reversing pantechnicon. 'Look at that – oh, sorry, sorry, I . . .'

'Uthed to it.'

'I tell you what,' Henry's fastidious eyes were fixed on the stained vest, 'it's *snow* white.'

'Oh thath by fabouwite.'

Henry gaped. He didn't ask: how do you know? He assumed that she preferred the sound of snow to that of ivory or polar, to dazzling, lily, chalk, fleece, blinding. Certainly, to blinding. He said nothing.

'We did *Thnow Fwhite* at pwibawy thchool. I wath a dwarf . . . I wath the talletht in clath and they thtill mabe me be a dwarf.'

Henry gaped again. He didn't ask: how did you avoid bumping into the other dwarfs?

'I like thnow fwhite betht of all. Cab I twy it ob pleath. Will it fit be? Neber wore a weddib dreth. You cab tell be fwhat I look like in it.'

Henry glanced at her, appalled. The accepted rules of decorum, the etiquette of respect for the departed – these had evidently not been learned by Miss Sullivan. Nor had respect for the bereaved, let alone deference to a boss. This was a temporary employee, a woman aged – how old was she? Her childish voice was a mask. Old enough, anyway, to know better, blindness or no blindness. Blindness was no excuse. It didn't absolve her of an obligation to courtesy, to the apparatus of restraint which anyone, anyone, not only a funeral director, will identify as a mandatory qualification of civilised adulthood. Checks and balances, checks and balances.

He nonetheless heard himself say: 'I . . . uh – it's my mother's. *Was* my mother's – yes . . .'

'Your mump woulb'mt mind – woulb thee. Mithith Gwuthtib's always thayib fwhat a kind thoul thee wath, your mump.'

Saved by the station.

Henry pulled into the forecourt, negotiated a wave of jaywalking commuters and stopped the car behind a taxi.

'Here we are then.'

'Eber tho nithe ob you to dribe me. You not goin to let me twy im then?'

A vehicle's horn yapped.

'It's a very unusual thing to be asked. You'll miss your train.'

The horn yapped longer.

'They all thaid after the play Teretha thould have been Thnow Fwhite.'

'That's – you're called Teresa? Teresa.'

The horn: this time a hand was held on it to produce a monotone squeal.

'Yeth. Tho fwhat?'

Bobby Camino was, without bidding or rehearsal, crooning in his head.

'It's, well it's funny. I've never met anyone called Teresa, not so far as I know – but when I was a kid there was this record . . .'

'Thath fwhy I'm—'

'Oi!' A corrugated jowl lunged into the open window: 'Cab rank.' A hand pointed with a tightly rolled tabloid.

'What?' Henry was distracted.

'Cab rank.' The eyes were tiny, the nostrils were richly furred caves.

'There,' Henry said, gesturing at the taxi in front.

'Thissis a *dedica'ed space*. Cabs only.'

'Sorry?'

The rolled tabloid was now a weapon. It was thrust again towards a sign on top of a standard: 'You're parked in my manor. You blind or wha'?'

Henry stared, speechless.

'*I* am,' said Miss Sullivan.

Jane growled.

The tiny eyes glanced at the bitch, the harness, the folded

white stick: 'Oh so you are. Well, I never knew it was catching. Come on – move!' The corrugated jowl wobbled in ostentatious disbelief.

Henry Fowler drove across the forecourt with furious negligence, inciting a cyclist to swerve and swear. He turned on to the road without braking, without looking. 'Jesus. How often does that happen?'

'All the time.'

'I can't believe it I really can't. It's just . . . What kind of person says that sort of thing. I, ah, I was going to say . . .'

'They think it'th you obe fault if you blime.'

'Look – if you want to try that dress on you're welcome. You're more than welcome,' said Henry in an access of deflected guilt and shame for his sex.

'Oh do you meab that? Thath fantathtic. When?'

'Well, I suppose you could now if you want.'

'You don' have to . . .'

'No, no it's the least I can do.'

He drove more steadily now, heading back home. He was going to point out some sights (pub signs, ancient trees) as he did to everyone, as he had so often to his children who were not his children that they anticipated him. But he remained silent. She's had enough embarrassment for the minute. She doesn't need reminding of all that she knows only by touch, smell, hearsay.

'It'th twue fwhat they thay.'

'Uh? What is?'

'That it'th by obe fault that I'm blime.'

Chapter Nineteen

One gram of apple seeds (pips) contains a 0.6mg secretion of the cyanogenic glycoside called prunasin which when digested reacts in the gut with the enzyme beta-glucosidase to release hydrogen cyanide. To obtain the fatal dose of 50mg at least 90g of seed must be eaten or, should the subject be hungry as well as suicidal, 20 kg of whole apples. For a job well done Dream Topping™ proposes a dose of 110g: an inadequate dose may leave the subject alive but brain damaged, liver impaired or blind. Cyanide attacks the retinal nerve.

Teresa Sullivan was not a failed suicide. She had never considered suicide even though the circumstances of her life might, in another child, another woman, have been propitious. Those circumstances included the legitimisation of the act by familial example. And if it's not thus learned it may be passed down, this genetic gift of willed death.

Her blindness was the result, rather, of prolonged subjection to apple cyanide.

From the age of twelve she had drunk between fifteen and twenty pints of scrumpy most nights for going on two decades.

This might be reckoned a slow suicide, but it wasn't, there was no volition. She had every reason to despair, and suicide is, according to the Catholic superstition she was raised and steeped in, a sin of despair even if eschatological nous demands that it should be classified as a sin of presumption. She didn't despair. She accepted her lot. It was all that she knew.

And if the arrangements and the harshly tiled corridors were unusual and if they were unlike those of her schoolfriends and, later, her workmates . . . well, Uncle Father Roy had always told her that she was special, that she was different from all the others. He hadn't told her that scrumpy could blind, that the pips are left in the mash, that despite prunasin's rapid evaporation a micro-residue remains and that whilst the accretion of that residue will improbably prove fatal it will very likely effect ocular impairment which will manifest initially with a diminution of night sight, then with a gradual turning of day to dusk and, in its tertiary state, with unalleviable omission.

Her mother Bridget had left her village near Galway within a month of feeling the first kick inside and before they might have begun to suspect. She did not doubt that her life there would have been perpetual disgrace, everlasting obloquy.

She had not told Sean Mullin. He was married and – witness how he had dammed her monthly blood – unreliable. He was, too, irregular in his observance, a drinker and a gambler. Besides, he was not the man for her. He never had been, save for that time on the treeless moor when she had stared beyond his ear at the seething black clouds in the sulphurous sky and all she had heard was the rasp of his rapid breath and she had felt him shudder in the moment of his vulnerability before those braggart ways returned and he complimented her on her decision to conjoin him.

She travelled to Britain. She confided in her brother Roy, begged shelter in the house of draughts on the Marches.

He said not yet, not until after the birth – for how would it look were she to arrive childless and then so soon for there to be the three of them. They didn't count the months these people. Even if they believed she was his sister they'd put two and two together . . .

So through those long months she skivvied in a Welsh hotel owned by a Major Malpas, a backslapper who when asked where the toilet was would reply: 'Off to destroy the evidence eh?'

During the week the men who undressed her in their head were reps. At weekends they were rheumy-eyed fishermen with whisky flasks to be filled through a funnel.

She resolved to love her child with her life. She would never give up her child the way Maria from Oporto who did the heavy lifting had. She planned her future whilst walking the precipitously rocky path beside the river, prodding anthills with lichenous twigs. She stood on the metal bridge and stared down at the water churning over the worn striped stones. When the time came she told Major Malpas that she had to return home because of her family, which was only half a lie. She believed she might be forgiven it.

She rented a furnished room in the Birmingham suburb of Balsall Heath.

Six days later she left. Not because the shared bathroom was filthy, nor because the tiny clothes she bought for her dearest love took on the room's clammy dampness but because after her first hospital appointment when she got off the bus at the ruddy public baths she saw, on the other side of the busy road, close as that, Sean Mullin's cousin Patrick Geoghan chatting away to a fellow in the queue at a chip shop. She put her head down and her collar up, scuttled into the vestibule of the baths and inhaled bleach fumes for half an hour before she dared head back to the home she had already decided to abandon.

She did not risk going before dusk even though it meant walking with eyes averted through the groups of rouged garrulous prostitutes gathering for their evening's work. They mocked her. They knew a prim virgin when they saw one.

The first stop on the first train was Kidderminster. She rued the wasted 3/6d she had put in the gas meter. It was the necessity of preserving her precious savings and of finding a room that very night which determined that that town should appear on the birth certificate of the 7lb 11oz child delivered without complications, father unknown. She elected ignominy for herself by giving her own patronym to the child of whose existence she hoped Sean Mullin would never learn, whom he'd never have a claim on if he did. She called her Bernadette Teresa, the first name for her mother, the latter for the song she loved to sing along to whilst peeling potatoes as a casual in a carpet factory canteen (perk: free seconds of carpet squares to insulate the cot with).

Back in her village Teresa would have been considered a presumptuous name in a family like hers. It was a name for the daughters of a hundred acres or more. She revelled in her freedom to take such liberties even if times were hard and she lived in fear that the contemptuous, suspicious National Assistance officers would discover that she undertook piecework for a tailoring firm which supplied funeral directors. There was always freezing fog along the canal where she pushed the battered pram. One afternoon she pushed it up the hill to the Bromsgrove Road. She marvelled at the riches required to afford the big houses with patterned bricks and fancy metal along their roof ridges. She reached a place where men on earth movers and bulldozers were working among uprooted laurels and mud Alps to flatten a building site. A sign said 'A New Home For Doctor Barnardo's Children'. She didn't walk that way again.

When Bernadette Teresa was seven months old her mother took her to live in the house of draughts on the Marches. A holy house it was, attached by a cold cloister to the great stone church whose spire was said to be visible from five counties in two countries.

The smell of God was the smell of Cardinal Red Polish. There was always Goddards for the plate and Duraglit for the brass, there was so much brass there never seemed to be an end to it. The tiles were back-breaking. After a year her hands were the colour of salted meat, calloused, cracked, so rough she hesitated to stroke her darling bundle with them.

Her big brother Roy was now Father Roy. He would become Uncle Father Roy when the little girl learned to speak. His congregation was sullen. The lanky few who spoke in a desiccated English drawl claimed recusant blood and forebears who had conspired in the Gunpowder Plot – an event they talked of as though it were within living memory. They referred to Father Roy Sullivan as 'our Maynooth chappie'. They regarded his clumsy attempts at ingratiation with amused distaste and were shocked by his greedy appetite for drink and food. He assumed that an invitation to a second helping was meant literally, he was too thick or thick-skinned to realise that it was merely a locution.

And while the congregation's majority (superstitious mumblers who worked in hop yards, orchards, maltings, cider mills, psychiatric hospitals) were respectful of their priest's office they were ill at ease with the man. His predecessor, the skeletal Father Gagini, scion of an Evesham market-gardening family, had spoken their language, had understood them, had lived as frugally as they did.

Father Sullivan weighed 24 stone by the time he suggested to his newly motherless niece that they share a bed for the sake of the heating bill, and for comfort too. He couldn't bear to hear her moaning like a whelp in her chilly room as she tried to excise from her memory the snapshot of her mother hanging from a bough in Young Vodden's drowsy orchard where sheep grazed and bees hummed and fruit crates to kick away were teetering temptations, stacked between the lichenous trees.

The noose: plastic-covered wire, baby blue. It put Teresa off washing lines for life.

Apples were different.

Sure, they were agents of pain. That death was indelibly bound to orchards, to trees ranked across slopes, to post-and-rail, to constellations of blossom, to boughs that sag beneath their red burden, to panniers full of fruit radiating smiles like the severed cheeks of happy, unorphaned children.

But apples were also solace. Let them ferment and they become a dependable friend. They also obliterated the pain they caused. They scrapped inhibition. they enabled her to talk aloud to her mother, as if her mother was in the room, beside her in the meadows and orchards, listening to the roster of her days, to her confidences and fears. They were vectors of sweet anaesthesia. Scrumpy was liquid forgetfulness, amnesia in a glass. It would become a demanding friend. Uncle Father Roy knew that. But he was never so mean that he discouraged her or warned her or refused her money to spend in taps where they turned a blind eye to her age and at the farms where Heale's New Missus, Nigger Llewellyn and Fancy Lewis filled her empty bottles and plastic jerrycan from barrels in barns and outhouses. She seldom went to Fancy Lewis's even though it was closer than the others because he was a known lecher and the holes in his rusting corrugated-iron lean-to reminded her of lepers' faces in mission magazines and, anyway, his brew was so sharp it scraped her teeth. The bottles jangled in bags hung from the handlebars. She stood on the pedals to push against the slope in ragged hedged lanes sunken so deep beneath the fields that she could only hear the kine lowing at pasture. She imagined even then what it would be to be blind and to deduce the bulky bodies and slow trusting eyes from the sound they made and from the taste of their milk and of the cheap cuts of their meat.

She was fourteen when she procured the first of her four abortions by drinking pennyroyal tea for six days. She had picked the grey-leaf herb in ditches where it lurked prostrate unable to bear its weight. She would have been shocked by its ultimate etymology: *pulegium* = that which drives away fleas. The foetus she sought to expel was more than a flea. It was a precious part of her whose brief existence she could never reveal to Uncle Father Roy lest it upset him. He was a man who coped badly with divergences from their homely routine. She was innocent of the renal, hepatic and neurological damage she might do herself. That night she drank scrumpy as never before, bled as never before. The blood flow stopped. She drank as never before for as long as they lived in the house of draughts.

The further south the orchard the more potent the fermentation. She knew from Nigger Llewellyn that three miles made all the difference: 'It's the sun what gives 'em strength.' She put on so much weight that the bed she shared shrank and groaned. She got a reputation as a drinker but not, like the other girls who drank, as a three-villages bike. Uncle Father Roy had instructed her that it was God's will that she should not sully herself and betray herself and debase herself by going with boys or men. Men were like Fancy Lewis – he always boasted, he always told. When she heard him telling that Ronwyn Jessup had nipples like a Massey Ferguson's starter button she gave him such a look that the snug went silent. Without looking up Fancy said: 'That's one who's not gonna lose her cherry. No one wants to go pumping up her tyres – Japanese wrestler.' She blushed red as a pearmain then waddled outside near tears. Wreaths of winter breath fogged her eyes as she stumbled back to the cold house, to the moulting hop-bines, to Uncle Father Roy snoring. She was a diligent student who wore an overcoat to do her homework. She sat at her table in the window chewing her pen cap, pretending that the sun in the western sky was a submerged fire beneath the perfectly blue surface of a salt lake surrounded by clouds that were rock formations crenellated and honed by a million years' winds.

It was the blinding lapis streaked with molten gold that she missed when they moved to a new house, new parish, new skies. Starlings swarmed over the Kentish Weald like iron filings. Their black flocks morphed from the letters of a forgotten alphabet to the shapes of fishes and cuddly toys. The central heating in the small-roomed, modern clergy house took some getting used to. She ascribed her headaches to the stuffiness. She took time to make friends at the Tech where she studied shorthand and typing with office-management option.

It wasn't till her second term that she met the Ramsey twins, Alf and Alf a.k.a. 'Alf and 'Alf a.k.a. the Dids, the Pikeys. They weren't like the other girls whose parents went 'up' to London every weekday and lived in gabled, paste-beamed houses. The twins wished to live in such a house. But they lived in a mobile home which was immobile save when shaken by the north-easters off the North Sea ('There's nothing between us and the Urals,' they cried as one). It rattled in those winds. It was stacked on breeze-blocks on Sheppey but was never blown off them. Alf and Alf's dad, Alf, liked to touch Teresa above the knee. She didn't mind once she was over the surprise, but she knew to squirm when his hand crept high, and he was a gentleman. His black hair was lustrous. He was proud to live in a 100 per cent metal carapace; metal was the product he broked. He told her a tale of her mother's and of Uncle Father Roy's country, of how convoys of Dids would park up in a village with their dogs and not move on till they were paid to. Ransom? she asked. Blackmail? It's a living, he replied. He told her another tale: they'd all park up *just outside* a village with their dogs and not move on till they were paid to. His wife, the mother of Alf and Alf, had gone out one day and not come back. She was that sort of Did.

It was, inevitably, Alf and Alf and Alf who told her that there was scrumpy in Kent after she had mentioned its primacy in her old life. They drank, all right, but they shared the sweet-tooth gene – Sambuca with a Malibu top, cassis and Bailey's. They didn't drink scrumpy because of who them that did were: the DSS cases in Sheerness, the no-hoper headbangers in Chatham's mean terraces. They were, though, generous and unproscriptive people. They fixed to take her to Lazaretto Farm where they had heard the pokiest stuff was made. It was a Saturday afternoon. Alf drove because Alf was banned and Alf was over the limit, could hardly stand, snored in the other front seat. They drove through avenues of hop poles. The malevolent cranes on Grain across the water dwarfed the patched farm buildings that she would come to know so well. They drove across marshes where water was differentiated from land only by the hulks' slithy ribs that protruded from its tidal mud. They drove along a causeway past the site of the disappeared lazaretto, a circular artificial island in the glutinous estuary separated from the land by a convict-dug canal: the turf was fervently green and rodent-cropped by the teeth of more rabbits than she had ever seen, they bobbed like balls of cotton and she felt ever so content.

Because Uncle Father Roy was a priest without convictions for driving offences the Archdiocese of Southwark had appointed him Chaplain to the M2 and the M20. He administered extreme unction to bodies broken in scrap sculptures in the fog, to concertinaed victims of unforeseen tailbacks, to somersaulters and hard-shoulder strays. But because he was now so fat that he had his own climate and each of his chins its own postcode, he and his 58-inch waist wouldn't fit into the rusty ten-year-old Punto that went with the job. He had to be chauffeured to death sites in big cars (Dennis Wendy Taxis Maidstone Ltd: a rosary was slung from the rear-view mirror). So as soon as Teresa passed her driving test she was able, whenever she wanted, to make her own way to Lazaretto Farm. She was never stuck for scrumpy. Nor for its distillate. Rowan and Annick were self-proclaiming antinomians, renegade industrial chemists, veterans of a thousand trips, former commercial synthesisers of LSD. They had stashed the profits, paid their debt to society (Winson Green, Holloway), sold up on Exmoor after their release and had relocated to Kentish isolation in the belief that this was a county whose police force was too overworked in the Crime Belt that extends from Chislehurst to Thanet to concern itself with a couple of myopic hippies making sheep cheese and cider. An incorrect belief, it turned out. Idle rozzers are always keen for easy prey. They tend to visit on the flimsiest of pretexts, they love a Christmas box in July. And because they were prone to watch the causeway to Lazaretto Farm from a copse beside the rutted field where races were held every Sunday in the stock-car season Rowan and Annick suggested that if Teresa slake her addiction at the farm she stay the night. The eyes in the copse knew precisely the point where the farm's property ended and the public road (and over-the-limit arrest opportunities) began.

She had never stayed in anyone else's house. She had never, as a child, been allowed to sleep over. She was astonished by the teenagers Hardin and Owsley; by their treatment of their parents as friends, by their effusive demonstrations of affection, by their disrespectful obstinacy, by their sexual candour.

In this house where she would eventually lose her sight she first lost her sense of clock time. She would stumble along the unlit corridors, bumping into teetering bookshelves and pictureless frames slumped against the walls, the legless tables, the collapsing settles. She would wake Saffron, the youngest child, and offer to take her walking on the marshes. Saffron would look at her alarm clock whose hands were grinning cats and tell Teresa that it was half past three in the morning and that she wanted to get back to sleep. An hour later Teresa, having returned meanwhile to a scrumpy barrel, is again in Saffron's room, oblivious of her last visit and eager to read the girl a bedtime story.

When she had gained her secretarial qualification Rowan and

Annick invited her to work at Lazaretto Farm. She milked ewes, forked manure, baited eel traps, hauled them filled with writhing silver life from vernal leets in the morning, skinned them, skinned rabbits, bottled damsons, picked apples, made the mash to make the scrumpy to sell to jacks from Chatham, to pongos from Brompton Barracks. She marvelled at the tidal mud banks rendered edible-looking by the setting sun. She composed a morbid litany of the names of the saltings and the creeks to make her spine alive: The Shade, Slaughterhouse Point, Ham Ooze, Bedlam's Bottom, Deadman's Island. And all the while she was drinking, drinking, staring at the sky to tell her mother there how much she loved this close-knit chaotic family and their wandering friends who arrived without warning, careless toking folk who believed in karma and hand-painted vans.

She returned to the clergy house often enough to keep Uncle Father Roy warm with her bloated body, with bottles of applejack which burned so much he needed more. When she was paid she was paid a pittance most of which Uncle Father Roy took for household contributions. That left her short but she never went with a lad for money, never went with one for love or fun, never went with one at all.

When Rowan and Annick couldn't afford to pay her at all she would find work as a secretary. Never for long. It was the people. They were chatty, lippy, prying. She could tell that they thought her a queer one. They exploited her diligence by giving her as much of their work as they dared so she had to stay late and all that was to be said for that was that she didn't have to partake in the communal ritual of the after-office drink: drinking was what she did alone, with her mother and her dreams.

It was during such a period, whilst temping in the claims department of a freight haulage company, that the initial sign of optic atrophy manifested itself. One Thursday lunch-time she walked across the office to look down into the yard where the liveried artics were loaded. They had changed colour. These must, she initially assumed, be vehicles that she hadn't seen before, part of an auxiliary fleet. Then she realised that the company logo and name were blurred. Had she not known that the marginally inclined capital letters spelled *GIBSON & MILLS* she would not have been able to distinguish the name.

There can be no doubt that the multiple vitamin deficiencies she suffered as a result of alcohol's ruseful ability to persuade the body that it is being fed, as well as drugged, contributed to the onset of the condition known, because it is observed in populations whose diet is reliant on cassava, as 'West Indian amblyopia' or 'Jamaican amblyopia'. That lunch-time when she looked at the soft-edged, chromatically amended lorries she barely nibbled her peanut-butter sandwich.

The drizzle she saw was fine, relentless, perpendicular, yet the asphalt yard didn't turn from matt to gloss, nor did the lorries' paintwork gleam.

Chapter Twenty

Henry Fowler was shocked by Teresa Sullivan's story, by her willingness to tell it to a stranger in such detail, with such dispassion, as if it had all happened to someone else, someone unknown.

Had she invented the pitiful creature who shared her name? Was this humiliating biography a nightmare fomented by her sensory lack? A masochistic compensation? Are the blind not blessed with heightened imaginative faculties just as they are with increased senses of smell and touch? If they make such efficient smoke alarms and masseurs maybe they are also consummate fantasists. But could Uncle Father Roy have been dreamed up?

He was shocked, too, that he should pay such keen attention to the way she bulged within and without his mother's wedding dress.

The stays were stretched. The upper bodice's hooks didn't reach their eyes. Her pudgy arms were distended by the puffed sleeves' tight cuffs. Neck folds lapped over elaborate stitching. He feared the dress might burst. It pulled at the seams to reveal margins of material that had not been exposed to light since the garment was made and whose hue was denser. Her grubby, once-white brassière's frayed back was exposed. Her spine's course was obscured by a rolling landscape of fat.

She curtsied. She twirled clumsily. Like a navvy executing a *ronde de jambe*: he immediately regretted his ignobility of thought. She was giving herself such enjoyment that she displayed a hefty grace. This was for her, not for him. He wasn't meant to be watching, wasn't meant to be torturing himself with invented remembrance of his mother's proud day and repining at this betrayal of her sacred garment. He was ashamed that the eyes he cast over the figure in the dress in the stale, dead bedroom were the eyes of a man observing a woman. Such eyes consume dance, and dance is the precursor of love. Henry was worried by himself. He feared too that she might detect his mute fascination, that his intentions might be misunderstood by Jane. The bitch was slumped against a pile of blankets, moistening them with her viscous slobber, but her eyes were open and she was watching Henry. Miss Sullivan stomped about. Was she essaying ballroom steps?

'Do I look ath lubbely ath your mump did?'

He said: 'Of course you do.'

She stood facing the drawn curtains as a sighted woman might a mirror. She wriggled, she plucked at the sleeves, smoothed the material across her buttocks and thighs, turned to scrutinise the profile.

'I can see that he'th gone neeb lettib out.'

'I suppose so . . . Yes.'

How, he wondered, could he so recklessly dishonour his mother? He was touched by the ingenuous presumption of suggesting it should be altered. Inside the near-dropsical body that demanded the garment's expansion was a near-child. Her wish to possess, uninfected by covetousness, was an expression of delight. It was an adventure prompted by want. This is what Henry told himself. He was fascinated by his slight act of altruism, by his readiness to put himself out during such difficult days. He wondered why he should have acceded to her request. There but for the grace of . . . He pitied her for her use of *see* even if it was merely figurative, unconsidered habit. Her blindness was unqualified. She couldn't see the disparity between her body and the dress that bandaged it. She couldn't see Henry.

He asked: 'What do you imagine I look like?'

She giggled and replied, clumsily coquettish: 'Tall, dar, hanthobe.'

'Two out of three.'

'Wish two?'

'Ah–ha!'

She turned towards him, all the better to scrutinise him.

She inclines her head, tilts it from side to side. Her movements are founded in forgotten gestural memory. She cannot see. She cannot see that Henry Fowler's erection is outside his trousers, that the thick vermicular creature from the deep is polished mauve for her, that it's emitting a leucous dribble. Only he knows how long it has been there, beyond his button flies, proud of the formerly containing black twill tailored in Kidderminster.

She cannot see, but she can sense the change in his breathing, the systolic pounding, the tension. She knows. She knows. The way she reaches out, searches for it: he might be seven years old again in his flannel shorts, tempting fate in a game of blind man's buff with Stanley in the blindfold.

'You're a nauthy one Mithtar Fowler. He feelth like a right prettyith fellow.'

Her left hand was coarsely vigorous. He was reminded of the way milkmaids practise on cows. Her right hand held to her gobbling mouth a cold faggot from the fridge.

He ejaculated on the straining belly of his mother's wedding dress. His mother was dead, she didn't feel a thing.

The stains were, immediately, someone else's, they belonged

to the past, to a past as distant as that in which he had smelled Ben's sweat-ringed squash shirt when he put it in the washing machine and had convinced himself that it must be OK because the boy, the future champion, was his son and he was a fertile father doting on his son's pubescent secretions.

Teresa insisted that she had to get home. Even though, she said, she hadn't shared his bed for years Uncle Father Roy fretted if she wasn't there. Bad things happen to the blind at night, she didn't want to cause him any worry, not with his heart.

It was the least Henry could do to take her, it was the gentlemanly thing to do. And, besides, he loved driving through the long suburbs at night, as hermetic in his locked car as his people in the safety of their bolted homes – what triumphs of cocooned privacy, what fertile groves for the pursuit of lives free of collective imperatives, for individuality and discreet hobbies. Here was the lamplit core of England's happiness.

Then there came a swath of inhospitable countryside: commons, fenced fields, bungalow smallholdings, scars of raw chalk, horses, coppices, water tanks in silhouette, a motorway whose roar alerted her to its proximity before he saw its chains of red-and-white light.

Some while after they had crossed it, on the edge of a straggling village where they waited at a junction for a gap in traffic, she asked him if he could hear a noise. He cocked his head. From somewhere in the night came a repetitive lowing groan. A far-off creature in terrible pain?

'Thas the paper mill. Know tha' noise anyfwhere.'

'Oh . . .' He laughed: 'That's all right then.'

'You look oppsit the gatesh.'

The mill entrance was marked by a presently lowered barrier and a brick hut at a gap in a line of poplars. On the other side of the road a multiply gabled late-Victorian house stood beyond a car park where a signboard was under-lit from such an angle that it was glaringly illegible.

'I don't think I'd want to stay there.'

'Uhnh?'

'Those hotels like that: they're always so . . .'

'Th'not 'n notel. Tha'th nurthing ome. Tha'th where I had Deneeth and Alith.'

'Where *what*?'

'Thath where I had my childrenth. The girlth: Deneeth and Alith. I talk to them eberyday.'

Henry gaped at her. 'I thought you said – you said you had to . . .'

'Yeth . . . But I thtill talk to them – Deneeth ith theven now, Alith ith fibe. They wen strwaight to heaven of courth . . . I tell them what I been doing. I think imaginawy children are better than weal oneth. No meth, no pith eberywhere, no nappieth etthetewar. And imaginawy oneths are pwettier.'

Henry heard her in disbelief. Was this an unfunny joke against herself? It evidently wasn't. She explained that her children were angels. They were fairies too. And fairies live in gardens because they seek 'a domethtic enbiroment'. They are also benign ghosts. They lead a better life than they would have done on earth. They stay young for ever.

She refused his offer to see her down the sloping path to the front door. Jane knew the way. There were lights on in the small house. A bulky figure moved in silhouette across a thinly curtained window. Teresa? – or was this Uncle Father Roy whose bed she claimed to no longer share.

He sat in the car with the engine running. He could discern broken fences, gardens' back ends, bent boughs, little sheds. A fox sauntered delicately across the road. Trees, there are quiet trees in the gardens: do they ever precisely repeat the pattern of their last gentle movement? He shook his head, blinked. He glanced at the illuminated instrument panel, wondered what he was doing here, thirty miles from Home. His memory of the journey he had just made was mostly erased.

Who was this infirm woman with a dog? What was happening to him?

Henry Fowler had not previously considered himself an imaginary father. But that precisely, he acknowledged, was what he was. He was less of a father than Teresa Sullivan was a mother. He drove slowly away.

The next night Henry Fowler wept. It was the eve of his parents' funeral and he wept because it was all done, because he had achieved the apogee of his craft, because that is as far as any funeral director can go in deploying the old skills that are ever more contracted out to freelance embalmers. How peace had come upon his parents – lifelike parodies of themselves, beneficent smilers. They both had teeth, though not their own, and those teeth were good, so take due advantage, let them grin in their rigidity.

That was the night Teresa Sullivan fucked him. It was a sympathy fuck, a response to his sobbing, a response he solicited. He imagined Lavender. Who, or what, did Teresa imagine? She wouldn't touch his face with her hands to get a reading of his features. Only the birth blind, she claimed, can make a construct by touch, because they have had a lifetime's experience uninhibited by the sight of a face, they don't know what an eye looks like. Henry was humilated by the sight of her manifold flesh slapping against his, by the realisation that her pubic bush was invisible beneath her sow's multi-bellies. Her weight upon him was immense. She clamped him by labial suction. Her genital musculature was prizewinning. He feared castration. She showed no respect for him as a man. His penis might be a simulacrum of a fascinum, made by chance of human tissue. It might be stubbornly engorged but her arhythmic bucking, her jolting lunges will surely twist it, tear it, uproot it from the sod of his body so that a gush of blood spurts from the rent left by her act of vaginal plunder. He was humiliated by his conduct, by this animal congress worthy of a freak show. He took pleasure in that humiliation, in his gutter cunning and exploitative self-abasement.

He was mutating. Henry Fowler was turning into someone different. He was no longer a father, no longer a son, he was no longer inhibited by familial obligations. Henry Fowler was a name that would soon be attached to a man free for the first time in his life to invent himself. He could paint over the old predetermined canvas. It was an exhilarating prospect, and one which rendered him fearful for he had led a life largely bereft of choice. Choice is a labyrinth, and – late in life – he was about to enter it, as Stanley would, perforce, have done, had, had . . . In that matter Henry Fowler had no choice. Some force was pulling him – towards an unknown locus, towards a revised destiny.

When they had finished Teresa asked him whether she should give him a hot lunch the way Uncle Father Roy liked her to. He had not previously heard the phrase. When she explained what it meant he was, to his astonishment, not repulsed. He was curious, excited. Moral fetters were to be unlocked. The warmth, the smell, the intimacy, the barely discernible clammy weight on his chest constituted a golden key, a clue to the many mazes of his future. And they linked him, too, to the child within the man, to the primal child who smears his nappy contents across his face. This formerly fastidious man suffered *nostalgie de la boue*.

When Teresa Sullivan walked about the old home that night it was as though she had eyes. He followed her, anxious lest she fall, bumping up against door jambs and never sure where the vase in the dark was. But she got the hang of a house in her dark as he never could. If a house had a soul she'd find it. If a house had a secret she'd find it. Wrapped in a towel she sat on a cushioned swivel chair at Henry's father's old roll-top desk with its now mostly cleared compartments, the desk that was a near-deserted universe of pull-outs and drawers. She ran her hand again across the wood's dried grain.

He watched her touch this instrument of his father's authority. Her fingers inventoried a Staffordshire figure, a porcelain menagerie, an ivory letter opener. She dredged in drawers for bent paper-clips, rubber bands perished to a crisp, erasers turned to stone, dried ballpoint refills, powdery scraps of paper, fluff, a button. Henry was stretching on a sofa in his unbelted dressing-gown when she tugged the bottom drawer to her right and pulled it out of its chest on to the worn carpet with a squeak, a thud and an exclamation: 'Damn and blath!'

The wooden stop which had held it in the frame was missing. Such stops which were until the 1920s precentor-jointed were habitually thereafter glued (and this was the case here: assume that the glue's potency had suffered from three decades of central overheating) Henry had explored that desk for as long as he could remember. When he was little it had seemed like a model of the world. When he was older he considered it the family museum with its aesthetically null, sentimentally charged keepsakes, the coronation mug for pencils, framed photographs, letters tied with string. His father, as fastidious a funeral director as ever lived, kept his pencils sharpened and his drawers locked. And Henry, an obedient son, had never sought to delve in those drawers. If they were locked it was for a reason.

'Wha' thith?' cried Teresa. Her right hand was examining the void between where the bottom of the fallen drawer had rested and the floor. 'Paperth.'

Henry grunted. He hauled himself from the sofa and padded across the room. He could feel a renewed penile engorgement. So soon! What a man he was. He kissed the nape of her neck, knelt, peered into the void which was contained by the drawer above, and the sides and bottom of the chest. The thin sheaf of papers had been long undisturbed. The accretion of dust was a felt layer. He turned from her and blew at it. Then he wiped it on the carpet. Then he looked at the first sheet, headed, in underlined majuscules:

<u>THE CHURCH ADOPTION SOCIETY</u>

4a Bloomsbury Square, London W.C.1

Telephone: HOLborn 1281/3310

APPLICATION FOR ADOPTION

Points on which enquiries must be made in the
case of every child proposed to be delivered by
or on behalf of a registered Adoption Society
into the care and possession of an Adopter.

'It's amazing,' Henry said, 'the way you can centre text with just a tab setting – you know, on a typewriter. Manual . . .'

What was this document doing under his father's desk? Where had the desk come from? No – that wasn't the right question, for it had been secreted between desk and floor:

EVERY QUESTION MUST BE ANSWERED

1

'Name and present address of child *Henry Dogg c/o Connaught Barracks, Woolwich New Road, S.E. 18*

Henry guffawed at the name. Then he looked at the next line:

Date and place of birth *7. 10. 45*
Royal Herbert Garrison Hospital, Shooters Hill Road, Woolwich

That was his own birthday. The answers were written with a fountain pen in a jagged old-fashioned copperplate. The numeral seven was crossed.

2

Is the child British? *Yes*

If baptised state date and place of baptism and denomination –

Why is the child being offered for adoption? *Because my husband, not being the father of the child, is not willing to support or maintain the child.*

3

Name of father *Unknown*

Address *Unknown*

Occupation *Unknown*

Date of birth *Unknown*

Religion *Unknown*

4

Name of mother *Vera Sophie Dogg*

Address *Connaught Barracks, Woolwich New Road, S.E.18*

Occupation –

Insurance number –

Date of birth *18. 6. 26*

Religion *Protestant*

Henry sat on the floor. His throat was constricted. He sweated. His heart was repeatedly throwing itself against his chest. His unsteady hands turned the pages.

I HEREBY GIVE NOTICE THAT

1 An application has been made by *Edgar George Fowler and Stella Mary Fowler of 17 Bedwardine Road, London SE19* for an adoption order to be made in respect of *Henry Dogg*.

Chapter Twenty-one

When I stare at strong light with my eyes closed the corpuscular tides seething in the lids are crimson.

That, Vera Sophie Dogg, is the colour of your snug wet womb where you fed me because you had no choice, succoured me against your will, deigned to let me squat for your two hundred and eighty days. Your body obeyed the dictates of its generative apparatus. Did you want the leeching burden excised? You have left me with nothing but a colour which I simulate with sun and bulbs. I have no face to fit the uterus I lived in.

But you could have extinguished me, made me an imaginary child. You spared me. I thank you for not having topped me so you could pretend intactness, immaculacy.

You hid me didn't you? You kept it from them just as you've kept yourself from me. How did you account for the expanding medicine ball? Did you plead weight gain, glandular mayhem, nutritional disorder, a craving for cake? Did you make sure there were always Dundee crumbs round your mouth? Did you build a disguise from dried fruit and flour?

There must have been those who knew. I am someone's grand-son. And someone's nephew, very likely. I am, without doubt, someone's son. I have a father. It's just that he's Unknown. But you knew him. Did you really not know his name? Did you marry Dogg without telling him you were bearing me? Did you hope to pass me off as his? He found you out. He did his sums. Smart Dogg.

Did my father hit you? Did he punch me? Did my father flit within hours of your bringing him the bad tidings from the doctor about the intruder who was going to replace the moon as your internal janitor then gaol you for a stretch of as many years as you had already lived? You were young, you were eighteen and a half when you conceived me.

Was it drizzling when you shuffled back from the surgery to the furnished room with the greedy meter? That's already one mouth to feed.

Men are quick to pack. They load that old valise like there's no tomorrow. The way to tomorrow is somewhere else, through the drizzle, through the autumn dusk, across the rusty old girder bridge, on the first train that leaves for an unknown town whose streets are paved with drizzle and there is no woman.

There are only women. Loitering in the lamplight down the hill from the station.

My mother wasn't one of those women. She didn't belong to the sisterhood of the lamplit. Please God tell me she wasn't that sort of woman.

So he disappears, supping in saloons with bonhomous fellows, forgetting. He'll have had no memory of me, no inkling of my sex, even. He might have been at the other end of the world by the time I was ready to be passed on.

Tell me you keened when I was taken from you. I know you wanted to keep me. Tell me that but for my father's fatal illness, but for his death from war wounds, but for your parents' objections, but for the money worries, you would have kept me. And I would not have been Henry.

They were such good people, Stella and Edgar. I was theirs and they were mine. They had no appetite for hurt. They should have told me. They might have chosen a picnic day, an ox-tongue-and-hamper day. My real father died for his King. In a night raid over Essen. Beside a bridge near Wesel. In a wood at Verdun. My unreal father had been excused a fighting role due to his asthma.

I dream of you Vera Sophie Dogg! You were young when you bore me. You're not that much older than I am. We're almost coevals now. We belong to the same generation. Is it from you that I got the blondness that is now besieged by grey?

Mama-mamamamama.

Were you eating when I sat down to eat, sleeping when I slept? My breath found its way to you and you felt a rush in your marrow, you recognised it and suffered a pang of maternal want.

We need to meet, to hug in a lachrymose tangle of regret and relief. You listened out for me. You blessed me as I snuggled in the depth of bed. The same stars shone for you as for me.

Who am I? I'm waiting for Shaun Memory to tell me.

If I am a bastard then I might as well be a royal bastard, a Royal Bastard with capitals and a bloodline to a distinguished traceable tree, noble as oak. Now there's a tree fit for a King to hide in.

I owe it to me.

Look at metempsychotics – you'll never catch them claiming to have been reincarnated from a navvy or a gravedigger. They're all former Kings, Pharaohs, Margraves – in the old days there were many chiefs and few Indians. Either that or only the chiefs are reckoned to have done well enough to deserve another turn. Unfairness extends to the afterlife too, it's inescapable.

I have forfeited all the years I have lived. I grieve for me, for my loss. I grieve for the deceived child I was. All children, I am told, fear that they are not their parents' child. All children save me. (And my non-children, my former children? What has Naomi told Ben and Lennie? Has she spilled the beans just as Freddie Glade – Freddie Glade! – spilled his queer seed in her? I'll bet she hasn't. Not her, with her fetish about *standards*.)

It never crossed my mind that I was not me, that I might be a ready-made, bought in to make up numbers. They spun for a child at dusk in the old mill's glassy pool where the water babies lived, the rejects who fed on algae and green weed. How often had they fished there before? Did they seek a son from early on? They married in the first month of 1933. It cannot surely have been twelve years before they sought to satisfy their want? Or were young undertakers different then?

Were there other versions of me? The precursors who might have been me but who were returned with a sigh?

I must not demean Stella and Edgar with the suggestion that their desire or duty to carry on the name (let alone the business) was what moved them. They were bigger than that. Their glee in my tiny advances was palpable. Their doting pride was unqualified. By the age of eight I could ride a bicycle. I learned to swim. I passed my exams. Congratulations on each count.

It's too late to ask whether she was barren or he infertile (that's one which can't be passed on). They possessed, in response to the one or the other's procreative lack, a united gift for parenthood. Begetting and nurture are not conditional upon each other. They may have been incapable of the sprint but they never flagged all down the marathon years. They took to parenthood, they adopted it as an ideal as surely as they had adopted me to be their fellow player in the masque of family life.

How could they have left me to discover my orphanhood in squalidly cached posthumous papers? Give them the benefit – by the time they were old they may even have forgotten where

I had come from, who I had been. They were that practised in self-delusion.

It's every funeral director's wish that his own funeral should be directed by his son. That goes without saying. I could not deny him even though I was intoxicated by the shock of what I had discovered.

His colleagues were generous after the service:

'You're your father's son all right . . .'

'You did him proud . . .'

'He was a great man, Edgar – and your mother, too . . .'

'The joy they'd have taken in how you done it . . .'

'Simple, rich – and just a touch different . . .'

'That was one of the finest jobs I ever had the privilege . . .'

'That was more than professionalism, that was filial devotion . . .'

'That was fit for a King . . .'

I embalmed the bodies of the man who was not my father and the woman who was not my mother to the best of my ability and was flattered that my prowess was acknowledged by his (and my) peers. He had taught me well. He developed my gift.

My funerary idiom was not his. Had we not shared a name no one would have discerned a connection. No one would have claimed to perceive a dynastic style. Couldn't they see the difference?

Little Cyril and Squinting Arthur and Mouthy Lawrie and all the rest who filed past with their hats to their hearts would have thought the less of Edgar had they learned that he was not the biological father of the mourning man who had lent him such a semblance of life.

They had their *own* sons – the purser, the bankrupt surveyor, the Dubai catering manager – who had neglected to follow their fathers' trade, who had turned their back on it because they lacked the gift, the will, the bent for the trade, properties which are not, then, merely passed on.

They were properties I owned. I could bring the dead to life, I bestrode the boundary. When they looked fearfully down at Edgar, with his babyish bloom, they regretted that when their time came to lie in the purple satin of mortality it would not be their sons who had dressed them but hired hands. That's what they rued. They believed that I was the blood successor to the Undertaker's Undertaker. I colluded in the lie about my provenance so that his name and memory – and hers – should remain unstained and his posthumous reputation attain perfection.

I need words that are full of hate, whose very utterance expresses cosmic contempt, which require no qualification.

A stroke of luck, then, that there is a ready supply of such words, all the words which the Chosen have caused to be coined against them throughout a millennium of usury, cheating, parasitism and looking after number one. Mothers may, down the years, have scalded, drowned, maimed, and starved their offspring but there is still no store of hostile synonyms for them. It's a lack that I really must attend to . . .

But no matter how zealously I seek such words I shall never be able to address the woman who pretended to have given me life with such justified hatred as I did Naomi in my last letter to her.

'Darling Oven Dodger . . .'

I wrote it for the sake of that form of address alone. The rest of it was simply nasty stuff which I expect her not to have read.

All the casual verbal offences which I railed against for more than twenty years are now mine to deploy.

When Teresa called the other day to tell me she was pregnant I laughed before she had even finished slobbering into the mouthpiece. She can have had no idea why. I sang her 'Teresa' – and repeated the line 'Your blue eyes tell me white lies'. I was glad of that line. I'm not going to be duped again. I put the phone down. Then I realised I should have changed it to 'blind eyes'.

I am nobody.

I can hear the irritation in Shaun Memory's voice every time I call. 'It's a slow process.' That's all he has to say.

Days pass and I am still nobody. I have nobody.

I haven't even myself.

What's in a name? Everything.

Me, I don't have a name, the one I bore was a chance mask, a slave name.

I am disappearing, I'm disappearing fast.

This is the last you'll hear from Henry Fowler.

This is not the last you'll hear from Me.

Jonathan Meades

Filthy English

A dog who stars in bestial pornographic movies describes the slippery slope towards aniseed addiction in 'Fur and Skin'. 'The Sylvan Life' is a story of rustling, hallucinogenic mushrooms and incest as they proliferate in the New Forest. In 'Spring and Fall' a rich and childless woman offers a sybaritic young boy a clandestine family life which becomes his downfall. The most extraordinary circumstances combine to provide the perfect alibi for a homosexual 'crime passionel' in 'Oh So Bent' . . .

Jonathan Meades has a black imagination. Not content with disarming his readers with an outrageous premise, he continues to tease their curiosity from one end of each story to the other. His is the kind of originality that comes along rarely, his characters the sort who lurk and linger round the back alleys of the mind.

Coming soon from 4th Estate

4th

Jonathan Meades

Pompey

Jonathan Meades's intensely distilled epic novel recounts scores
of stories: of a pygmy hunt, an assassination, a crucifixion; of a
human blood bank and a man with metal in his head and a dentist
with nasty habits; of sick sex, ill winds, malignant diseases; of the
Voys, the Halals, the Puppymen.

Most of all it tells the story of a flaky pyrotechnicist, Guy
Vallender, and of his four progeny, chief among them Poor
Eddie, who was quarry, whose gifts were otherworldly, whose
gruesome fate was perhaps transcendent. The action stretches
seamlessly between the mid 40s and the mid 70s; its many
topographics include Brussels, Salisbury, the Teutoburgerwald,
the Congo. But the dominant setting is the titular city – a
nightmarish brick grid set on mud and populated by garish
freaks. It is here that the characters move to their unique and
inexorable ends.

Pompey is a witty, gripping, emotionally harrowing work of our
most viciously inventive writer – part hallucinatory adventure,
part unhappy family saga, part perverse tragedy of fundamental
delusion, it is persistently, hurtfully entertaining. Heed the
author's warning: 'After using this book please wash your
hands.'

Coming soon from 4th Estate